Praise for Rex Burke

Sometimes the Universe drops the exact right book into your life at the exact right time … From the first pages, had me engaged and smiling.

KRR Lockhaven, fantasy author

I can't wait to be able to read the final entry in the Odyssey Earth series.

Shazzie, Fantasy Book Critic

I completely, wholeheartedly recommend this gem of a book.

Rebecca @ Indie Book Spotlight

[For] fans of Pratchett and Douglas Adams who like SciFi stories with a sense of humour and a 'slice of life' feel to them.

Sue Bavey, book blogger, Sue's Musings

STAR BOUND

Also by Rex Burke

Orphan Planet

Twin Landing

Star Bound

STAR BOUND

Odyssey Earth
Book 3

REX BURKE

ISBN: 978-1-916694-03-3

This book is also available as an eBook.

Cover design: Chris Hudson Design, chrishudsondesign.co.uk

Acknowledgements: Huge thanks to my beta-readers Sue Bavey, Lisa Rose Wright (and S!) and Karl Forshaw for help in shaping the final journey. To Shazzie, Kevin and Rebecca for their amazing support throughout. And to Elaine, the Juno to my Jordan, my shining star.

Contents

Buckle Up for the Final Ride   9

1. Sign   13
2. Money   28
3. Moisture   41
4. Loss   53
5. Textbook   60
6. Caves   77
7. Daisy   91
8. Hot   104
9. Mates   117
10. Sisters   126
11. Normal   137
12. Video   147
13. Bunker   156
14. Sorry   166
15. Bacon   179
16. Eyes   185
17. Armada   196
18. Impressionist   205
19. Cruise   217
20. Dice   226
21. Sonic   237
22. Speech   244
23. Switch   252
24. Deep-freeze   265
25. Swayze   275
26. Photograph   288
27. Bounty   304

28. Geneva 317

29. Wings 326

30. Casablanca 343

Like This Book? 351

About the Author 353

Buckle Up for the Final Ride

I'm going to assume you're not starting the 'Odyssey Earth' series here at Book 3? That would be mad – like watching the fourth film of a space saga first. No, hang on, bad analogy.

What I really mean to say is, thank you very much for alighting here at the final volume, but it really would be much better if you went and read *Orphan Planet* and *Twin Landing* first. Because then I don't have to recap quite so much – and I can tell you, a whole *ton* of stuff happened in those first two books. There were some good jokes, too, you'll miss those otherwise – though I'm not averse to rehashing some of the best ones, as you'll soon see.

So, welcome back, and here we go.

You'll know by now that Book 2, *Twin Landing*, finishes on a lot of cliff-hangers, which you either like or don't like as a writer's ruse. You're here, so I'm going to say it worked, but I promise I won't make a habit of it. I just really wanted everyone who had made it through the story thus far to keep reading.

Our 'orphans' from *Orphan Planet* – the six teenage kids and Jordan Booth – have been surviving on the twin planet they call Dave. And they finally manage to get a signal back to the *Odyssey Earth* ship, which is great news, as everyone back at base now knows they're still alive. In the meantime, they've been out exploring, and their castaway home has started to give up its secrets – strangely behaving soil and trees, a creature or two, and a dramatic hideaway cave full of alien handprints.

Elsewhere, things have not been going well on the colony planet, New Earth, thanks in part to the machinations of one Donald Sprake – the funder and founder of the whole mission, who had secreted himself away on the ship. Not only that, he seems to have brought along his own twin, teenage daughters, Bel and Jet – you might say kidnapped – and they are really not happy about that.

Juno, the captain, is in a bind. She'd like to send out a rescue party to fetch the kids back, but Reeves, the AI, has bad news. The life-support system keeping a thousand crew in hypersleep appears to be failing, and there's a massive, magnetic storm approaching the twin planet.

While Juno does her duty and prioritises the mission, her second-in-command, Susannah, takes matters into her own hands and steals one of the remaining landing-shuttles. She takes big Dave with her

– the quartermaster, not the planet – and Bel and Jet sneak on board, too, to get away from their father.

And while they are on their way to try and rescue the ship kids and Jordan, the villainous Sprake plots his next move …

That's you all caught up, so now, let's get everyone *Star Bound*. I hope you love reading it, as much as I enjoyed wrapping up the tale.

Sign

ORDINARILY, when you piloted a landing craft from orbit to planetfall, you could check the calculations with the mothership AI. And you also generally had time for a quick cup of tea and a chat with the captain.

But as Susannah had taken this lander from the *Odyssey Earth* against orders, cut all comms, and flown three million miles across uncharted space, she only had her own skills to rely upon. And they'd run out of tea days ago.

Back on the *Odyssey Earth*, she had been part of a team – First Officer, second-in-command, following well-worn protocols. This situation was different, and what happened next was going to be all on her – but it was why she'd come.

First things first. Susannah popped a switch and the small comm-sat disengaged from the lander, unfurling its spindly arms as it moved steadily away from the craft.

Fingers crossed.

Her target, the twin planet, hung below them – blue and green, in a sea of black – and it looked as if she would be able to coast in and pick her spot. Whether anyone was there or not – Jordan, the kids – she didn't know. But hope had brought her this far, so – fingers crossed again.

"Everything all right?" said Dave, as he attempted to shoehorn himself into the bubble seat beside her in the cockpit.

Dave. Fellow mutineer. One of the *Odyssey Earth*'s quartermasters. A sort of human hillock on legs. He tried valiantly to sit down, but it was like the Incredible Hulk attempting to cram himself inside a two-door Smartcar – in the end, Dave gave up and stood behind Susannah, looming over her as he studied the navigation screen.

"Define all right," she said.

"You tell me, Suze. You're the pilot. I just go where I'm told."

That was true, as it happened. Tillie – the colony ship's other QM, Dave's other half – had pretty much ordered him to go and rescue the kids, while she stayed back and foiled the pursuit. And as Tillie was built like a brick outhouse with biceps, you didn't tend to argue with her.

Plus, Dave loved Tillie and, accordingly, did what he was told, like any sensible man would.

"Let's see. Still no comms with the ship or New Earth. There's something going on that's interfering with transmission and reception. I've launched a satellite, see if we can't find an approach that might cut through."

When they had first taken the lander, a couple of weeks ago – taken, stolen, liberated, choose your verb – Susannah had deliberately cut the comms and locked out Reeves, the ship's AI.

Let's face it, they were doing something that they had expressly been told not to. They were only going to be shouted at by an angry captain. Told that they'd let her down, the mission down, and most importantly, themselves down. Ordered to come back. Shouted at a bit more.

Far better to get to the twin planet as quickly as possible, and then restore communications, announce the start of the rescue mission, fetch the kids and Jordan, and return home triumphantly. And hope that that would reduce the amount and volume of the shouting.

Only, having tried to switch them back on, the comms weren't working, so Susannah's plan – such as it was – was already unravelling.

And that wasn't the only problem.

"The beacon signal is patchy, too. Which is even more of a worry."

The explorer pod beacon. The reason they were here in the first place. The emergency transmission from the twin planet, received on the *Odyssey Earth*, that had told them Jordan and the kids were still alive.

Probably still alive.

Perhaps still alive.

Anyway, the signal had been enough for Susannah to plan a break-out rescue mission, take – sorry, liberate – a lander, and fly for fifteen days across the solar system. And now, just as she was about to plot a landing trajectory, the beacon signal kept glitching.

It was still there, pulsing away, but it wasn't consistent. Faded in, faded out. Stopped, started again. More atmospheric interference mucking around with the lander's systems.

"Probably because of that," said Susannah, pointing at a wispy, frosted band on the nav screen, and then nodding out of the cockpit at a crackling swirl of dark clouds that obscured part of the planet below them.

"Is that normal?" said Dave, as flashes lit up the stratosphere.

"Who knows what normal is around here. But it's in our way. Last fix for the beacon is right under that big, black cloud."

"So, what's the plan, Suze?"

Susannah had got to know Dave better over the last couple of weeks of confined flight. She'd known him for seventeen years, of course – crewmates on the *Odyssey Earth*'s long voyage across the galaxy. But he and Tillie had tended to keep themselves to themselves down on the cargo deck, happy amid the vast inventory of stores, while she – as Dave put it – "lived up at the pointy end, with the brass."

She'd known him, but hadn't really known anything about him. And now that she knew lots more about him – favourite music, hardcore punk; favourite curry, *jalfrezi*; favourite film, *The Bridges of Madison County* – she really liked him. She could see what Tillie could see, which was that Dave was not only kind and unflappable but trusted people implicitly, unless they gave him a reason not to.

Dave trusted Susannah's skills as a pilot. He wouldn't have come along otherwise. He trusted that she would have a plan, and he'd go along with it, without question, because he also trusted her (to a point – "I'm sorry, *tikka masala* is not a proper curry, Suze. We'll have to do something about that when we get back.")

She laid out the plan, which was, admittedly, less in the way of a carefully formulated scheme and more of a bullish dive through hazardous electrical storms above an unknown planet.

"Avoid all the flashing and banging, I reckon. Go in the long way round, get under the storms, hope we pick up a strong beacon signal, and take it from there."

"It's a fingers-crossed scenario then?"

"That it is, Dave, you are correct. Holding on tight might be an idea. Praying, too, if that works for you."

"What about the girls?"

Ah yes, the girls. Bel and Jet. Turned up mysteriously on the *Odyssey Earth*, having been tucked away anonymously in the hypersleep chamber, and now along for the ride to escape their snake of a father, Donald Sprake.

Until now, Susannah had been working on the principle that, if you were going to go and rescue six teenage castaways from an alien planet, what difference did it make if you added another couple of teen stowaways into the mix? Probably, no one would even notice.

And she liked Bel and Jet, having got to know them as well over the last couple of weeks. Teenagers, obviously, and thus fundamentally absurd, self-absorbed, and all-knowing. Just as it should be. But they were very different from *their* teenagers – the ship kids, born on the *Odyssey Earth*, raised alone in space, on a one-way voyage to the stars.

Susannah – at almost fifty – could just about remember what it was like to be a teenager, and she knew that the ship kids were not your usual specimens. How could they be? Accidents of birth on a colony ship, their childhoods and teenage lives had been nothing like hers, or the rest of the crew's. There had been nothing normal about their upbringing.

Bel and Jet were different, in so many ways. There was a confidence about them, a sophistication, that came from their monied background. Mother a former model, estranged father a multi-billionaire. They had a life experience that the ship kids had only read about or seen in films – independence, holidays, luxuries, pets, parties, girlfriends, boyfriends.

They'd never been on an interplanetary landing

shuttle before, though. They didn't understand anything about space flight – they were still getting used to the idea that they were in space at all, having been drugged by their father and put into hypersleep aboard the *Odyssey Earth* without their knowledge.

Now they were on board the lander, it was fair to say that they were cowed by the view – of millions of stars across billions of miles. They had been relieved to reach the planet below them, but Susannah thought they didn't need to know that the landing might get a bit hairy.

Anyway, they were asleep, of course. Getting their regulation, teenage, sixteen hours a day.

"Let's wake them up after we get through the next bit. They'll be happier when we're closer to the ground."

Fingers crossed.

———

Three day-cycles ago, the Family had seen the first sign – the sign of the coming change.

As always, it had started on the jagged heights above the valley – on the hard, stone peaks they called the Old Ones. Solid rocks and crags that had lived forever and would last forever.

The sign always came from that direction, from on high, where the peaks – the Old Ones – girded the thundering spray of the Falling One.

The Old Ones themselves never changed – how

could they? – but the age-old stones played their part, as everything played its part.

From nests and perches in the rocks and crags, sheltered among the Old Ones, the High Ones launched themselves, spreading their wings and riding the thermals. And because it was time – because change was coming – the High Ones swooped down into the valley, diving deeply, buzzing the ground, before climbing again, and then diving once more.

Climbing and diving. Again and again.

This had been the first sign, as always. Three day-cycles ago now.

The Family raised itself from the ground, touching palms to the earth, leaving fingerprints in the soil, before standing upright. Thanking, acknowledging, connecting.

The Family was one and it was many. It spread along the lower valley, from the cauldron at the foot of the Falling One as far as the endless expanse of the Rippling One, where the land dissolved into salty water and the sky began.

They were one, two, three – they were many – and they were Family.

The High Ones swooped down once more and the fourth day-cycle began – the last one, the important one.

Four digits on a hand, four day-cycles. It was time.

The rain had already come once, sweeping over the top of the Falling One, bringing first blooms to the valley. Bringing life to the ground. The ground that supported the Family. The ground that connected everything.

Soon – now that the sign had come – the rain would arrive in earnest. In great waves, in downpours and floods. The valley would soak.

And then the sparks would come from the swirling clouds above – the Dark Ones, who tore in on high winds, firing strikes onto the soaked ground. The ground that connected everything. The ground that was given new life for the next great cycle, as the water from the Falling One and the sparks from the Dark Ones combined.

By then, the Family would be gone. Today was the fourth day-cycle of the sign. It was time.

Time to retreat to the high ground and wait for the rains to end. Time to prepare for the next cycle. Time for thanks, for acknowledgement, for connection.

It was always the same, once the sign had been seen. How could it not be?

They would take the route down the valley towards the Rippling One, as a Family, both one and many.

Then the turn at the edge, where the land dissolved and the sky began, to follow the trodden path leading far away from the valley.

And the slow climb inland, into distant peaks, which harboured sheltered caves. Where the Family would rest and be thankful that the sparks struck the ground and not them.

A short time later – four digits on a hand, four more day-cycles – the Dark Ones would rise back into the sky, higher and higher until gone altogether, and the rain and the sparks would be no more.

Once again, it would be time – time now to leave the caves and descend from the peaks.

Time to embrace the rushing waters of the Winding One as it led the way to the jagged profile of the Old Ones.

Time to pick a way down on stone steps, under the skirts of the Falling One.

Time to leave the Family's mark inside the hidden shelter – one and many. Leave their mark on the walls, as a message to the Old Ones above that the Family had returned, and that things would never change. How could they?

And then time to make the final descent into the valley, where there was life in the ground, and the ground connected everything.

The sign had come.

It was the fourth day-cycle.

It was time.

———

Susannah did her best, but the lander dropped into cloud cover as soon as they hit the planet's atmosphere.

"Hold on, this might get a bit – " she shouted, before a massive bump rendered the rest of the sentence out of date.

Two heads popped up behind her. Bel and Jet. Alien planet turbulence. Better than any alarm clock, apparently.

"Sweethearts, you need to strap yourself in back there. Do it now."

"What's happening? Are we going to crash?"

"Of course not!"

Fingers crossed.

"But please, strap yourself in. Dave! Come and sort them out, would you?"

"Come on, girls. Let the nice lady fly the spacecraft. Nothing to worry about. It's just weather."

The nice lady didn't like the look of some of the clouds approaching at speed, where flashes of multi-coloured light were snaking between the darkest areas. Susannah checked the nav screen, which was just a hot mess of dancing white lines. Marvellous – currently flying blind, too, as well as being tossed around like a dark load in a heavy wash cycle.

Well, she knew what she could do about that. She'd had enough of gentle cruising speed anyway. She was a pilot. She was supposed to fly things, not get wafted around by weather. So – let's fly. Which in this instance meant increasing the speed, gaining back some control, and getting out of here into calmer skies.

The technical phrase was, "Seeing what this baby can do," and it involved pointing the lander downwards and going very fast.

Susannah did that for a bit, held her breath for a bit more as the cloud seemed to go on forever, and then breathed a big sigh of relief as the lander popped out high above a shining ocean. The nav screen resolved itself as the interference dissipated, and Susannah could trace a distant coast and, further inland, a range of high, jagged peaks.

"Nice one, Suze," Dave shouted from the back. And "Told you we'd be all right," the latter comment presumably to the girls, because he hadn't told Susannah anything of the sort. In fact, she knew he'd had his eyes closed for most of the descent, not to mention his fingers crossed.

She'd give him that one, though. It had been a bit hairy. Could have gone either way.

Behind her, she could hear unbuckling, and then the three of them crowded together so that they could all see the view ahead.

Susannah dropped lower again and skimmed the craft a few hundred feet above the surface of the sea, enjoying the sensation of some real flying. It was clear ahead, and the coastline was coming up fast.

"We're here!" she said, happily.

"Where, exactly?" said Jet.

"Doesn't have a name. We've just been calling it the Twin. About three million miles from New Earth and the ship. Similar atmosphere, environment, geology, everything. Probably formed at the same time."

"And you know where we're going?"

"I do now." Susannah pointed at the nav screen. "See that little light? Winking away? That's the explorer pod transponder. That's where the kids are. We hope so, anyway."

She punched some numbers into the console, and the lander climbed slightly and then slowed as it passed from ocean to land.

Now they were flying over a low coastal plain, where many arms of a river emptied into a rippling sea. It was a dull, overcast day, under high clouds, but channels of sunlight illuminated patches of green and brown far below.

They were too high to make out landforms or details – perhaps marshes, perhaps woods? In the distance, a chain of mountains formed a natural barrier at the end of a broad valley. The peaks were shrouded in dark clouds, and Susannah noted more ominous flashes.

As they raced towards the mountain range – a metallic dart in a leaden sky – the girls gasped. The curving stone face ahead of them was split by a vast waterfall, tumbling down hundreds of feet in a deep, green sheet that was almost indistinguishable from the surrounding rock. The top of the falls was above the line of the craft, and higher still, the clouds boiled and flashed.

Susannah banked the lander. "We're going up into that, so time to hold on again."

"What's the plan, Suze?" said Dave, not for the first time.

"The pod and the beacon are that way, couple of

hundred miles. I've got a strong lock, and this is the best approach we've got. Don't worry, I'll take it easy. Nav readings are showing that it's calmer on the other side of the range. We'll be fine."

This time, Susannah didn't even bother saying, or thinking – fingers crossed. They'd come too far to fail now.

She was a good pilot, and she knew what she was doing. She'd always known what she was doing, from the minute she boosted the lander from the *Odyssey Earth*'s launch bay. She was rescuing their kids, and the weather wasn't going to stop her.

She punched more numbers, and the lander soared up and into the storm.

———

The Family moved down the valley, away from the Falling One and towards the Rippling One, where the land dissolved into salty water and the sky began.

The fourth day-cycle had begun. The High Ones soared from the peaks one last time, diving down into the valley. Then they climbed back on strong, beating wings to the rocks and crevices of the Old Ones, high above the deep green curtain of the Falling One.

The Family looked up, watching the last of the High Ones – just specks – cruise into their sheltered nests. A straggler, much larger, adjusted its approach and climbed steeply, before it, too, disappeared into the tumult.

Then the Family turned, one and many, and left the valley behind. The High Ones had all retreated. The sign had been delivered. The new cycle was underway.

It was always the same, once the sign had been seen. How could it not be?

2

Money

"WHAT'S HE DONE NOW?"

'He,' being Donald Sprake – stowaway billionaire, monumental pain in the stars.

'Done' – because all he ever did was do things that were a monumental pain in the stars.

And 'now' – well, because it had been at least a day since his last pain-in-the-stars manoeuvre, and Juno was sure that the Major's sudden appearance and worried expression was indicative of yet another thing to be concerned about.

"You won't like it."

"Let's just take that as read."

Nothing Sprake did was conducive to the general wellbeing of a fledgling planetary settlement. It was, however, usually to the benefit of a disruptive billionaire.

"He's opened a bar."

"He's what now?"

"I say 'bar,' he's installed a counter in one of the accommodation units, from which he's currently selling drinks to the crew."

While she didn't doubt the Major – her extremely reliable righthand man – there were at least two things wrong with that sentence.

"What do you mean, 'drinks?' We haven't got any. Not yet, anyway. That wine of Gerald's was – well, it wasn't wine. Surely no one wants to keep drinking that?"

Gerald – the reclusive botanist. Hadn't been seen around much since the commemoration ceremony a few weeks ago when, at short notice, he'd manufactured an alcoholic drink notable only for its high gag-reflex quality. The settlers had planted a vineyard since then, with archived heritage vines, but they were a full year away from first harvest and even longer from anything drinkable. Juno had heard rumours of a still, but the Major had so far failed to uncover any evidence.

"He's got something from somewhere. I can produce the comatose engineers, if you like."

"Give me strength. Is that where they've been? I wondered why work had stopped."

"Two are destined for enormous hangovers when they wake up, so they'll be out of action for the rest of the day. I found another one asleep in an excavator by the half-dug swimming pool."

"We don't have a half-dug swimming pool."

"We do now."

Juno sighed in exasperation. "And this is why

alcohol and alien planet colonies don't go well together. We agreed, we all did. High days and holidays only for the first year, until things settle down."

"Well, Sprake, it seems, disagrees. I'm told it's like the Tatooine *cantina* down there come nightfall, though I'm not familiar with the establishment myself."

"You also said 'selling' drinks? What does that mean? Dare I ask?"

"I haven't actually seen any money change hands. But there's a price list posted at the bar."

"There's *money*? Where have people got money from? *Why* have people got money?"

Given that there was nothing to spend money on, on a starship, and nothing to buy on an otherwise uninhabited alien planet. No one had money. Which idiot would have brought money with them?

"You must have noticed the construction on the eastern perimeter? It's not on the plans. I think it's Sprake – getting people to do things for him."

"He's *paying* them?"

"Somehow, yes. I think so. And then they're using the money in his bar."

"Right. Show me. He's gone too far this time."

Juno and the Major strode out across the site, towards the accommodation units at the end of the main thoroughfare.

'Thomas,' Juno reminded herself, and no longer simply 'The Major,' now that she'd got used to him. She'd had him revived from hypersleep a few weeks previously, in need of a wingman to assist on the ground while she tried to establish humanity's first galactic outpost here on New Earth. He'd been a bit stiff and formal at the start – and it wasn't just his military manner either.

Back on Earth, he had been a recognised space hero – Juno had perused his records – and maybe that had something to do with it. Juno was used to slightly odd, single-minded space pilots – after all, she was one herself – but there had been more to it than that.

He had seemed distant at first. Aloof. Juno even wondered if he'd been playing a part, presenting himself as a character. There was the whole endless business with talking in David Bowie song lyrics, for a start, and she still wasn't sure that he hadn't been playing an elaborate joke on her.

Come on, really, out of all the ex-astronauts they could have employed, they'd sent her a 'Major Tom'?

However, the Major had thawed over the last couple of weeks – following Susannah's dramatic lander hijack and rescue mission – and he and Juno had been thrown together, as they dealt with one crisis or another. Perhaps he had just taken a while to adjust, after coming out of the cryo process? Juno had seen enough hypersleep revivals over the years to know that it affected different people in different ways.

He'd mellowed, certainly. "Call me Thomas," he'd said eventually, once they had decided to dismiss the whole 'Captain-Ma'am' form of address. He was a stickler about 'Thomas,' mind. Didn't like to be called 'Tom,' and was still adamant that he'd never heard of this Major Tom Bowie chap that Juno kept asking about.

So 'Thomas' and 'Juno' it was between them, and she had come to recognise and appreciate his very solid qualities. He was straightforward and reliable, and if he said he'd do something, he did it. Thanks to him they had a fully operational airstrip and workshop, a goat-proof perimeter fence, and a working stone quarry, not to mention the vineyard, which had also been his idea.

A competent, trustworthy man, who wasn't threatened by her status – Juno liked that and, increasingly, she liked him.

The thorn in their mutual side was Donald Sprake.

Look, no one enjoyed having unexpected guests to stay. Even if he'd been a cuddly billionaire, out to do good in the universe, Juno would have resented the underhand way he had sneaked himself on board what she regarded as *her* ship, and which Sprake – who had paid for it – constantly reminded her was *his*.

As was the planet, New Earth, apparently. His scientists had found it, his mission had reached it, and they were all lucky to be here – that was Sprake's general gist.

For Sprake wasn't a cuddly billionaire. He was a Grade A, top-of-the-range, Nasty Piece of Work, who had drugged and kidnapped his own twin daughters – putting them in hypersleep alongside himself, to be woken upon arrival at New Earth. He had his reasons – he had expounded upon them extensively – but they all boiled down to his extreme narcissism and the fact that he was a Grade A NP of W.

It was possible he wasn't even a billionaire. Who knew if his companies or stocks had rebounded, back on the old Planet Earth – it was coming up for twenty years after all, since he'd left clandestinely under humiliating threat of liquidation.

And even if he was still loaded, it didn't matter. Out here, as settlers of New Earth, everyone started with the same zero balance – the same chances, the same opportunities. No one cared what you were before, or what you had done. It was the single most compelling reason why around twelve hundred people had been persuaded to give up everything and embark on a one-way mission to the stars.

Two hundred crew, a thousand in cryogenic hyper-sleep – all with their own reasons, a clean slate and nothing to lose. Juno included.

Sprake, though, was upsetting the applecart, ruffling feathers, and generally cutting a swathe through all available metaphors. He'd been a monumental pain from the minute he'd arrived, and if you thought that seeing his daughters flee the solar system rather than be on the same planet as him would put a stop to his gallop, you'd be wrong.

If anything, thought Juno, he'd got worse. He didn't seem at all perturbed by the – hopefully temporary – loss of his daughters. He barely mentioned them, and certainly never enquired about Susannah's rescue attempt, now at the end of its second week. Not that there was anything to tell him. There had been radio silence since the lander had made its hurried escape.

Sprake had taken his daughters on a whim, for spite, Juno was sure of it, just because he could. And now he'd moved on to the next thing occupying his unpleasant, reptilian brain.

Juno didn't know what that thing was. But Sprake was not making life easy for them. What had started off as general questions about the settlement process – in his role as an interested party – had rapidly become a torrent of comments, suggestions and even orders. Sprake thought that everything should be done bigger, better and faster, and he seemed under the misapprehension that he was in charge.

Whereas, in fact, Juno was. By common consent, by protocol, and by letter of authority, issued by – oh, the irony – Sprake's company, Odyssey Enterprises, at the outset of the mission back on Earth.

And Juno didn't want a cocktail bar on New Earth. Not right now, and certainly not one operated by Sprake for reasons unknown but undoubtedly nefarious.

And yet it seemed she had one, given that she and Thomas were now standing outside one of the accommodation bunkhouses, which had a rough sign hanging from a nail on the outer door that said, 'Atmos-Beer.'

"That's actually quite cl– "

"No it isn't, Thomas."

"Quite right, of course. After you."

The bunk room was empty, save for two grey-faced

crew members, out for the count but snoring loudly on their beds.

"We'll deal with them later," said Juno. "So, where's this bar?"

"Well, it was here – at the back there, anyway, in the lounge." The Major gestured to the rear of the bunkhouse, where some hand-built trestles supported a ship-printed length of resin counter-top. "They were using that to serve drinks from. Can't you smell it?"

"I suppose so. Although this is a men's dorm. They all smell like this."

"Good point. You'll just have to take it from me, this was in full swing an hour ago."

"What was he serving?"

"I have no idea of the precise vintages. A brown liquid in large cups, and a white liquid in small cups."

"And you're sure he was selling it? I don't see the price list."

"He must have taken that, too. It was pinned right there, you can see the hole."

Juno looked around and shook her head. Could Sprake *be* any more aggravating? On current evidence, the answer was probably 'Yes.'

They turned for the bunkhouse door, which stuck as they tried to push through it. There, on the other side, was Sprake, removing the bar sign and tucking it under his arm.

"Juno, Major!" He didn't seem at all disconcerted to see them. "Didn't have you down as morning drinkers. You're a bit late, I'm afraid. Or a bit early I suppose."

"What *are* you doing, Sprake?"

Regarding names, Juno had gone the other way with Sprake. He'd started off as Mr Sprake – he was, or had been, technically her boss, after all – and then Donald. And Sprake himself had tried, unsuccessfully, to get everyone to call him Don. But in the last few weeks he'd forfeited every right to familiarity, as far as Juno was concerned, so Sprake it was. You could spit it out satisfyingly, too, depending on how annoying he'd been, and the marvel of it was that he didn't seem to notice or care.

"Getting the sign. I need it for tonight."

"Not that. Let's start at the beginning. Why – how – are you running a bar? It's entirely inappropriate. Not to say irresponsible. You should have come to me."

"And you'd have said yes?"

"No, I'd have said no. I shouldn't have to spell it out. What do you think you're doing?"

"Let me ask you a question, Juno. How do you think it's going? The whole planet-settlement thing?"

"What's that got to do with anything?"

"Everything. I told you when I got here, I'm a big-picture guy. You and Lofty here" – he nodded his head at the Major – "are so busy organising everyone's lives, you don't see what's going on around you. You're good at it, don't get me wrong, but you need to lighten up, cut people some slack."

"And that's where you come in, is it? Lightening things up? Cutting slack? That's what this is?"

"The natives are restless, Juno. They had all those years on a spaceship and, now they're here, you've got them working even harder than ever."

"Everyone understands the situation, Sprake. We all signed up for it. Not you, obviously. You just sneaked aboard, not a care in the world. But the voyage was only the first part of it. We only get one shot at this. We have to do it correctly, follow the plans and protocols – that your company drew up, incidentally. It is hard work. The first year *will* be hard. But we'll be in a much better place next year, and everyone gets that."

"Are you sure?"

"I don't know what you mean."

"I'd say that not everyone is as keen as you think to keep grinding away without some R&R. This little pop-up bar was filled to bursting last night, and some of them were still at it this morning."

"Which is why it's such a bad idea. Where are you even getting alcohol from, anyway?"

"You've got a planet full of chemists and what-not. They just needed a bit of a nudge and a secret ingredient or two."

"I don't even want to know what that means. And the Major here thinks you're selling the stuff?"

"I wouldn't say 'selling,' exactly."

"What would you say?"

"An exchange of favours, perhaps, facilitated by the transfer of polymer-printed transactional vouchers."

"Cute."

"People like the old ways, Juno. Makes them think of home. Makes them think this could be a home."

"It *is* their home!"

"Then you need to give them something familiar. Something enjoyable. Look, I'll hold my hands up and say we should have thought through the planetfall scenario in more detail. But we are where we are, and we need to be adaptable. Try something new, see if it works – it's the only way forward."

"Well, this isn't it. It's got to stop."

"I don't think so."

"Excuse me?"

"I told you, Juno. Big picture. You really can't stop this, not unless you want a lot of unhappy crew members on your hands. I didn't exactly have to force drinks down them. Well, maybe the excavator guy – though he did lose the drinking game fair and square."

"This isn't funny, Sprake. I'm serious. This has got to stop. I'm going to call a crew meeting and read them the riot act. Then we'll see."

"You do that. Tell you what, you explain to everyone how they have to keep working hard, living in bunkhouses, showering in lukewarm water, and eating under canvas. Put on your little quiz night if you want. And I'll put on a two-for-one session at Atmos-Beer, and we'll see who gets most takers. You might not like me, Juno, but I know people. And maybe they don't like me either, but I understand what drives them and I get things done. It's really what my businesses have always been about – understanding human nature. I can tell you now who they're going to side with."

"Is that a threat?"

"Just an observation, Juno. I'd let this one go, if I were you. It's a pop-up bar, it's just a bit of fun. Every bunkhouse down the street wants us to put on a night. Why go upsetting everyone? We need them happy, I'll keep them happy."

Juno watched him stroll off down the thoroughfare between the bunkhouses. Was that insufferable man whistling?

The worst of it was, she wondered if he had a point? Maybe not about the bar itself, she still didn't think that was a good idea. They'd lost a day's work on one sector already.

But it was proving to be a bit of a slog, building a settlement from scratch. It had certainly been an easier life on the ship – less arduous, more comfortable. Proper showers. Clean sheets. Tastier meals. Maybe she was driving everyone a little too much?

Not only that. There had been a palpable lift in mood when the *Odyssey Earth* had first intercepted the distress message from the twin planet. Knowing that the kids might still be alive after all had been a powerful motivator. People had even seemed to understand that it wasn't just a simple matter of going to fetch them – the logistics weren't that straightforward, and Juno had been wrestling with possible solutions.

Then Susannah had pulled her little stunt, and after that things had been tense, to say the least. Juno wasn't blind or deaf – she knew that, mostly, people supported Susannah's rescue mission. Heck, so did she, although she could hardly say so, given the number of rules, regulations and promises that had been broken.

But as the hours had turned into days, and the radio silence had continued, the wave of optimism had subsided. Had they lost even more crew members – not to mention another precious lander – to fate or accident?

Heads had dropped. Juno had heard the mutterings. It was not a happy camp.

Sprake was right about that, if nothing else. Damn the man.

3

Moisture

"MY HOUSE, MY RULES," said Reeves.

"I'm not going out there. It's absolutely lashing it down."

"Then you'll just have to hold it in."

"You wouldn't even know. And the others don't mind."

"We do, actually."

"This pod's sensors are rudimentary, it's true, but I certainly would be able to detect excess internal moisture."

"If it is moisture."

"Gross."

"Bryson, it better just be moisture."

"Stop talking about it. You're just making it worse. Dana, tell them."

"Everyone, stop talking about rain, waterfalls, running water, gushing streams, thundering rivers and torrential floods. Bryson is trying to be a big boy."

"Dana!"

"I want to go as well now," said Poole.

"Unbelievable."

"The male human bladder can hold up to twenty-four fluid ounces of liquid," said Reeves. "Bryson, how many fluid ounces of liquid do you currently contain?"

"I don't know! How is this helping?"

"Humans feel the need to urinate when their bladder contains fifteen fluid ounces, so by common reasoning we may infer that – "

"You're going to be detecting moisture in your circuit boards in a minute. See how that helps you."

Jordan closed his eyes. Usually, he just let it wash over him – though probably not the best choice of phrase, given the circumstance.

Which was that this was the second night in the last few days that they'd had to seek shelter in the explorer pod. The weather – searingly hot and dry since they had first arrived – had turned. Temporarily, seasonally, permanently, they didn't know. But no sooner had Dervla, Poole and Bryson returned from their expedition downriver, with tales of their own monsoon experience, then things had changed back at Camp Castaway, too.

Just clouds and grey skies at first, which had been a novelty, all the same. Then an isolated downpour, which they endured under their dripping, canvas sleeping shelters, and then cleaned up afterwards as the sun shone the next day. Then nothing for a few days, except for more blue skies and warm weather.

Now, though, the nights were different, with lurid sunsets giving way to pulsing green, purple and blue smears and swirls which lit up the sky like it was alien abduction week on the SciFi Channel. Everyone was captivated by the sight – majestic and mesmerising, all at once, and as impressive in its way as the vast carpet of stars they had previously been able to see.

Dana had tried to give them scientific chapter and verse about the phenomenon of the aurora, until Poole had said "Bore-ora, more like," and another campfire evening had dissolved into a squabble. But Jordan had been astounded by the deeply coloured waves in the night sky, and looked forward to each new manifestation. They appeared regularly for a few nights, interspersed with calm, dry days, and everyone relaxed.

Until the clouds returned abruptly and the rain simply sheeted down and didn't stop for twelve hours. The same thing happened again a few days later, accompanied by distant rumbles and vivid flashes of lightning far away on the horizon.

Their camp – such as it was, a few shelters, a makeshift kitchen area, and a bubble workshop – couldn't cope. They hadn't built for the weather – or, rather they had, just for shade from the piercing sun rather than for protection from a full-on rainstorm.

Everything got soaked the first time, and was later painstakingly dried out on hastily erected stick-frames. When it started to rain the next time, they moved all the things they wanted to protect inside the pod, and ignored Reeves, who was forever bleating about microbial contamination and air-filter congestion.

On that occasion, they tried to keep themselves dry under their shelters, but the rain was so strong it battered the structures and tore away sections of canvas. The airlock-style workshop at the pod entrance that Manisha had so carefully constructed was badly damaged in the first pelting wave of water.

Eventually, they had given in and huddled inside the pod – each of them soaking wet and miserable enough to give Reeves short shrift when he complained they were fogging up his instruments.

Which brought them to tonight, when they all had all dived inside the pod the minute the rain started. That meant, at least, that they were dry. But they were not comfortable, and no one was happy.

Especially Reeves. And now, it seemed, Bryson.

To be fair to Reeves, the pod was not designed for its current use as a storm shelter. It was a simple, cone-shaped module – just tall enough to stand up in, with perhaps a fifteen-foot diameter.

With its racks and shelves, and built in Med-Lab, it had accommodated a surprising amount of gear and supplies before being launched from the *Odyssey Earth* many months ago. When the castaways had reached it, it had undoubtedly saved their lives, and when it had been emptied of equipment, the pod itself was quite spacious.

Reeves had co-opted it as his personal fiefdom – the only place, he said, that he could be certain his essential computational capabilities wouldn't be compromised. He had a thing about keeping it free from dust.

Dust. Jordan shook his head, as the rain thundered down on the pod roof. If only.

The pod had two wing-like doors that could be closed against the elements, and when they put most of the essential gear back inside, it still seemed like there was plenty of room. Of course, that was before they also tried to cram in seven humans. There was just about enough space for everyone to slouch down in something approximating a sleeping position, as long as no one moved.

Or wanted to go to the toilet. Not that there was a toilet.

There was a hand-dug trench latrine about fifty yards from the pod, though the last downpour, a couple of days ago, had turned it into a rather distressing quagmire. At this point, Jordan suspected, there would no longer be much of a delineation between latrine and camp. It probably didn't matter where Bryson pointed himself – what was a few more fluid ounces of moisture in the great scheme of things?

"It's only rain," said Reeves.

Jordan sighed. The actual Reeves – the Full Reeves, the Proper Reeves – would have known when to stop.

The most advanced AI ever created – a self-learning, self-aware, virtual human simulacrum – *was* idiosyncratic, but he only ever had the ship's, and the kids', best interests at heart. They all liked teasing each other, but at least you could ultimately count on Reeves being the grown-up in the conversation.

Not this version of Reeves, though. The Budget Reeves, the Discount Reeves, the one they had got free in a nav screen when they had been catapulted off the *Odyssey Earth* during a meteoroid strike. This diminished version of Reeves was as bad as the rest of them. It was like having a seventh teenager in the gang, even more of a know-it-all than the others. And he couldn't help himself.

"Easy for you to say," said Bryson. "You're tucked up in here. You don't have to go to the toilet."

"Such an inefficient system, I've always thought," said Reeves. "Possibly one day, evolution will sort that out for you. In the meantime, I repeat, it's only rain. Human skin has a low permeability. The keratin in the epidermis forms a protective – "

"Stop talking!"

"I'm just pointing out that no harm can come to you, if you were to – "

"No harm! You haven't ever been out in it, Reeves. It's really painful. When we were out on our trip – "

At this, there was a chorus of jeers from the others.

"Here we go, the trip again. You didn't discover rain, Bry. It's not like no one's ever got wet before."

"Yeah, Bry. You got wet that time you nearly drowned, remember? You've definitely been wet before."

"As I was saying," Reeves continued, "keratin in the

epidermis forms a protective layer that creates a natural barrier – "

"Right! That's it! Shut up, all of you."

Jordan's voice carried above the sound of the rainfall.

"If it's like last time, the rain is going to ease off and then stop in another hour or so. Bryson, can you wait until then?"

"Suppose."

"Anyone else? Right, good. Honestly. Ridiculous, the lot of you."

"I don't need to go to the toilet," said Reeves, "if that helps."

"You're as bad as the rest of them. Instead of winding up Bryson, why don't you apply your giant brain to the important things. You said you'd had some thoughts?"

"You mean the geomagnetic storms, the pheromone-responsive trees, the germinant-reactive soil, the protein-dense mycelium mat, the alien zoological specimens, and the apparent presence of four-fingered beings on a planet you had previously considered uninhabited?"

Indeed, thought Jordan. Those things.

———

The rain slowed, then stopped, as predicted, by which time most of the pod's occupants had fallen into a deep sleep of tangled limbs and echoing breaths.

Except for Reeves – Jordan never knew what Reeves did, when everyone else was asleep. Or when everyone else was awake, for that matter. Was he on standby? In sleep mode? Or – a more unnerving thought – simply waiting in silence, fully conscious, listening, observing, monitoring, until something or someone sparked a response?

And except for Jordan, too. He hadn't slept particularly well since the three of them – Dervla, Poole and Bryson – had returned from their epic overland journey.

Given the things they had seen, and the news they had brought back, Jordan was surprised that anyone could manage a full night's sleep. Ever again. And yet, there they were – demonstrating a remarkable facility to fall asleep in the most uncomfortable of positions or locations. Jordan had been sixteen, back in the day. He must have been able to do that himself once, and wished he still could.

Only, important things tended to give him sleepless nights. Four-fingered aliens, for a start. That really had been a conversation-stopper around the campfire that first night back. Evidence that they were not alone – that creatures unknown, with human-like hands, had made their mark in a hidden cave on their accidental home.

This was the sort of extra-terrestrial contact that humanity had long been seeking. And while Jordan might previously have been curious about such a discovery made by intrepid explorers on a distant planet, it was altogether a different matter when it happened in the cave next door.

That was only the half of it, of course. There was the zombie soil. Giant space cats. Overly protective trees. Biblical flooding. It was bad enough when it had just been those weird, spiny 'rollies' and purple apples, and the soaring sky creatures that at best were local vultures and, at worst – well, that was the point. Who knew?

Here they were, stranded on an uncharted planet which had suddenly and emphatically revealed its full 'alien' side. And Jordan was the only one who seemed to be unduly bothered by any of this.

Reeves, he could tell, was quite energised by all the recent evidence and information.

"Until now," he'd said, "it's been a big day for me if someone wants to play chess."

He'd analysed the soil that had rejected the archived Earth seeds that Karlan had tried, and failed, to grow. And he'd sampled the matted ground cover that Dervla had brought back from the expedition.

Some sort of fruiting fungal mat, was Reeves' working hypothesis, connected by an underground, information-carrying network of filaments. The trees were probably part of the same eco-system. And the mat itself was extraordinarily high in protein, which itself opened up another series of fascinating possibilities ... and it was at about this point that Jordan usually lost the thread of what was being proposed, and Reeves just said, "Look it's a big mushroom that talks to itself, that's all you need to know."

"I'll be the judge of that," said Jordan. "I don't think I needed to know that at all."

As for the handprints in the cave – if it had just been Poole, or even Bryson, that had reported them, then you might have thought they were mistaken. Or that they were playing some elaborate practical joke. But Dervla had seen them, too, and Dervla was sensible. Yet there was no physical evidence for Reeves to examine, and he seemed sceptical. They had been on this planet several weeks now, and had seen no other signs, anywhere else. No indication that there were four-fingered folk gaily running around, plastering their handprints on things.

"If only you'd brought back some of the cave residue," he'd complained. "I might have been able to run tests on samples of the pigment. From what you say, it seems like the cave has been in use for a long time. There might have been DNA traces. I could have sequenced – "

"Dust. You're complaining that we didn't bring back cave dust? I thought dust was the last thing you wanted around you? Excuse us for not filling our pockets with dust. We were kind of busy, what with having discovered aliens and all."

Poole had said this matter-of-factly, and Jordan realised that the others took their great discovery – if that's what it was – in the same way. They didn't seem at all surprised, or afraid, that there might be creatures

– things, beings – with hands and fingers on this planet. Jordan got the impression that Dana, at least, would have been disappointed if there hadn't.

Whereas he had grown up on Earth, where little green men had resolutely failed to appear for thousands of years, the ship kids had spent their lives travelling through the stars in the company of scientists who thought it just a matter of mathematics that alien life existed somewhere. There was simply too much universe, and too many potential life-supporting planets, however distant, for aliens not to exist. Intelligent life was out there. We weren't alone, we just hadn't found anyone yet.

And now, we had. Or at least Poole, Bryson and Dervla had. They just couldn't prove it.

They were all for going back, of course, and gathering the proof, only the rain had put paid to that for now. However gung-ho they were about it, even Poole had acknowledged the danger in taking the buggy anywhere at the moment. They had almost had a washout on their previous trip, and if anything, the weather seemed to be getting more extreme and unpredictable.

Just keeping the camp together was going to be a task in itself. If the rains continued to fall, they would have to rethink their living arrangements. Move to higher ground, maybe? Find shelter? They couldn't all live in the pod. They could barely get through the night in it.

It was another, more immediate thing to worry about – to keep Jordan awake at night. He envied the sleeping bodies around him. Didn't know how they did it.

He closed his eyes, and tried at least to doze, against the backdrop of the white noise of the storm outside.

If someone had told him, twenty years ago, before he was cryo-frozen on the *Odyssey Earth*, that one day in the future he'd be more concerned about the rain than about the possible presence of alien lifeforms …

The water continued to drum against the pod roof.

The waterfall the kids had discovered sounded nice, though. He'd like to see that. Nothing alarming about a waterfall …

Eventually, Jordan slept, and later woke with a start when he realised that the rain had finally stopped.

4

Loss

"WHAT DO YOU THINK HE WANTS?" asked Juno, not for the first time.

"I have no more information than you," said Reeves.

"I thought you were supposed to be all-seeing, all-knowing? What d'ya see? What d'ya know?"

"I don't have sensors all over the camp. Just in some of the communal areas. We agreed, as you'll recall. It's not like on board the *Odyssey Earth*. Twenty-four-hour surveillance is no longer required, now that the worst the crew can do is fall down a hole and not accidentally blow up the ship."

"I know. I'm just frustrated. He doesn't make it easy."

Juno and the Major were lounging in the New Earth comms rooms, discussing Sprake. Reeves was patched in from the ship.

It was quite the regular coffee-morning meeting,

only with Noffee – the mission's artificial coffee substitute – which meant that it was just like having normal morning coffee, except not as nice. If you stirred the Noffee absent-mindedly, and didn't breathe in too deeply, you could almost convince yourself that it was just really bad coffee.

"Thomas can probably find out more than I can," said Reeves.

"I've tried. He's a slippery chap. Our little chat made no impression on him. The bar popped up again last night in another of the bunkhouses, and he was nowhere to be seen. It sems he has a couple of helpers running things now."

"Where was he?" said Juno.

"I don't know, I couldn't track him down."

"He must have been somewhere in the settlement?"

"Then he's laying very low. I looked in every building."

"What do you think we should do?"

"I'm not sure there's anything we can do. He was right about one thing. It would be more trouble than it would be worth to try and shut him down. He's proving *very* popular in certain quarters."

"Because he's plying them with booze!"

"He is. But it does seem to have calmed down a little. It was nothing like the first night, nowhere near as wild. I think people like the social aspect. Work has gone as planned today."

"So, we should just let him carry on?"

"As I say, I'm not sure you have much of a choice.

Are we going to turn up mob-handed and put a stop to it? I'm not sure we'd currently be able to raise a mob to help us."

"I don't like giving him an inch. I don't trust him. I feel that if we let him get away with this, what's next?"

"As my brother always used to say, 'Don't look where you don't want to go.' Perhaps we should simply wait and see?"

"Didn't know you had a brother, Thomas?"

"Why, yes. Much older. In the services, too. More of a rocket man than me. Always away a terribly long time before touchdown brought him home again. Sad, sad situation. Hardly knew him, really."

Juno looked quizzically at the Major.

"Rocket man?" she said.

"Yes. Test pilot chappie. Full of good advice, whenever I did see him."

"Right." Juno rolled her eyes and shook her head. He'd moved on from quoting Bowie, then. "Reeves, what do you think?"

"I think Thomas is right. We currently have larger concerns."

"The hypersleep chamber?"

"I'm afraid the projections are not encouraging."

The *Odyssey Earth* had launched with a live-aboard crew of two hundred, most of whom had now relocated to New Earth to help with construction and settlement.

The ship remained in stationary orbit above the planet, and there were still just shy of a thousand people in the vast hypersleep chamber – all scheduled to be revived, according to a strict rota, over the next twelve to eighteen months.

However, Reeves had been running the numbers since they had arrived at New Earth, and had uncovered an alarming fact. The cryo-system was in danger of failing.

While the cryogenic process hadn't been entirely experimental, and had been proved to work, it had never been tested for a significant period of time. The Odyssey Enterprises scientists who devised it had said it was rated for a twenty-year mission, twenty-five at a push. The seventeen-year voyage to New Earth kept the system well within the limits, though Sprake's company made sure that everyone had signed enough waivers to stop them complaining in the event of a failure. What complaint a human puddle might make, and to whom, at some unspecified future point, was never quite clear.

As it happened, they hadn't had a single problem with the system while en route. Not one accident or fatality. The only death on the mission thus far had been that of educator, Sam Smart – from an undetected, pre-existing cancer. They had revived upwards of fifty people over the years, Sam and Jordan Booth included – again, all without complication. The Major had been one of the most recent to undergo the process, and Sprake and his daughters after him. The system had worked perfectly.

But now, there were definite signs of degradation.

Nothing so far that Reeves hadn't been able to fix or bypass, but the indications were that the process was compromised. He didn't think that there was an immediate danger of catastrophic failure – that was extremely unlikely, in his view – but he couldn't guarantee the indefinite integrity of the hypersleep process. The signs were not encouraging.

In fact, the signs were quite upsetting. Reeves had been wondering how to break the news.

"I regret to say, Juno, that we have had our first cryo-pod failure."

"No!"

"Yes, I am sorry. From one of the early admissions – BQ-235. I am still conducting investigations, but it seems – "

"Name? That was a person, Reeves. Don't give me the pod number, give me the name."

"Apologies, Juno, of course. The critical failure was in the pod containing Jepson Glennon, microbiologist. Born, Cambridge, 1975. Entered hypersleep, 2006. Died, yesterday, Ship Year 18, Earth Date, 2024."

Jepson Glennon. Juno mouthed the name, quietly, as she sat up straight, looking blankly at the wall opposite. She blinked back tears.

Jepson Glennon. She didn't know him, of course. She only knew a handful of the people who had volunteered for hypersleep – a couple of distant ex-colleagues, a notable name or two from the scientific world. But, as captain, they were all her crew, whether awake or to be wakened.

Jepson Glennon had had a life on Earth that she knew nothing about. Parents, family, friends. At – what? – thirty-one years old, he'd signed up for humanity's greatest adventure. A life on New Earth – experience, discovery, friendship, love – ahead of him. And now, nothing. No one back home would ever even know. And no one on the ship, among the crew, had ever met him – would ever miss him.

It was the saddest, the emptiest, the most wasteful of ends.

Juno cleared her throat. Thomas, she could see, was also deeply affected. A fellow hypersleeper, there but for the grace of – well, there was no grace here, and Juno imagined that Thomas was having his own thoughts about Jepson Glennon.

"Thank you, Reeves. That's very upsetting. I'll inform the crew. We will remember Mr Glennon together – he was one of us. Is there any immediate danger of further – failures?"

She hesitated, as it seemed a harsh word to use about the ending of a human life.

"There are no systematic faults that I can see. I am still investigating. But, as you know, the system degradation is real and unpredictable."

"Understood. We'll revisit this later, I need to think. Tell me some good news, at least?"

Reeves was happy to. He had been waiting for this moment, as much as anyone.

"Of course, Juno. Do you hear that?"

He overlaid a local solar system chart on the shared

screen and switched up the volume. A slowly repeating 'ping' cut through the air.

"That's a relay from Susannah's lander. It came back online a short while ago, from a satellite above the twin planet. It's not the lander itself – still no reliable signal – but I think they launched and tripped a signal from this satellite before making their descent. It's been fifteen days, which was the planned flight time. They've made it, Juno. They have reached the planet."

Textbook

SUSANNAH HAD BEEN RIGHT about the storm clouds. Once above the thundering falls and over the mountain range, conditions had rapidly improved. It was clear enough to bring the lander in lower and follow the river upstream, racing through a wide valley with the distant smudge of more mountains on the horizon.

"Not long now," she said to Dave, nodding at the nav screen, the craft winking ever closer to the pulse of the signal from the explorer pod.

"You think it's definitely them?"

"It must be. What else? Who else?"

"Doesn't mean they're all OK, though, right?"

"I know that." Susannah grimaced. She hated the thought that it might all be for nothing. That not everyone had made it. That they still might be too late.

"Sorry."

"No, don't be. You're right, let's not get ahead of ourselves. Locate the pod first, then we'll see."

Dave moved out of the way so that Bel and Jet could peer through the cockpit, down onto an alien planet, flashing by at high speed. Winding, sparkling river; rocky outcrops that formed a gorge; patches of woodland; grassy meadows. Wild, natural, unkempt – not a straight line, not a stone wall, not a power cable, not an evident human hand.

"Looks like home. Not London, but you know, the country," said Jet.

"When did you ever go to the country? No Abercrombie & Fitch in the country, you know?"

"Funny, Bel. I've been to the country."

"You went to a spa in the Cotswolds with Mum. That's not proper country. Not like when I went – "

"Not the so-called camping with your mates again. You slept in a double bed in a safari tent with a fridge full of Bacardi Breezers."

"At least I got mud on my shoes."

"Trainers. You got mud on your Moschino trainers. You never shut up about it."

Susannah had thought the twins might be overwhelmed by their imminent arrival on a different planet to the one they had been born on, but not a bit of it. Time to focus minds.

"Girls, look, straight ahead, there."

The nav screen wasn't showing anything else other than the pod location, but she had glimpsed an anomalous grouping ahead. Just specks on the ground, really

– could be single trees or outcrops, at this height and distance she wasn't sure. But as they roared closer, and the sun glinted off a slightly larger structure, Susannah felt hope rise in her chest and then, finally, she knew that they had reached the right place.

"See, down there!"

Bel and Jet pressed their noses against the cockpit screen, straining to see, craning their necks as the lander flashed over a clearing by the river.

———

With the storm over, the sheltering castaways had emerged from the pod, bleary eyed in the morning light.

Dervla and Manisha wrestled with the frame of the workshop bubble. It sagged badly at one end, while some of the covering material had slipped into water-logged bunches on the muddy ground.

Poole was checking the buggy – wet and out of power, but otherwise unscathed. Karlan and Dana were going through the inventory of supplies, mostly still inside the pod, where they'd been placed for protection. And Bryson was absent, last seen walking awkwardly away from the pod, with the distracted air of a man who wished he hadn't drunk a pint of tea before a job interview.

Jordan yawned. It was carnage. Water and mud everywhere. Reeves was already making his usual huge fuss about contamination – he could hear him, through the open pod doors – and while they were all dry and clean, if irritable through lack of sleep, they would soon all be wet and filthy again. And still irritable.

At least the weather had cleared up. The growling thunder and dense, dark clouds that had forced them inside the previous night had been replaced by blue skies and a warming sun. The storm had swept past them, heading upriver – Jordan could see high, distant clouds, miles over towards the direction of their old, crashed lander. Beyond that were the mountains they had cleared on their hair-raising approach to the planet – mountains that would soon be battered by high winds and driving rain.

They could simply dry everything out, and put the camp back together. They had done it before, just a couple of days previously. It's not like there was a huge amount to rebuild in any case – a few frames, some stretched tarpaulins, and a pile of stacked cases.

But it wasn't sustainable. They couldn't go on like this. With no idea of how long the storms might continue. Open to water damage, and possibly even lightning strikes.

They were far enough away from the river not to have to worry about flooding, but the camp didn't stand on particularly high ground. Each downpour made it more sodden.

They were going to have to move. And what that meant about the pod – well, Jordan didn't know. They couldn't possibly move that. And it sheltered all the important stuff they owned, as well as Reeves. They'd never hear the end of it if they tried to leave Reeves here on his own.

An hour later, the camp was looking more like a home again and less like Glastonbury the day after.

The sleeping shelters were back up, and the bundled reeds they used as mattresses were balanced across packing cases and drying in the sun. Everything they had on was spattered with mud. They were aching from their night on the pod's hard floor, groggy through lack of sleep, and their faces and hands were streaked with crud from picking things up off the claggy ground.

On reflection, it was still exactly like Glastonbury the day after.

"Jordan!"

Reeves was roaring from inside the pod. He could safely be ignored. He'd only want him to clean foot-prints off the floor, or some other menial task – which, Jordan noted, he never asked any of the others to do.

"Jordan! Poole! Anyone!"

Right, must be serious. Mud in the old quantum processor or something.

"What is it? We're not exactly having a party out here, you know? We have got things to do."

"Poole's nav screen. Is it in here? Did he have it in here last night?"

"I suppose so. I'm sure he did. Why?"

Jordan was certain he did. Poole had looked after the detachable navigation screen from the crashed lander since they had first arrived. Kept it by his bed every night, checked it every morning. The others had either given up thinking about it, or forgotten, but Poole – through habit or hope – scanned the screen daily.

In sweep mode, it locked onto the location of the pod and showed it as a blinking icon on the screen. It didn't show anything else, because there wasn't anything else with a signal for millions of miles – and probably trillions, if as Jordan increasingly suspected, the *Odyssey Earth* had been destroyed in the same accident that had cast them away.

"See if it's in here. I need to check something." Reeves sounded impatient.

"All right, calm down. What's the rush? It's not exactly a priority."

"Jordan, please."

Reeves never said 'please' to Jordan.

"OK, look, I've got it." Jordan found it on one of the cargo racks, above where Poole had been trying to sleep. "He probably just left it in here, until things dry out a bit more outside. What do you want it for?"

"Slide the power on, let me just connect, and – oh." Reeves was silent.

"Oh? Good 'oh' or bad 'oh'?"

"Look at it, Jordan."

Jordan toggled the screen and saw the blinking icon.

Icons.

"Oh."

The good one, then, apparently.

"Is that – ?"

"Yes. Incoming. Imminently."

They heard the lander before they saw it. A dull, distant roar from way downriver, that could have been rolling thunder, until a paunchy, reflective, silvery craft appeared high in the sky. The noise increased as the lander approached, and the seven of them stood stock still on the ground by the pod, faces raised to the sky.

The lander flashed overhead and then moved off upriver, away from the camp, before circling back round for another pass.

"Holding pattern," whispered Dervla, more to herself than anyone else. "Looking for a landing spot." She'd done the same manoeuvre a hundred times before on the *Odyssey Earth*'s sims.

After another circle, the lander moved further away upriver, almost disappearing into the distant clouds. After an excruciating minute, as the noise receded, and those on the ground started to look wildly at each other, back it came – slower and lower, closer and closer to the camp, before hovering half a mile away over flat, plain ground, and then dropping the final thirty feet or so, landing on hydraulic feet.

"Textbook," said Dervla. And she and the others started to run.

———

Jet looked out from the back of the lander as Susannah dropped the cargo ramp. It seemed to take an age to unfurl and hit the ground.

Maybe not like home exactly, thought Jet, as the foreground and then more of the scenery came into view. Not like England, anyway. A wide, uninhabited river valley – meadows and higher ground. Distant peaks. It reminded her of the trip that she, Bel and Mum had made to New Zealand, two years ago.

Actually, not two years ago. She'd been in what they called hypersleep, hadn't she? That New Zealand trip had been almost twenty years ago now. Jet still found that a weird thought.

And here was another one. This wasn't England, or even New Zealand. This was a different planet. Her second, in fact, after Earth. Third, if you counted New Earth, which she had seen from a spaceship but hadn't yet set foot on.

Jet thought that all that probably trumped any showing-off about the Koh Phangan Full Moon Party from the girls back home. Mum hadn't let them go to that – and here she was, on planet three by the age of seventeen.

"Ready, girls?"

Dave grinned. All four of them were now on the ramp, looking out across a grassy plain. They had landed on a slight elevation. The camp – they'd seen it from the air – lay half a mile or so away, closer to the river. And charging up the slight incline were seven figures, in a whir of waving hands and screaming voices.

"Let's go say hello to the natives."

Dave jumped down, followed by Susannah, and ran

to meet them, while the two sisters stood back, uncertain as to what to do.

Jet watched the huge, burly man scoop up the first two to reach him. They fell to the ground in a tangle and two more figures piled on, laughing and shouting.

Susannah opened her arms to two more and clasped them tightly – they were girls of about her own age, and Jet could see they were crying. Wailing, really. Susannah's shoulders heaved as she flexed her arms around the two of them, and all Jet could hear was her saying, between gasps, "I can't believe it, I can't believe it."

An older man stood back, wide-eyed, his hands tented around his nose, holding back tears. Jordan, presumably? Jet had heard a little about his story on the journey across, and even from where she was standing she could see that he was shaking – his head and shoulders were rocking in short little bursts.

Dave shrugged off a pile of bodies and turned to Jet and Bel. "Girls! Come over here. Come meet the babies!" Then suffered a flurry of playful slaps from two extremely puppy-like boys, long-haired and whippet-thin, who clung onto his arms like they were hugging a tree trunk.

Susannah stepped out of her own hug, touched the two girls' cheeks, wonderingly, and then moved forward to stand in front of Jordan. He stood there, blankly, tears now streaking his face, too.

"It's all right, Jordan," Jet heard her say, as she

pulled him to her. "It's all right now." And then after a second or two, Susannah added, quietly, "Thank you."

Jordan shrugged, seemingly lost for words. Dave loomed up and pounded his arm in delight.

"Jordan, man! Fancy seeing you here!"

Jet watched the circle of people form, and then split, and then reform, as different configurations came together to laugh, cry and hug. Now the lander engines had powered down completely, she could hear the strained voices, the half-finished sentences and questions, the sheer emotion that flowed across this alien hillside.

She saw Dave hold out a clenched hand to one of the girls and then unfurl his fingers.

"From Tills," he said, and the girl caught a breath and sobbed as she took a small brooch from the big man's hand. "She knew you'd be OK," he said. "She wanted you to have this, she's thinking of you all." The girl pinned the brooch to her top and then clasped her hand over it, pressing it close, gulping back more sobs.

"I see you all dressed up for the occasion?" said Dave. "Spring break party, was it?"

The seven castaways stopped for a moment, looked down at themselves and then at each other. Damp, mud-streaked clothes, grass stains, smeared faces, hair in all directions – like there had been an explosion in a compost heap. Someone started laughing, and within seconds they were all helpless.

"Haven't you heard, mud's all the rage in this part

of the galaxy," said one of the boys. "This is the look I like to call – 'Brown Steel'."

"Idiot!"

"Orange mocha frappuccino!" shouted at least three mud-spattered teenagers, hysterically.

"These," said Susannah, over her shoulder and over the hubbub, "are the kids from the ship. Our babies. Bel, Jet, meet Dana, Dervla, Manisha, Poole, Bryson and Karlan. They're usually *exactly* like this, by the way."

Susannah stepped aside and six heads turned to look at Jet and Bel for the first time.

Jet half-raised a hand, palm out, and smiled, and everyone looked at each other. She saw quizzical looks, some confusion, an open mouth or two.

"Hi," she said, as she took in the line-up. "I'm Jet."

She and Bel had heard so much about them over the last couple of weeks, but she wasn't sure that she had ever expected to meet them. The rescue mission had seemed like too much of a long shot and, truth be told, for Jet the greatest attraction of jumping on a runaway space lander had been the chance to put some distance between her and her father.

The stories about the ship kids – the babies, the sprogs – had been just that. Stories, about people they had never met – like being invited to show an interest in the children of your parents' friends.

But here they were. Three girls, three boys. Looked to be her and Bel's age, though Jet knew from Susannah that they were maybe a year younger.

Tanned limbs, mostly. Hair that had grown out. Some scratches and bruises. A mismatch of T-shirts and cut-offs. One of the boys – the one who'd made a joke about the mud – was barefoot. They all looked lean, athletic – the way they had *run* up that hill. A strong gaze from a couple of the girls, a catch of the eye and then a quick look to the floor by a boy. A longish, awkward silence.

Apart from the mud – and the fact that this was an alien planet and not the sixth-form common room – it was first day of term, all over again.

Eventually, one of the girls stepped forward. Confident, hand out, bright smile. "Hi! I'm Dana."

She pointed back at the others, introducing them. Some came forward and raised a hand. One – Manisha, the one who'd taken the brooch – looked down at her own muddy clothes and grimaced slightly. Jet could see her wiping her hands on her side, muttering something under her breath.

"And that's Teach," said Dana. "Jordan, I mean."

"We've heard all about you," said Jet. "This is my sister, Bel."

Jordan looked at Susannah. He seemed as confused as everyone else.

"Who – ?"

"It's a long story. But Bel and Jet are part of the crew now. They're with us."

"They were in hypersleep?" Jordan made the jump before anyone else. "But – "

"Like I said, long story. It can wait."

"Susannah?" Manisha had approached and taken Susannah's hand. "Are we going home?"

"Yes, honey. That's the plan. Soon as we're prepped."

"The *Odyssey Earth*? It's all right?"

"Told you!" said Poole.

"When did you ever tell us?"

"I knew the ship hadn't been blown up!"

"Don't say that!"

"Don't start, you two." Dana turned on them. "Sorry," she said to Jet. "We're not used to visitors."

Jet smiled. "Don't worry. I know we must be a bit of a shock, too."

"Dave, where's Tillie?"

"Is the Cap all right?"

The questions piled in until Susannah clapped loudly.

"OK, enough. I promise you, everyone's fine. All in good time. But how about you show us around?"

"Good plan," said Jordan, who seemed to have collected himself. "We've got to go back and tell Reeves anyway. We left in a bit of a hurry."

"Wait, what's that?" said Susannah. "Reeves?"

"You must remember? Self-aware techno-brain? Artificial insult-o-meter?"

"How is Reeves here?"

"Well, I'll let him explain that to you. It's very boring."

"You've got Reeves? Here? With you?"

"Part of him. Mostly, the annoying part. Come on, I'll show you."

————

The campfire crackled and flickered, and Jordan looked about him, with a rising sense of something, deep inside. Hope? Joy?

A year ago, he hadn't known any of these people. He still barely knew Susannah. And now there were two more new faces. But this felt like the start of something. Whatever happened now, at least someone had come to look for them. Someone hadn't given up on them.

For the first time in a long time, Jordan felt that he belonged.

Dave sat between Poole and Bryson, nudging them in the ribs now and again as they roared with laughter at some joke or other.

"You know we named this planet after you?" said Poole, and then embarked on a lengthy defence in the face of catcalls, with Dave smiling genially at him.

Susannah had Manisha close by – the girl had barely let her out of her sight – and Dervla was trying to bring Bel into the conversation. Dana and Jet were talking intently.

They'd finished cleaning up the camp, and had then washed themselves in the river and changed their clothes. That had seemed to brighten everyone's mood. Dave had proved to be an absolute force of nature – putting structures back together, helping as directed and then carrying down some supplies from the lander. He was the only one, Jordan thought, on either side, who hadn't seemed overwhelmed by the arrival of the rescue party. Ex-marine, made of stern stuff, no doubt – though the mere mention of Tillie tended to melt his harder edges.

Earlier, Jordan had shown Susannah the fish traps down at the river, before bringing back a catch for dinner. She had been impressed, and told him so.

"You made these? Never had you down as a bushcraft guy," she'd said.

The camp had dried out and the evening sky was beginning to show its most recent colours – blue, green and purple, with flashes of yellow and red. No rain tonight at least, thought Jordan, and a spectacular show for their visitors, as the aurora pulsed and flickered.

Susannah had already said she was going back to the lander later to sleep, the new girls too. Jordan thought a couple of the others might go with them, but Dave announced his intention to sleep out under the amazing sky and – surprisingly, perhaps – most of the castaways were happy to stay put, too. They had got used to it. Being outside, under an elemental, alien sky. Even himself, Jordan realised.

"I've always liked camping," he'd said to Susannah, and she'd laughed.

"I did not know that about you, Jordan. Guess you were the right man for the job, after all."

"I'm not sure about that."

"I am. You kept them alive. We'll never forget it."

"But how did you find us?" said Manisha, one more time, as the conversation ebbed and flowed around the fire. She fingered Tillie's brooch again, as if tethering herself to the distant ship – to the people she'd thought she had lost.

"We got your message, of course."

"Thank you, thank you very much, you're all most welcome," said Dana, raising herself up and performing a half curtsey, as the others variously cheered and whistled. "No, really, you're all too kind."

"Clever," said Dave. "Your idea?"

"Me and Reeves, to be fair. Well, Reeves figured out the technical bit, how to rig the pod's transponder, and I did the words."

"It *was* very funny," said Susannah. "Very you."

"What words? It was just an SOS," said Poole. "What's so funny about that?"

Dana raised her eyebrows theatrically. Karlan shook his head at Susannah, making a cutting sign under his chin.

"What?"

"He doesn't know, does he?" said Manisha, gleefully.

"Know what?"

"I could have just sent an SOS, but where would be the fun in that?" said Dana. "In any case, an SOS might have come from anyone."

"Who else was going to be sending out an SOS?"

"You never know, do you. You're the one who

thought the *Odyssey Earth* had been downed by an alien missile."

Manisha couldn't contain herself. "Dana's message said, 'Oops, wrong planet.'"

"I suppose that is quite funny," said Poole. "Funny for her, anyway."

"'Oops, wrong planet,'" continued Manisha, "'Poole is an idiot!'"

The crowd around the campfire erupted.

"Dana, you little nerd!" wailed Poole. "You broadcast that to the entire universe?"

"It's not like the universe didn't know you're an idiot already. I was just confirming matters with our alien brethren. Anyway, it worked, didn't it?"

"Dork."

"Why, thank you." Dana curtseyed again and sat down to a round of applause by everyone else, and to continued grumbling from Poole.

"So, now what?" said Jordan, when the laughter had died down. "What's next?"

"I reckon it's time to go home," said Susannah. "We didn't exactly have permission to use the lander, they'll be wanting it back. What do you say?"

6

Caves

"WHAT'S IN THESE, ANYWAY?"

Gerald lugged another case from the trolley into the back of the cave and set it on the floor. Sprake manoeuvred it into position next to the others – half a dozen, robust, lockable packing cases, stacked three by two. He fussed over them, and then dropped a dark, waterproof cover over the top. From the low cave entrance, a few feet away, the cases melted into the background, invisible.

"Donald?"

"Just stuff, Gerry. Don't worry about it."

Gerald wasn't worried about it. He *was* worried about someone calling him Gerry, which implied a level of familiarity that Gerald didn't have with anyone. No one on the ship had ever called him Gerry, and he'd known them all for years. He'd first met Sprake a couple of weeks ago, and still couldn't bring himself to call him Don, as invited.

Don, Gerry. Where would it all end?

"I'm not worried. But they are in one of my caves."

"*Your* caves?"

"You know what I mean."

That was the grey area here.

Gerald – being someone who preferred his own company, and didn't want to be called Gerry – had slowly extricated himself from the construction process underway at the New Earth settlement. There was so much going on that no one had really noticed the absence of a crochety botanist. The Garden on the orbiting ship – Gerald's old stamping ground – was under new management, and as long as Gerald kept an eye on the planet's fledgling polytunnels and reported on progress now and again to the captain, he had found he could come and go as he pleased.

And what had pleased him, in the first few days on the new planet, was finding a series of rock shelters about a mile out from the main settlement, screened by trees.

Here, Gerald had set up a shadow camp, just for himself, which by now was a fully self-contained hide-away where he could live and sleep. He had food, supplies, shelter, a proper bed, cooking facilities, a power unit, solar lighting, and even – after a bit of Heath-Robinson pipework from the nearby stream – running water.

The caves gave Gerald an escape from the ever more crowded settlement. No one else knew they – or he – were there, which was how he liked it. His camp, his caves.

Until Donald Sprake had followed him one day, tracking him silently to the main cave entrance. "Wondered where you kept disappearing to," he'd said. "Nice set up. You're an interesting chap, aren't you, Gerry?"

At which point, Gerald was determined to slink off into the hinterland and find another retreat, where no one could bother him, except Sprake had moved quickly to reassure him.

"I won't tell anyone," he'd said. "Your secret's safe with me. Who needs to know? Why don't you show me around?"

Gerald knew who Sprake was, and how he'd made his appearance on the ship. By now, everyone knew. And if he'd wanted to sneak himself inside a flying coffin and trust that someone would wake him properly all those years later, then good luck to him.

He'd heard the rumours about his daughters, too, though as Sprake never mentioned them, and no one else had actually seen any daughters, Gerald wondered how much of that was true.

Gerald also wasn't bothered about *who* Sprake was. Whether you were a billionaire, boffin, or biochemist – all human adults were potentially idiots, as far as Gerald was concerned. Money didn't really come into it, especially not here on New Earth. Sprake was just Sprake, and he seemed affable enough.

"Nice caves," he'd said, as Gerald had given him the tour, and then had been as good as his word, because after he'd gone, no one else had turned up at the camp. Sprake kept the information to himself and left Gerald alone for a few more days, before arriving early one evening dragging a large case.

"Store this for me, in our caves?" he'd said – and Gerald had let the 'our caves' bit go. But several more days later, here they were, stacking half a dozen cases into a side-chamber, Gerald wondering if perhaps he'd made a mistake.

"Nothing I need to know about, then?"

"Gerry, honestly. It's just some personal things from the ship. I don't plan on being up there anymore – it's easier to have them down here with me, and I need somewhere safe and dry to keep them."

Gerald remembered the single, small case that every crew member had been allowed to bring with them on the *Odyssey Earth*. A few essentials and mementoes – memories of an old life on Earth. He supposed the luggage allowance was different if you actually owned the company. Or, as Sprake kept intimating, without actually saying, if you owned the ship and the planet, too.

To be honest, Gerald didn't really mind or care. Sprake's business. What's the worst that could be in there, anyway?

And it wasn't like Gerald hadn't stretched the boundaries of what was and wasn't communal, since he had arrived on the planet. Looking around him, most of the stuff in his camp had been filched from the settlement's cargo depot when no one was looking.

"Fine, just wondered, that's all."

As long as Sprake kept his side of the bargain, Gerald figured he could store what he liked in the caves. It was his planet, after all.

It was frustrating for Sprake, having to duck and dive on a micro level. He liked – needed – to be able to get things done quickly. Macro things.

Back on Earth, if an idea had come to him in the middle of the night, he would be up and out of bed, if he'd gone to bed at all, working the phones and messaging systems. He could never understand why sleepy-sounding employees didn't just get it, immediately. It was obvious what the next step was; how the big idea could be implemented. Yes, it was day-urgent. Come on, this was going to make everything so much better!

Other people had ideas, too, Sprake knew that. But his edge – commentators said genius, though he didn't – was in unravelling the knots and putting those ideas together. He'd always been good at that. Not innate genius, just hard work.

Look at Odyssey Enterprises – a ton of brainy people with good ideas, but it was Sprake that had driven them on. Look, he'd literally put a trans-galactic, colony-ship space programme together – no one else had managed to do that. And the markets had liked him, until they didn't, but so what? Idiots and algorithms, that's all markets were.

Obviously, he hadn't liked losing almost everything to stock-market runs and the predatory circling of his ex-wife's lawyers. But it was less about the money for Sprake – though he didn't see why Nadia should get most of it – and more about the threatened loss of his pet project. The stupidity, the short-sightedness, of those trying to unravel the marvel of science, engineering and human ingenuity that was the *Odyssey Earth*.

He'd had to move quickly, and had gambled on an escape plan – another midnight idea that he'd put together in haste. And as most of his gambles paid off, Sprake hadn't been at all surprised to wake up safely many years later on the *Odyssey Earth*. Success is what happened when people did their jobs reliably and efficiently.

Bel and Jet, though? That had been a different kind of impulse decision. He hadn't given Nadia, his ex, their mother, a second thought – hadn't really considered her feelings for years. She'd get over it, he supposed, as he had had to get over not having the girls around when they were growing up.

Still, it had all been a bit spur of the moment. He didn't regret it, exactly, but he wasn't sure why he had done it, either. Probably, a therapist could tell him. Did they have one in cryo? Sprake made a mental note to check.

Anyway, not his immediate problem, since the girls

had made themselves scarce. Not much he could do about them right now, so – prioritise, organise. Much against his own theory of work, Sprake realised he was going to have to sweat the small stuff before he could start on the big stuff.

Which brought him back to Gerald and the caves.

The caves would do for now – Sprake had no concerns about Gerald, and if he started asking questions again, he could always offer him a little something.

But the caves were not the answer. The new compound *was* – the one that was being laid out at the edge of the settlement. The one that Sprake was variously persuading, cajoling or plain bribing certain crew members to help him with, whenever they had some spare time or could lay their hands on more material.

Some of them didn't even need much persuading. It turned out that if you simply asked for help, and waved a flip-screen or two, people assumed that the structure you had them working on was part of the settlement masterplan. And if they started asking questions – well, everyone had a price, even if they didn't know they had.

The pop-up drinks' nights had worked wonders in that respect.

As an experiment, Sprake had handed a few of the guys some actual money, a bunch of notes each, after they had dropped some gear off at the site. Paper money? They had all laughed their heads off, thinking it was some kind of billionaire joke. Yeah, good one, Donald.

But he'd insisted, laughing with them. Humour me, he told them. Bring the money along to the accommodation block tonight.

In the meantime, he'd worked on a couple of the chemists, biochemists, astro-chemists – whatever, didn't matter, they all had white coats and seemed to know what to do once he'd provided the starter kits. Hey presto, designer homebrew for distribution to an emerging domestic market.

The chemists had been puzzled by the offer of cash, but it was amazing how much work they were prepared to put in for a single, vintage, 1978 Darth Vader action figure. And Sprake had half a dozen of those in their original boxes.

Come the night of his first pop-up bar, 'Atmos-Beer,' Sprake had no doubt that it would be a success. He'd spent enough time in the rough-and-ready settlement canteen, picking up on half-complaints and moans about the workload.

Everyone who turned up that night got a drink – but the guys who came in carrying his cash exchanged it for another, and another, and another. And over the next couple of days, Sprake had had a steady stream of visitors to his rapidly expanding construction site asking if he needed anything building, fetching, carrying or appropriating.

Out went the cash, out went the drinks, and in came the gear and labour.

It's what Sprake did. It's what he had always done, on one scale or another. With minimal outlay, he'd engineered a closed-loop economic system that put him another step ahead of everyone else, and closer to his goal, which for Sprake was always the point. He knew the Major was sniffing about, but he thought he'd be able to continue evading him. Gerald's hideaway cave retreat was perfect for that, and Gerald wasn't going to say anything – he was as anxious as Sprake to remain undiscovered and off-radar.

And, in any case, once his new compound was in business, Sprake wouldn't need the caves anymore.

He was going to pause the bar nights for a while, too. Not because of anything Juno had said the other day, but because Sprake knew that there was no advantage in saturating a market. Keep everyone waiting for a day or two – remind them what they were missing. No harm in building some anticipation.

Meanwhile, the captain had actually called the meeting she had threatened, so Sprake thought he'd go along to that – take the temperature, see what other opportunities might arise.

He was enjoying himself, Sprake realised. Being hands-on with the small stuff? Not so bad after all.

***

This felt like an important moment, thought Juno, as she looked out over the assembled crowd. Almost everyone present, waiting to hear what she had to say.

Despite what she'd told Sprake, she didn't think she'd be reading the riot act. Maybe he was right about what everyone needed. Maybe not. But the information about the potential issues with the hypersleep crew had been sobering. They all deserved to know. But first, the good news.

"We think that the lander has reached the twin planet," she said. "I know you've been anxious about that. We all have."

There was a swelling noise – some clapping, a few isolated cheers, but mostly an indistinct undercurrent of people talking amongst themselves. Some raised arms, and lots of shouted questions to which Juno had no answer.

It wasn't like the last time, when Juno had announced that they thought the kids were still alive, marooned on the twin. Then, it had been sheer relief – a release of pent-up grief that had turned in an instant to giddy hope.

But since then, Juno hadn't had anything positive or encouraging to say about the kids or their potential rescue. At first, they had had no workable plan. And then, when their hand was forced and Susannah had taken the lander, they had had no news. No contact with the castaways on the planet, no signal back from the lander, and increasingly poor reports of climatic and atmospheric conditions.

Even now, two weeks later, with a satellite apparently in orbit, and a signal received, Juno had little else she could tell them.

"You mean you don't actually know if the lander has got there or not? You don't know if everyone's safe? If they're coming home?"

There was more grumbling, as Juno confirmed that all they knew was that the lander had triggered a signal, presumably before a descent.

"How long before we know anything else?"

"A couple of days, I'd have thought," said Juno. "Unless the conditions improve, it looks like they can't make contact until they're back off the planet. If they find everyone safe and well, they'll make a quick turn-around, I'm sure. Once back off the planet, they should be able to contact us. And then, with any luck, it's another two-week shot back here."

"That's a lot of guesswork."

"Well, it's the best I can do. This was not exactly a planned mission. You know what happened."

"We know that if it was up to you, no one would have gone out to rescue them at all."

It was just a single voice, clear above the general hubbub, but it silenced the crowd.

Juno flinched.

There, someone had said it. The thing she had worried about the most. The thing she knew a lot of them thought. The thing she had wondered about in the longest, darkest of nights. The thing that, as a captain, with responsibility for more than just seven castaways, she feared was true.

And this had been her attempt at leading with the good news.

"I'm sorry if you feel like that. I only ever have the best interests of the mission at heart." It sounded weak to her, but she could see others nodding in agreement or sympathy, which was something to build on, at least.

"You know me," said Juno. "I've always been straight with you, about everything. I think you know that. Which is why there's something else I want to talk about."

She laid out the problems that Reeves had identified with the hypersleep life-support system. Short story, there was another decision to make, because the longer they left everyone else in hypersleep, the more likely they were to face individual, and then multiple, failures.

"And by failure, I mean what happened to Jepson Glennon. His pod failed, he didn't make it. You didn't know him, but he was your crewmate, your colleague. You should have got to know him – maybe some of you would have been friends with him. Others of you would have worked with him, lived with him, found out what he liked. I've looked at his record. He was thirty-one, I can tell you that. He was one of our next generation. He studied at Cambridge. I can tell you his height, his shoe size, his hair colour. I know that his parents were still alive when he left."

Juno paused. There were almost two hundred people before her in the crowd, and the silence was absolute.

They had been lucky so far – extraordinarily lucky. Only one person had died during the entire voyage, Sam Smart. That had hit them hard enough – Juno could still remember the tears and sorrow at the commemoration ceremony, held when they had first arrived. But her death had been an accident – an error – a missed cancer diagnosis. This was different.

This was a crew member lost to the technology that they all relied upon. This touched them all. This spoke to the deep fear that many of the crew had about the hypersleep process. Lying there, asleep in the dark, for year after year, knowing and feeling nothing, until awakened – or not. After all, you'd never know. It would be as if you'd died on the very first day you entered hypersleep. Received a random death sentence from a smiling medic with a hypodermic needle.

"It's embarrassing how little else I can tell you about Jepson," Juno said. "You should have had the chance to get to know him. We all should. He shouldn't have died. And there are almost a thousand other Jepson Glennons in the cryo-hold. We can't play roulette with their lives. They should all have the same chance we've had. They signed up for the same journey."

"What are you saying, Captain?"

Another lone voice. A different one, and this time, Juno could see and hear who it was. In the enveloping silence, everyone could. It was Sprake, from somewhere in the middle of the crowd.

Was this supposed to be helpful? Juno doubted it, though she took the question at face value and answered it honestly, because she could never do otherwise.

"We need to think about the revival protocols. They've been paused while we look into this, but we may need to wake people up faster. And very soon. We owe everyone the same chance for a new life on New Earth. That was the promise we made them" – she emphasized the 'we,' looking directly at Sprake. It was his company that had recruited them. All of them.

At this, the chatter started again, as people turned to each other to digest what they had heard. The mood had changed, but Juno could still hear concern in the air.

The Major appeared at her side and touched her arm.

"Was that all right, Thomas, do you think?"

"It was hard for them to hear, Juno. But you got them back on side. You did well. You always do."

7

Daisy

"I MAY BE MISSING SOMETHING HERE," said Jordan, as they all stood around the explorer pod, its doors spread wide open.

"Almost certainly," said Reeves. Jordan heard Poole and at least one other person snigger at that, but he pressed on.

"Look, it's not like this hasn't been fun. Entertaining, anyway. You, in your little pod, doing your little sums. Us, out here, doing all the real work."

"What's your point, Jordan?" said Susannah.

"Why do we need to take him back with us? There's a proper Reeves back on the ship. And it's not like you needed him to fly out here to rescue us. You did that all by yourself."

There was a sharp intake of breath – not by Reeves, but by Dana, while Manisha said, "What?" very loudly.

"I don't understand how it works, that's all. The

Reeves you know – the one you all grew up with – is back on the ship. This is just another version. And we don't need him to fly the lander. Or have I got that wrong?"

"Another version?" Jordan could hear the disbelief in Manisha's voice and realised that perhaps he had gone too far.

"All right, not a version, exactly. I get it, he's still Reeves. But he's not the real Reeves."

"We're not leaving him," said Dana, firmly. Jordan could remember her saying something similar before, when they had first arrived, with a slimmed-down version of Reeves, which then got slimmed down even further, before being upgraded into the pod – and, by this point, Jordan had lost all track of how many Reeves there were, or if it even mattered.

"I'm just saying," he finished, lamely.

"Well don't," said Dana. "He's coming back, and that's that."

"Actually," said Reeves, "Jordan has a point. I am not technically required for the return journey, and I would be able to continue operations here indefinitely using power from the solar arrays. I would miss you, of course – most of you, anyway – but you really mustn't worry about me. What's important is that you all make your way back to the ship successfully, where I'm sure I'll be delighted to see you."

"There you go then," said Jordan.

"I'll be absolutely fine. Really, I wouldn't want anyone to be concerned on my behalf."

"Don't be silly, Reeves, you're coming."

"I wouldn't want to be a burden. I have everything I need here. Who knows, perhaps I'll learn to enjoy the dust. Please, don't worry about me one little bit."

"Oh, for goodness' sake, he's just milking it now."

"It's your fault, Teach. Honestly, why would you even say such a thing? He's coming with us, and I don't want to hear another word about it."

———

For his own part, Reeves was in two minds about the procedure.

He did want to be released from the wholly inadequate confines of the pod's comms system, where he had been forced to reside since they had first reached the camp. No offence to the lowly explorer pod, with its extremely limited capacity and lack of external sensors, but it had been like living in a deprivation tank furnished with dial-up internet.

He definitely wanted the far superior upgrade that the operating system of the newly arrived lander represented. He still wouldn't be fully himself, but he'd have room to live and work, and would finally be able to sense something.

Who knows – be still his beating binary code – he might even be able to get back to solving the Twin Prime Conjecture, once he didn't have to worry about people traipsing dust into the pod.

However, to get from pod to lander required another short journey in the detachable nav screen.

The last time he'd done it, his imprisonment had lasted four days, which had seemed like four millennia, and he'd felt sick the whole time. This time, he was only going to be carried up the hill the half mile or so to Susannah's lander, but it did mean disengagement, transfer and a hard reboot, and all the potential dangers that entailed – from memory scrape to full drive failure.

Hence, the two minds.

"That's a quantum joke, by the way," he said, "because my identity, while single and discrete, is also able to operate – "

"We get it," said Jordan, hovering in the pod, keen to move this along. "Right's, who's got the hammer?"

"Don't tease him," said Dana. "You'll be all right, Reeves."

"How are we going to do this?" said Susannah. She stood in front of the console inside the pod, holding the detachable nav screen and several cables.

"Might I suggest, very carefully and with steady hands," said Reeves. The console lights flickered as he spoke.

"Nurse, the screens."

"I'm glad you're finding this amusing, Jordan."

"What's the worst that can happen? You can hardly become any more annoying."

"Stop it, you two."

"Is that so? I could become impaired to the point

that – oh." The pod's console lights flickered and died, as Susannah made the connections.

"Reeves? Everything all right."

"I'm afraid, Jordan. My mind is going. I can feel it." Reeve spoke in a wavering voice.

"Very funny."

"Daisy, Daisy, give me your answer do, I'm half crazy – "

With Reeves now singing away, Jet, standing at the back, tugged at Dana's arm. "Is this supposed to be happening?"

"Don't worry about him, he's always like this. Well, not always. Mostly with Jordan."

"Detonation in T-minus thirty, twenty-nine …" – all the console light started flashing in earnest – "twenty-eight – "

"Pack it in," said Susannah, straightening up and turning around with the nav screen in her hands. "Right, Dana, here you are. He said you're the only one he trusts to carry him."

Reeves' voice was now coming out of the nav screen. "Twenty-seven, twenty-six …"

"Are you sure it's all right?" said Jet.

"He's just quoting from *2001: A Space Odyssey*," said Jordan. "And that's how much I have been scarred by all this. A year ago, I wouldn't have known that. Amazing what being woken up on a spaceship and then stranded on an alien planet with a glorified streaming service will do to you."

"Ooh," said Reeves, from the nav screen. "Noughts and crosses. I'd forgotten I had that."

They marched in procession up from the camp to the lander, Dana out at the front, holding the nav screen tightly to her chest, Jet in lockstep beside her.

"This is surreal," she said. "I've never met a – well, I don't know what to call it."

The nav screen coughed.

"He," said Dana. "Not an 'it'. And you call him Reeves."

"Sorry, I didn't mean – "

"It's all right, he takes a bit of getting used to." Dana rapped the screen. "Especially when he behaves like this. Although, to be fair, this isn't him. Not properly. Because – "

"Because he's a self-aware, quantum-level, ship-resident AI that had to be down-rated and partitioned in order to function in operating systems with lesser capacity?"

"Exactly!" Dana, surprised, smiled at Jet. "Jordan still doesn't get that."

"I like her," said Reeves.

"Pleased to meet you," said Jet, tapping the nav screen lightly.

Ten minutes later, Susannah made the final adjustments on her cockpit monitors. Most of the others had remained outside, soaking up the morning sun on the lowered ramp at the back of the lander, but Dana had insisted on being there as the switch was made.

"Ready?"

There was silence, and then a hum as the system rebooted.

"Reeves?"

If he had to explain it in a way that humans would understand, Reeves would have said that he could feel a warmth that had been lacking since he had first been popped out of the other lander by Poole, all those weeks ago. He felt – not complete, only the version of himself on the *Odyssey Earth* was complete. But fuller, better, more nourished, and all the other entirely inadequate metaphors he would have to reach for if asked to explain it to a human.

"Come to me, my little qubits. Entangle away, you beautiful, superdense coding protocols … "

"It worked then?"

"Hello, Susannah. Hello, Dana. You are both looking lovely today, if I may say so."

"Thank you, Reeves. Nice to have you back."

"And it's nice to be here. Now, if you wouldn't all mind going off to play, I have a lot of catching up to do."

———

"Is that Reeves singing? How many times has he played that now?" said Dave.

Music drifted out of the back of the lander. Susannah could hear the verse start up again, accompanied by a surprisingly soprano echo, half a beat behind – "I study nuclear science, I love my classes – "

"REM, isn't it? He loves that song. I think he's happy."

"And how about you, Suze?"

She looked out over the patch of grassy meadow, where Bryson was huffing and puffing at a pile of sticks, trying to light a fire, to jeers from the others. They had moved the evening meal up to the lander, where Dave had promised them a rip-heat curry from the supplies, and Karlan had nearly hyperventilated with excitement at the thought of a meal that wasn't based on fish or nuts.

She watched the young people talking animatedly, Dana trying to bring the two newcomers, Bel and Jet, into the conversation – always the thoughtful, sensible one. The boys would break off now and again to charge around after each other in an overemphasized display of bravado.

They were excited. They were going home.

"I'm happy, too. When I think of all the ways this might have gone."

"Not me, Suze. Every confidence."

"That's kind of you to say, Dave. But really, I should never have dragged you into this."

"Let's be clear, Tills dragged me into this. And I wouldn't have had it any other way. Who else was going to come and get them?"

"Do you miss her? Stupid question, of course you do."

"You might not think this to look at me, Suze – "

and Dave did a spread-hands, look-at-me gesture – "but I'm quite a big brute of a guy."

Susannah laughed.

"But if there's one thing that gets me up in the morning – one thing that makes me disobey orders and jump on a hijacked lander to go on a fool's mission – it's that little lady." He arched his eyebrows at the word 'little' and Susannah laughed again.

"So, yes, I miss her. But I knew you'd get us here, and I know you'll get us back, too."

"Fingers crossed."

That again. They would have to carry on being lucky, that much was certain.

In the meantime, Susannah was enjoying the novel experience of being off the ship.

The sky was another bruised blanket of indigo, aubergine, and emerald green, occasionally pierced by white flashes that lit up the distant hills. She had no idea that night-time could be so beautiful. Spent so long in a cockpit of one sort or another, looking out at stars – beautiful, but in a more clinical kind of way – that she'd forgotten about the attraction of earth beneath her feet, skies above her head.

Maybe – when she got back, assuming Cap didn't just chuck in her isolation before a court-martial – she'd take that ride down to New Earth. See what she'd been missing.

But until then, she had this. The kids, safe. Sprake's daughters, slowly coming to terms with their lot, making friends. Dave, alarmingly loved-up and chuffed to have a planet named after him. And Reeves, disconcertingly happy. Things could be a whole lot worse.

Later, after dinner, they sat in a circle around the fire. Eleven of them now, almost a village. A hamlet, anyway. At the end of the universe.

"It's like the Northern Lights, the *aurora borealis*," said Bel. "We saw them last winter. Mum took us to Norway. It was just like this. Electro-magnetic something or other."

"Energised particles slamming into the atmosphere, deflected by the planet's magnetic field," said Dana, automatically, to a loud snore from Poole.

"After the Roman goddess of dawn, Aurora, and the Greek god of the north wind, Boreas," said Jet, almost absent-mindedly, smiling at her sister, remembering the trip the previous winter.

Not last winter. Long years ago now. Maybe Mum had been to Norway again since then, wondering where her daughters were, wondering if they were seeing the same skies? Which they couldn't possibly be. Jet dropped her head and stared into the fire.

"They seem to be doing all right?" Dave indicated the twins, with a nod of his head. "I thought they might find all this a bit overwhelming. They've only just got used to being here, with us. But they fit right in, I reckon."

Susannah looked at Bel, laughing at something Poole had said or done. Two weeks earlier, Bel had been woken up after years in hypersleep, on a spaceship trillions of miles from Earth – put there against her will, or at least against her knowledge, and asked to accept that she could never return home. She had been almost catatonic at first, and then hysterical. Look at her now. And there was Jet, trading facts with Dana and taking everything in her stride.

It showed a resilience that Susannah envied – and that she thought their own ship kids didn't necessarily have. A rich-kid resilience, a confidence when confronted with new people and situations. These were girls who went to Norway to see the Northern Lights, who had been to New Zealand, who had flown in planes and helicopters. Sure, this was deep space, halfway across the galaxy, but Susannah wondered if it didn't just seem like another exotic holiday to them.

Bryson had finally got the fire going, and Jordan had left him to it and came and plonked himself down beside Dave and Susannah.

Here was another one who had surprised her. She had heard all about the trek from the crashed lander, and the establishment of the camp – the fires, the fishing, the shelters. Susannah would have put her money on it being Dana, or possibly Dervla, who would have stepped up to save them all. She hadn't known Jordan very well on the ship, but Bryson saving *him* from drowning, rather than the other way round, had seemed a much more likely scenario.

Yet Jordan had gone from out of place on the *Odyssey Earth* to entirely in the right place, at the right time. They – she – owed him a huge debt of thanks.

"So," said Jordan. "Home? The ship, or New Earth, you know what I mean. Tomorrow?"

"Or maybe the day after. We're still letting Reeves get acclimatised to having a giant brain again."

"And are we going to talk about the aliens, before we go?"

"Your supposed four-fingered folk?"

"If it was just Poole … but Dervla was pretty convincing."

"No other signs, though? While you've been here?"

"No – but I don't suppose we've been looking. Just getting through the days, you know? And it's not like there isn't tons more that's weird about this planet. I mean, just look at the sky. And then there are the trees, the soil – all sorts of random stuff. I haven't even shown you the self-propelled plants."

"Don't you want to go back, Jordan?"

"It's not really 'back' for me, is it? I never got 'there' in the first place."

And maybe that was it, thought Susannah. She had never understood how anyone could have put themselves into hypersleep, as Jordan had done – submitted themselves to oblivion like that.

She'd had years to commit to the mission and anticipate the end result. For Jordan, though – bang, and there he was, awake on a ship he'd never wanted to be on. And then, bang again – crashed on a planet he'd never expected to be on. She could see how that might mess with your mind, although he seemed to have coped.

"I've got used to it here, I suppose," he said. "It's not really what I'd pictured, when I thought about being on New Earth. But it's not terrible, either. I'd like to know more about it. I don't want this just to have been a mistake. How many times do you get an opportunity like this? I guess I'm torn. The longer I've spent here, the more I realise you only get one life."

"Did you just YOLO me, Jordan Booth?" Susannah fixed him with a quizzical eye, and then winked.

"I believe so." Jordan laughed, when he realised how it sounded.

"Either way, we won't even get to live once if we don't go back now. You've no idea of the trouble we're all in – though Juno might forgive us if we can bring everyone back safely."

"How can I be in trouble? I haven't done anything!"

"Well, you did all sneak onto one of her landers and then crash it. And I stole another one. I'd say we've both probably got some explaining to do."

8

Hot

"THIS IS where you've been living? All this time?"

Dervla was walking Bel and Jet through the camp the next day, with the others bringing up the rear.

"Apart from the first few days. We crashed – about forty miles that way. First time we'd ever flown in the lander."

"Well, Jet crashed Mum's Jag the only time she drove that, so I wouldn't worry about it."

"Hey," said Jet. "It was hardly a crash. I dented it a bit."

"You drove a sports car?" Dervla had run the ship's sim games a million times – X-wings, cargo trailers, high-performance bikes, rally cars. She thought she'd probably be good at driving. "We've got a solar buggy," she said. "But Poole's a pain about it, hardly anyone else ever gets a go."

"What is he? Your brother?"

"Something like that. None of us are related, but we are brothers and sisters I suppose. Family, anyway."

"Sounds complicated."

"Not really. I mean, we grew up together. Anyway, you're twins. You don't look alike, though."

"I'm the oldest," said Jet. "By five minutes. Bel's the baby."

"Baby, yourself. At least I can drive properly."

"And this is where you sleep?" Jet was moving between the shelters, running her hands along the top of the frames.

"No room in the pod, unless it rains."

"Bathroom?"

"The river."

"Toilet?"

"Don't ask."

Dervla could see raised eyebrows between the two girls, and felt oddly embarrassed. She hadn't had cause to consider it before, but for the first time began to think what it must seem like through others' eyes.

She looked – they all looked – scruffy, dowdy and unkempt compared to Jet and Bel. Even though the two girls were wearing similar clothes – actually, now Dervla looked closely, some of *their* clothes from the ship – there was an air about them. Confident, sophisticated. The sort of girls who had a mum with a sports car. Not the sort who slept outdoors in their worn, torn clothes and washed in the river.

They even spoke differently. Dervla had heard them use words to each other which, even if she recognised, she didn't understand in context. How any of their castaway experience was 'sick or 'wicked,' for example, was beyond her. Bel and Jet seemed quicker and slicker all round, as if talking in code. What was a 'Brangelina'? Dervla had no idea.

There was a buzzing noise behind them and the buggy flashed past, Poole at the wheel, Bryson in the passenger seat. They called out to the group, circled the camp, and then brought the buggy up close and braked sharply. Poole looked smug, and folded his arms, Bryson grinning beside him.

"We've got a buggy," he said.

"Congratulations." Jet looked amused.

"Have a go, if you like."

Dervla bristled. "You never say that to me. Could you *be* any more obvious?"

"What? Just being friendly."

"Showing off. It's like you've never seen a girl before."

"Not a proper one, no," said Poole, flushing red, but indicating both Dervla and Dana.

Dana shot back. "I'm not sure that's the clever retort you think it is. Would you like to tell us a bit more about your lack of experience with real girls?"

"Forget it, come on Bry." Poole gunned the engine and roared off.

"Sorry about him," said Karlan. "He is a bit full-on."

"I don't know, he's sweet," said Jet.

"Sweet? Are you kidding?"

"And what about you?" said Bel.

"What about me?"

"What experience do you have with real girls?"

Karlan looked confused, and then embarrassed, before muttering something about needing to check his garden.

Listening to all this unfold, Dervla was torn.

In a way, she felt even more of a country clodhopper, watching Jet and Bel run rings around the boys. They barely had to utter a sentence to reduce them to gibbering wrecks. It was impressive, there was no denying it. She didn't have that power over them – she wished – but then again, how could she? It was just Poole, Bryson and Karlan, for goodness' sake.

On balance, Dervla felt, it rankled. If anyone was going to humiliate and undermine the boys, it should be her, Neesh or Dana. The boys might be idiots, but they were *their* idiots.

———

The first strike hit the ground near the camp kitchen.

The sky had been darkening for a while, but the heavy clouds hadn't been accompanied by rain, so the group had carried on getting things ready, prior to carrying up some supplies to the lander.

Manisha and Karlan had taken what they needed from the pod, refilled it with the gear they were leaving, and secured the doors. The buggy was parked outside – that needed dismantling and putting back inside in pieces. They were leaving that task for Poole, and would come back with him tomorrow for a final sweep, before take-off.

Poole and Bryson were already halfway up the hill, carrying boxes, with Manisha and Karlan behind them. Dana and Dervla were walking back from the river with fish for dinner that night – they were going to show Jet and Bel how they prepared them at camp, before bringing up some cooking gear to the lander. Everyone liked sitting up there, with the elevated view, and the bulk of the lander behind them. It was a reminder of home, in a way – of safety, of security – for them all.

A bright flash lit up the sky, and Dana watched a bolt arrow down into the camp, a couple of hundred yards ahead of them. A huge, rolling boom followed, and as she looked up she could see more flashes within the clouds, sparking from one area of the sky to another.

"Lightning!"

Jet and Bel were standing closely together, and heard Dana's shout. They looked up, mesmerised by the sight of the sky, which was now a crackling sheet of sparks and flashes.

Another bolt struck the camp, this time on the far side of the pod, where Karlan had tried to establish his garden. There was another almighty bang, and a tangible fizz in the air.

Dana could feel the hairs rising on her forearm, as she looked at the ground beneath her feet. It had dried out a lot over the last day or two, since the last all-night downpour, but parts of the camp were still damp and muddy – and it was even wetter here, closer to the river.

"We need to move now!"

Dana started to run, passing Jet and Bel, who were still immobile – eyes wide, mouths open, as they looked skyward.

"Come on!"

The pair of them started to move, and Dana looked back for Dervla.

"Derv! Move!"

Now, all four were running, following Dana who was out in front and leading them on a circle around the edge of the camp.

She had thought about sheltering in the pod, but it was full of gear again, and anyway, the buggy was stationed right outside the doors. She didn't fancy being wedged between pod and buggy, wrestling with the doors, while electricity was being flung around from on high.

Drier ground would do for a start, so she kept on running, up the hill, towards the lander, checking behind to see that everyone was following. Higher ground wasn't the greatest option, but she didn't see they had a choice. The lander was their best chance of protection.

Another flash, and turf exploded about fifty feet from Bel, who was trailing behind in last place. She yelped and fell, and then scrambled back to her feet as Jet turned to help her.

"No!" Dana was waving her hands wildly, from further up the hill. Her voice barely carried above the deep boom that rumbled across the valley. "Keep away from each other!" She pointed up into the sky and then towards the lander, still a few hundred yards away. "Keep apart, but get to the lander!"

Dana could see that Jet got it straight away – safer to stay apart. She gestured at her sister, and both put distance between themselves and ran as hard as they could. Dervla, meanwhile, was coming in from another angle up the slope, and all four were unconsciously switching directions as they ran, as if they were under sniper fire.

The noise was relentless, a rolling churn of thunder, and Dana could hear more cracks as lightning strikes hit behind them.

When she looked back one last time, the camp was capped in deep, bruised-purple clouds. Flashes speared into the ground, and she saw two of the sleeping shelters take a hit and disintegrate.

Poole, Bryson, Manisha and Karlan had made it to the lander and disappeared inside, up the loading ramp. Dana ran past the boxes that Poole and Bryson had dropped and kept going until she reached the foot of the ramp. Dave was standing a few feet in, imploring her to come inside, too, but Dana waved him off and watched as the final three converged on the lander.

There were two more strikes in quick succession, on the heels of the runners.

Along the ridge beyond the lander, more flashes rained down in sequence as the clouds tumbled closer. Dana flinched as one huge rumble erupted overhead, and then a few seconds later there were strikes that tore up the hillside just thirty feet away.

One after another, Dervla, Bel and Jet charged up the ramp and into what Dana hoped was safety. They collapsed on the cargo deck, panting and wheezing. Dave hit the manual ramp button and the booms and cracks – now almost constant – were muffled slightly as the ramp sealed shut.

———

Six hours later, there had been no let-up. The lander occasionally groaned under a particularly violent shock-wave and the bang would echo up and down the length of the cabin.

Out through the cockpit window, the higher ridge was visible, lit by a criss-cross of lightning bolts that played across the valley below.

All eleven of them had moved further into the lander, away from the cargo area, whose bare panels and racks somehow seemed exposed. Instead, they had spread out in twos and threes along the opposing seats in the main cabin, trying to make themselves comfortable.

"And this is entirely safe, in here?" said Jordan, who

was still not convinced. "What with it being metal, and everything?"

"I wouldn't say 'entirely,'" said Reeves. "How about 'mostly' or 'probably'? And how many times do I have to repeat myself? Metal does not attract lightning. I have already explained the nature of a Faraday cage. The electricity – that's the sparky stuff, Jordan – travels along the outside, thanks to the conductive mesh, while surge shielding protects the circuitry from burn-through. In the meantime, the craft's static wicks – "

"Please make him stop saying things like 'surge' and 'burn-through.'"

"If you doubt my hypothesis, you are welcome to go outside onto the open land into what I like to call the 'Kill Zone.'"

"That's enough, Reeves," said Susannah. "None of us are exactly happy about this situation. It is rather unnerving."

"I don't understand how they could let certain humans into space, no less, without even the most basic understanding of physics."

"I understand the physics of on-off switches. Shall we try that?"

"Settle down, you two. Honestly, you're like children."

"He started it."

Another crack outside shook the lander, which brought silence to the cabin.

"Any more intel, Reeves?"

"I am sorry, Susannah. The current conditions

mean that I am unable to broadcast or receive. Atmospheric data remains scrambled, but the electrical storm appears to be widespread and enduring."

"We're stuck here, then?"

"Until the conditions change, yes. I do not advise going outside, it is unsafe."

"Nice one, Sherlock."

"At least it's better than the pod," said Manisha.

"Amen to that," said Dana, warming to the topic and addressing Bel and Jet. "Honestly, nightmare. You have no idea. No space to move or breathe. Foul."

"I can imagine."

"Not unless you've got brothers, disgusting brothers, you can't."

"I don't know," said Bel. "They don't seem so bad. Some of them, anyway," she said, shooting a look at Karlan, oblivious, sitting a few seats down.

Manisha heard and saw, and looked horrified. "What's happening?"

"He seems nice, that's all. Karlan, I mean."

"K? Well, I suppose he is nice, mostly. But not – surely – ?"

"You can't see it, you're his sister. But he's hot."

"Oh, please, no."

"I don't mean that you should think he is. But, look, he is. Poole, in a way, too, actually."

"No, no, no, no. No, stop it."

"I'm just saying – "

"Please don't."

"Bel!" said Jet.

"What? I'm just saying."

"You don't have to say everything that comes into your head."

"At least I say what I think."

"What's that supposed to mean?"

"Well, this got interesting very quickly," said Dana. "What do you reckon, Neesh?"

"I feel icky. I can't listen to any more of this."

Dana laughed. "Hilarious. It's cheered me up no end. Poole, hot. Whatever next?"

"Don't listen to Bel," said Jet. "She shouldn't have said anything. We hardly know you."

"Look, it's fine," said Dana. "We've lived what you might call a sheltered life."

"Sounds like it. Born on the ship. You're all, what? Sixteen? Seventeen?"

"Sweet sixteen."

"And no boyfriends? Girlfriends?"

"See Jordan, down there? He's the most eligible, closest in age to us on the entire ship. Thirty-something, going on fifty after the cryo. Most of them are much older. Though I think there are some in their late twenties in the freezer."

Jet studied him for a second or two. "Jordan's the youngest? He's ancient. No offence."

"Welcome to our world."

"Well, that would mean, if you wanted, he'd have to – with one of you – "

"Exactly."

"Unless, I suppose, you wake up one of the younger

ones in hypersleep."

"Which just seems creepy, we can all agree."

"God." Jet made an appalled face.

"She certainly moves in mysterious ways, especially when deciding to impregnate randoms on a trans-galactic spaceship. She might be omnipotent, but She didn't really think it through."

"You're funny."

"Why, thank you. Now tell me more about the Earthling heat-attractiveness quotient. Does it have a minus scale?"

"Boys or girls?"

"Let's start with boys, we haven't heard about Bryson yet. Then we'll see."

———

The barrage of noise and light continued all day and into the night. Sometimes louder, brighter, more immediate; receding at other times, but always present.

Reeves reported at least three direct strikes on the lander's fuselage – after the first he had shut down all external sensors, and isolated the comms and life-support circuits, just to be on the safe side.

It wouldn't make any difference while they were on the ground, but they'd need everything in full working order once they were off-planet. It meant pulling the power to the internal fans as well, and the recycled air inside the lander soon became stale.

They all made themselves as comfortable as they

could, which meant an initial fight for the four hammock beds that had been slung in the cabin for the outward rescue journey. Susannah and Dave left the gang of squabbling teens to it, and hunkered down up front in the cockpit bubble, where they could keep an eye on the changing conditions.

Jordan took up a berth on the floor, somewhere in the middle of the cabin, where he didn't have to see the distant – or not-so-distant – flashes.

Dave picked his way through the cabin at some point and shifted boxes around in the cargo area until he found some food supplies. He distributed rations, made sure everyone drank some water, and then the cabin quietened again as the night wore on.

The noise must have stopped eventually, because everyone slept.

And when Dave finally awoke – to daylight and blue skies – he got Reeves to restore internal power and pop the cockpit door.

"Coming, Suze? Looks like it's over."

9

Mates

JUNO HAD MADE HER DECISION. Time to wake up the Stiffs. Although she'd have to get the Med-Bay team to stop calling them that.

If she pulled some crew back from the planet to the ship to assist, they could start reviving the hypersleep contingent in batches.

The Med-Bay staff could cope with ten at a time, probably more once they were underway and had got into the swing of things. Thaw them out, tickle them pink, and send them down to New Earth – that's what they had signed up for, after all. Let them pitch in and get things really moving down on the planet.

The only limitations were how many they could revive at a time, and how quickly they could transport them to the surface.

Juno had almost a thousand people still in hypersleep. Ten at a time, every few days – that was going to take up to a year. And Reeves couldn't tell her how long they had before the pods started to fail – or even if they would fail en masse at all. A year might be far too long to wait, or the whole thing might be an unnecessary enterprise.

Well, she couldn't worry about that. She was working on the basis that she was saving lives and ensuring the future of the mission, and that would have to do.

If the system turned out not to be fatally compromised, all that would have happened is that she'd have woken up a few hundred people a year or two early. Juno could live with that – address all complaints to the management in triplicate, and check the small print on your contract.

All that said, getting everyone down to New Earth wasn't going to be straightforward. Currently, they only had one lander, which seated twenty people plus flight crew. And running that constantly, full of new settlers, from ship to planet and back again, was asking for trouble. They were already behind schedule on shipping down gear, food and supplies, since Susannah and Dave had purloined the only back-up craft.

Not for the first time, Juno was torn between admiration for a friend's heroic venture and frustration at having to be all captain-y about it.

Let's see. OK then, the revived hypersleep gang could stay on the *Odyssey Earth* at first. There was plenty of room, since most of the original crew had decamped to New Earth, and everything on board was still fully operational.

In truth, the ship was large enough to cope with the entire mission crew if it had to. They'd need to repurpose some of the deck space, ramp up production from the Garden, and think a bit more carefully about power and water, but the *Odyssey Earth* was robust enough to manage. At least until Susannah came back with the other lander.

And she wasn't even going to think about Susannah *not* coming back.

So, that was it. Start waking up the Stiffs. Sorry, the valued, comatose members of our community.

The Major was on board with her decision, as she knew he would be. Very supportive, as always, and as keen as her to get started.

"The sooner the better, under the circumstances," he'd said, before adding, cryptically, "Don't let the sun go down, ma'am, that was always my brother's advice."

That brother again, that she wasn't sure existed. Reliable but certainly unusual, our Thomas, thought Juno, but she could live with that.

She checked in with Reeves and then punched the first series of revival orders through to the Med-Bay team on *Odyssey Earth*.

"Am I doing the right thing, Reeves?"

"It's difficult to answer that question, Juno. My calculation is that you are not, at present, endangering the mission by doing so."

"That's not exactly the full-throated support I was looking for. Thomas was much more positive."

"It's a balance, Juno. You are erring on the side of

caution. That cannot be criticised. However, the full consequences of early revival cannot yet be known."

"I might be making a mistake?"

"You are human. It goes with the territory."

"Ah, the subtle dig. Just once, Reeves, I'd like it if you could restrain yourself, and tell me that everything is going to be all right."

"Everything is going to be all right, Juno."

"Well, now you're just saying that."

"I thought that's what you required?"

"Yes, but not like that. Properly. Reassuringly, because you believe it."

"You'd like me to adopt a belief system incorporating a predeterminist position regarding actions born of decisions brought about by the random firing of neurons in an adult female brain?"

"Forget it."

"I didn't mean to upset you. I still find human emotions confusing."

"After all this time?"

"The longer I have spent with humans, the more confusing it gets. You really are all very puzzling."

"Right back at you."

"How about this, Juno. Your decision is logical, Captain, based on the current evidence."

"*Star Trek*, really?"

"I find it helps, in any situation, to ask what Mr Spock would do. In this instance, I think that you are giving the individuals in hypersleep the best possible chance to live long and prosper."

Gerald wasn't much of a one for small talk. Or, usually, any kind of talk. It only encouraged them. Before you knew it, you'd be having to remember people's names and ask how they were doing, and Gerald generally didn't care how people were doing.

He did make an exception for a few of his fellow crew members. Obviously, the captain – you couldn't not answer the captain, if she asked you something, those were just the rules. She usually stuck to need-to-know questions, and rarely strayed into the getting-to-know-you side of things, which he appreciated.

The jury was still out on her new security officer, Major Chatwin, but from what Gerald had seen and heard, the Major was also a man of few words, which suited him down to the ground.

Sprake talked a lot, but – even Gerald had noticed – didn't seem to listen, so even though he saw more of Sprake than perhaps he'd like, he accepted the relationship as purely transactional. Sprake wasn't going to turn round one day and ask him how he was feeling, that's for sure.

That left Tillie and Dave, the mission quartermasters, who completed the set of people that Gerald didn't mind talking to.

They had lived self-contained lives on the ship, in much the same way that Gerald had – he in the Garden, they in Cargo – and, in as much as he admired anyone, he admired the way they dealt with the rest of the crew. Straightforward, if you didn't mess them around. Blunt, if they needed to be. Borderline violent, if you asked for it. He'd enjoyed many an afternoon watching them terrify nuclear scientists who'd had the temerity to sign out a set of adjustable spanners and not put them back in the box correctly.

Dave, however, was currently loose somewhere in the galaxy on an illicit rescue mission, which meant that Tillie was back on the ground, running the New Earth cargo depot on her own. And because Gerald needed something from the depot, and because he liked Tillie, he did something he rarely did.

He asked how she was doing.

"All right, Gerald. All right." She folded her arms on the counter, like two slabs of beef on a butcher's block, and leaned forward.

"Any news from Dave?"

"There is not, Gerald. Two weeks now. We know they got to the twin planet, you heard the captain the other night. Other than that, nothing."

"They'll be all right."

Gerald didn't know this to be the case at all, but it was the sort of thing you said, when you asked how people were doing.

"Not just Dave, though, is it?" said Tillie. "The big lump. There's Suze, put her life on the line like that. Sprake's daughters – nice girls. Not to mention our kids. There's a lot riding on that lander making it there and back in one piece. It would be nice to know what's going on."

Sprake did have daughters, then. Gerald filed that away. The man had never mentioned them, and while Gerald couldn't imagine having children of his own, he had been close enough to the ship kids for their loss to affect him.

"Is it true that you sat on Sprake?" Suddenly, Gerald very much wanted this rumour to be correct.

"I assisted him off the lander, while Dave and Suze were trying to get away. He was not as cooperative as he might have been, so I may have relaxed onto him." Tillie had a faraway look in her eye, as if recalling a fond memory. "He is not a nice man," she continued. "I would steer well clear."

This was the trouble with chatting, thought Gerald. One thing led to another, and before you knew it, you were conflicted about revealing the presence of a not-nice man's secret boxes in your hideaway cave. He decided to say nothing, because while he liked Tillie, and thought that Tillie probably liked him, he didn't want to be relaxed upon by a giant quartermaster at any point in the near future.

"I could do with a couple of things," said Gerald, changing the subject. This was the delicate part. He was running low on certain supplies, and Tillie's store was the only place to get them. "The captain has asked me to – "

"Are we going to carry on pretending that I don't know about your little camp, out beyond the woods?"

"Um … "

"It's all right, I don't mind. I know you've been

carting things out there. Thomas – the Major – saw you. He came and asked me if I knew about it."

Gerald was mortified. It seemed that Sprake wasn't the only one keeping his secret.

"Why haven't you said anything, to anyone else?"

"Let me tell you something, Gerald. We've known you, what, for over seventeen years now? There are a lot of people from the ship that keep themselves to themselves. Dave and I included, you know that. Everyone has their reasons. But not everyone was nice to those kids – not everyone made time for them, when they were growing up. And definitely not their parents. But we saw you with them, Gerald. The captain, too. Why do you think she gives you such a long leash?"

"I just wanted a place that was away – "

"Doesn't matter, I don't need to know. You're a good bloke, Gerald. We all need a place of our own. Dave and I basically lived on Cargo. You should have seen the stuff we nicked over the years – helped that we were in charge of it all, I suppose. Anyway, bottom line, you need anything, you ask me or Dave. You don't have to sneak around with us."

"I don't know what to say."

"You don't have to say anything. That's what mates are for."

Gerald gave Tillie his list and they loaded up a handcart between them, and then he waited until the cover of dusk to wheel it back to his camp.

Gerald had never thought of himself as a good bloke before. He wasn't sure he was one. And he didn't know that he'd had mates, though he also wondered about that as he made his way back to the caves.

Did good blokes do favours for people that the good bloke's mates sat on?

That was something to think about.

10

Sisters

THE CAMP WAS GONE.

From a distance, it all looked fine – the pod, glinting in the sun – but as Jordan got closer, he began to see the havoc that the electrical storm had wrought.

Fire-blackened stones that once ringed the campfire area lay split and scattered across the ground. There were scorch marks here and there, and a metal trivet that had somehow been missed in the previous day's pack-up, was embedded in the ground, yards away from the fireplace.

Only three of the seven individual sleeping shelters remained intact, though even those had fallen timbers and scattered reeds. The other four – a close grouping – had been torn apart, with material strewn far and wide.

Jordan walked through the remains. There was still a faint, burning smell in the air, and no longer any moisture in the ground, at least here in the camp. He could see some of the others picking up what was left of the workshop bubble, whose struts were piled on the ground – there were sheets of singed canvas hanging from a surviving frame.

"Are you all right," said Susannah, coming up behind him. "There isn't much left, is there?"

"I've never seen anything like it."

"Me neither. Some storm. It's like a bomb hit it."

Jordan rolled a few of the fire stones back into a circle, and then straightened up. He felt strangely affected by the devastation.

Of all the places he'd ever lived – parents' house, student halls, flat-shares, his own home back on Earth – why would this castaway camp mean so much? It was nothing – found and foraged material, some rough-and-ready construction. It had barely been comfortable. It couldn't even keep them safe.

But it had been a home, even if just for a few months. And maybe it had felt different, because it had been the beginning of something?

Every other home had meant an ending – his parents' house, empty after their deaths; his own house, a shell that he rattled around once he'd pushed everyone else away. Even his randomly allocated room on the ship – 3-4, number four on Three-Deck – had been a dead-end, occupied only briefly, given with one hand and snatched away with another.

But here? Bed Two, Camp Castaway, Twin Planet – Jordan had started something here, and he felt its loss keenly as he walked among the wreckage. He'd helped make this place. Who knows what it might have become, if their rescuers hadn't arrived – or perhaps it, and they, wouldn't have survived much longer? Either way, it had been as much a home as anywhere else in his life.

Susannah tapped his shoulder, as they heard a shout from over by the pod. Some of the others must have shunted the buggy aside, because Poole and Bryson were wrestling with the pod doors, one of which was buckled and misshapen.

"Direct hit," said Dervla, as they approached.

Jordan could see scorch marks on the exterior, and a pile of gear on the floor inside. Poole and Bryson wrenched the broken door off and threw it to one side, and then forced open the second door, folding it back on itself. The others peered in as Dana stepped gingerly through, picking her way over blackened boxes. It looked as if someone had set a fire inside.

"No power," she said, punching buttons on the shattered console. Poole joined her and prised off a panel, crouching down for a better view.

"Cabling, all burned out." He traced his hands under the console, and then pulled more panels away, one after another, around the pod interior. "The whole lot." He held up smeared, sooty hands.

"The Med-Lab?"

Dana pulled hard at the covering shutters, exposing the equipment. There were cracked and shattered vials on the shelves, and the scan-screen was heavily chipped and scarred where the diagnostic arm had swung loose against it.

"Wouldn't matter anyway, without any power."

"Well, this officially sucks," said Bryson.

"Lots of this stuff is salvageable." Dana was moving boxes and containers, and opening lids and latches. "And we got some of it up to the lander yesterday. This was mostly camp gear, for if anyone came back."

"The Med-Lab, though? And the comms console."

"I know, that's not good. But look, everyone's all right, and we've got the lander. We're leaving anyway."

"Good job. Because my bed seems to have been blown up." Poole stood at the pod door and gestured at a pile of wood splinters and burned reeds.

"How can you tell? Looks pretty much like you left it every morning."

"Amusing."

"I aim to please."

———

Karlan had wandered away from the pod and was staring out over the camp.

"Are they always like that?"

"Who? Oh, yeah, mostly." He looked quickly at Bel, and then looked away again.

"A brother-sister thing?"

"I guess."

"You don't join in much, though, I've noticed."

"Poole's all right. Mostly. Dana can't help herself,

though. Always needs the last word."

"A bit like Jet."

"It is? How come?"

"I don't know. Older sister thing."

"You're twins, though, aren't you?"

"You better believe that five-minute age gap is important to her."

Karlan looked at the ground and shuffled his feet. "I've got to go."

"OK."

"I mean, I don't have to. But I've got this garden. I was going to check on it. Silly, really, but I've got some seedlings, well, there might be some seedlings, and – anyway. You can come if you like. It's over there. Just, you know, past … " Karlan eventually stumbled to a halt.

"Are you asking if I'd like to come up and see your seedlings some time?"

Karlan flushed red, again, before Bel took pity on him.

"Come on, show me," she said.

He led her around the back of the pod, and walked her over to the patch of land he'd previously tried to cultivate with seeds from the explorer pod cache.

"Only, they didn't take." He explained about the several attempts he'd made, when he thought an animal or birds had been digging them up. And he told her about the all-night vigil he'd undertaken, again to no avail.

"Weird."

"I know, right? We think it's something to do with the soil here, and the particular way that the indigenous plants have developed. Reeves reckons it's all connected, and I think he might be right."

Karlan became more animated as he told Bel the theories, and also the things that the others had observed on their expedition the previous month.

"So, I took seeds and cuttings from plants that already existed here," he said. "That broccoli stuff grows wild, look." He showed her the patch that was next to his seedbeds. "And I found other things, too – fruits, nuts, at least that's what they look like. I wanted to test them out, see if Reeves was right, so I replanted a couple of weeks ago using native plants."

"And?"

"Let's see. To be honest, I'd be surprised if anything survived, after the storms and the lightning."

Karlan looked around. There were strike marks – burns, churned-up earth – as far as the edge of the pod, twenty yards away, but nothing beyond. His raised beds were still intact, though the netting cover he'd tied in place was sagging here and there.

"Probably the weight of the water, when it rained," he said, peeling back the cover. "Hey, look."

Bel crouched down to see, as Karlan gently touched some of the obvious green shoots and sturdier cuttings.

"I never got anything to grow here before." He turned his face to smile at her. "I think Reeves and Neesh are probably right. They figured it out. Somehow, the soil – the planet –can tell."

"You're really into all this, aren't you?"

Karlan straightened up. "I suppose. Yes. But not just this," he said quickly, thinking that gardening was probably not the sort of thing that Earth girls were interested in. Not in the films that Sam Smart had shown them, anyway. No one in *The Breakfast Club* or *St Elmo's Fire* was into gardening. Ferris Bueller didn't take a day off school to plant out his begonias.

"What else, then?" Bel looked amused.

"Music, I guess … "

"You are? Cool. You had music, did you? On the ship? Sorry, stupid question."

"We have *all* the music. Reeves does, anyway, and then Sam – she was like our mum – got us into it. Not all of us. Poole has no idea, don't ever listen to his playlists. But, yeah, music. I do my own stuff, too."

"You do? That's so cool. My mum would love that. She was a model, and then in a band for a while. She's big into vintage Eighties' girl-bands, new wave, all that stuff. Not vintage for her, I suppose. Named us after the singers in her two favourite bands. The Go-Go's – "

"You're a Belinda!"

"I know, right? After Belinda Carlisle. What can I say, I prefer Bel. And what if I told you that my sister's real name is Joan … ?"

"I can see why she goes by Jet. Should have two Ts, though, right?"

"You know, you're the only person that's ever got that. That's how she spells it but no one else ever does, drives her mad."

"Told you, music. That's me."

"So you did. Music and gardening. You're quite the unique combination, aren't you?"

———

Back at the pod, Susannah and Jordan were pulling out damaged gear, while Dana was assessing what could be saved and repacked. Poole and Bryson were checking over the buggy, which – remarkably – appeared to be undamaged.

"You're back," Dana said, as she spotted Karlan and Bel.

"The seed patch is untouched," said Karlan, "and there's new growth. Neesh, you were right."

"It's the cosy couple," said Jet. "Nice day out at the garden centre?"

"Yeah, good one, sis. It's actually quite interesting, K said – "

"K, is it now?" said Manisha, ears pricking at the shorthand.

"Very cosy, it seems."

"All right, settle down – Joan, is it? Or Joanie, maybe?" said Karlan.

Jet flashed a dark glance at Bel, who smiled sweetly.

"What's that, K?" said Manisha, heavily emphasizing the 'K.'

"Nothing," said Jet quickly. "It's nothing." She looked around and changed the subject. "What's next?"

"This is all very entertaining," said Dana. "But if

you crazy kids have finished, I could do with some help down at the river. We left some of the fishing gear there, and a couple of water containers. It might all still be down there, it's worth a look. We should pack everything up if we can."

She set off towards the river, Jet following, with most of the others eventually trailing after them, and Karlan and Bel at the rear.

"Sorry about her."

"Don't worry. I've got sisters, too, remember? They're all a nightmare, at times."

They came to a halt at the muddy water's edge, where Dervla and Manisha were already retrieving scattered items that they had overlooked the previous day.

Karlan looked out at the river, tumbling past, remembering the first time that they had ever seen a river, shortly after they had arrived. Remembering how cold it was, how fast it ran. Just a few short weeks ago, but it seemed like another lifetime.

Bel and Jet were talking to each other, laughing. Just like that, thought Karlan. He never really understood what was going on when Derv and Neesh got fired up like they did, and then were back to besties the next minute. And now here were two more into the mix. Another change, just like that. It was going to be hard to keep up.

When you were a kid, life seemed like one long day, without end. You got older, but nothing much changed. Eat, sleep, play, repeat. Hang out with the sibs, watch films and talk music with Sam, work in the Garden. On the ship, the sun didn't even come up and go down. One long day, and nothing much changed – ever.

Until now, when you didn't know if you were going to get through the day without being zapped or flooded. Shocked or soaked. Teased by strange girls you didn't know or mocked by equally strange girls that you did know. Life, thought Karlan, was proving to be a whole lot more complicated off the ship.

"Dana?"

Karlan had spotted her further up the riverbank, standing apart from everyone else. She was looking away from the river and didn't turn round when he called. As he got closer, he could see that she was upset.

"Sam," she said, simply, and Karlan followed her gaze and saw the pile of stones.

Sam's Place, that's what they had called it. A small clearing by the river, away from the camp, where they had built a stone cairn in memory of the woman who had raised them. They'd come down here a few times over the weeks, to add another stone to the pile, to sit around a fire, or just to look up into the night sky at the stars that Sam would never see.

The cairn was their connection to Sam and the ship, their reminder of another life, their anchor.

The lightning must have struck it head on. There were shattered rocks to all sides – some of the bigger river boulders were split clean in two, and Karlan could see fragments spread along the ground in all directions.

"We can build it up again," said Karlan, starting to

roll a couple of the stones back towards the jumbled pile.

"Don't," said Dana, wiping her eyes. "It was just so that she could be with us. But we're leaving now, we have to. It's all destroyed here. She can come with us instead. We'll build her a new cairn on New Earth. That's where she – we – were supposed to be, after all. It's time to go back."

"If you're sure."

"I am. It was just a pile of stones."

They carried the gear back between them to the camp, where Dave had come down from the lander to join Susannah and Jordan. As the kids approached from the river, he stepped out to meet them.

"Bad news, I'm afraid," he said.

"You've run out of curry?"

"We have to leave Poole behind?"

"How is that bad news?"

"Good point."

"Reeves can't get the air-con to work?"

"I am not spending two weeks in that lander without a steady flow of internal air."

"I can provide a steady flow of internal air, no problem."

"Bryce, you really are foul."

"Guys!" Susannah shushed them. "Listen to the man."

"The lander isn't going anywhere," said Dave. "Seems like we took a hit, after all. It doesn't look good."

11

Normal

"SO, WE CAN'T JUST - "

"No."

"And there isn't a way that – "

"No."

"What about the – "

"No."

"Well, that's all I've got," said Jordan.

"You've been most helpful, as always," said Reeves.

"Isn't this your fault?"

"And most amusing, as always."

"You were supposed to be protecting everything, I thought? With the surge thingy? And the bundle-shield thingy? And the diverter thingies?"

"You see what I've had to put up with?" said Reeves to Susannah. "This high-level scientific discourse is simply exhausting. It's as if Stephen Hawking is here in the cabin."

"Rude. I'm only trying to understand the problem."

"David." Reeves raised his voice, so that it carried down through the open hatch in the cockpit floor. "Would you care to take over? I'm feeling faint with the effort."

Dave popped his head up through the hatch. His face was streaked with soot marks.

"All right, Jordan. How much do you know about avionics, electromagnetism, and conductivity?"

"As much as the next man."

"Let's say you're the next man."

"Nothing then, obviously."

"He can tell you what Vikings ate for breakfast," said Reeves, quietly.

"What's that?"

"Nothing. Carry on, David, you're doing very well."

"Tell you what, stick your head down here, have a look."

Dave ducked down again, and Jordan crouched and peered into the hatchway. Dave had shuffled a couple of feet along an access chamber, which had been built for an average-sized human and not one chipped off the side of Mount Rushmore. Even if everything was working normally down there, Jordan doubted things would run properly with an **XXL** quartermaster wedged in place.

Jordan followed Dave's outstretched arm.

"You see this black panel here?"

"Yes."

"And then, you see when I take it off, like that, how it's empty?"

"Yes."

"Well, it's supposed to be white, and it's supposed to be full of little wires."

"Ah."

"And then, you see all these other black panels?"

"Right, I get the picture. But you can fix it, right?"

"I could, if I had replacement units. All the tools I'd need are in the pod. But I don't have any units, because — "

"Because this was a one-in-a-million strike," said Susannah. "And because we stole this lander, and because we're two weeks and three million miles away from the only workshop that has replacement units."

"And without the units … ?"

"The electronic flight displays, comms and atmospheric sensors won't work. We can take off and fly but we'd be flying blind. We can't find the satellite and talk to the *Odyssey Earth*. And we have no idea what the weather's going to do. And the weather, as you may have noticed, can be brutal in these parts."

"They all do seem like big problems."

"You said it."

"So, without being able to replace the parts that were burned out after we were hit by lightning, we're stuck here? Again?"

"That's about the size of it."

"I do believe he's grasped it," said Reeves. "I'm still working on the comms link, and have some suggestions about how we might proceed, but as for flying, I'm afraid there isn't an obvious solution at present. Perhaps if we – "

"We just need replacement parts, then?"

"And he's back," said Reeves. "Dave, you will have to start your explanation again from the beginning. Imagine you are talking to a mollusc; I find that helps."

"Yes, Jordan," said Susannah, more patiently. "Can't fly without the units, like I said."

"Well, I know where there are some," said Jordan.

There was a slight noise from the cockpit console, which could either have been a crackle of interference or an AI snorting.

"The lightning strikes may, of course, have affected the neuro-circuitry in the underdeveloped human brain, it's always a possibility. I'd need to see a slice of the cerebral cortex. I don't think he'd miss it."

"The lander," said Jordan. "The other one. The one we arrived on."

"I thought you said you crashed it?" said Susannah.

"I didn't crash it, Reeves did." Jordan carried on speaking over objections from the console. "But it didn't burn, it just sort of crumpled. Reeves and Poole said it was never going to fly again, but that doesn't mean the parts aren't any use. Does it?"

"Jordan, you little beauty!" Dave's head popped up again from the hatch. "He could be right. Got to be worth a look."

"How do we know it hasn't been struck or damaged since?"

"We don't, unless we go and see."

"Jordan, what do you reckon?"

"You're asking *him*?" Reeves sounded incredulous.

"You saw it, after the crash? Could be a chance, right?" said Susannah.

"Well, it's just an idea. What have we got to lose?"

"I am not going back in that nav screen," said Reeves. "Don't even think about it. I've just got comfortable in here."

"Who says you need to come? This is a job for feet and fingers. You can stay here, twiddling your switches."

Outside, talking to the kids, Jordan was surprised how readily everyone accepted the situation. He had expected disappointment, at the very least – maybe devastation, given that they had all thought they were going back to the *Odyssey Earth*.

But the arrival of the others – Susannah, Dave, Bel and Jet – seemed to have energised them. They hadn't been abandoned, after all. Someone had come for them. And this latest setback didn't seem to concern them half as much as it concerned Jordan. In fact, they were buzzing once they heard about the plan.

"Because you know they trust you, right?" said Susannah.

"You could have fooled me."

"I've known them all a long time. Dana, she listens to you the way she does me, or Dave. And she's no one's fool. Poole – he says you're 'all right,' and believe me, that's high praise."

"He does? When did he say that?"

"They told me about your trip here – your trek from the lander. You saved Bryson's life. You kept them going. They respect that."

"I was just doing – "

"Doing your job? Not really. It was a lot more than that. And they know it."

"I've just got Reeves to convince, then?"

"Reeves? Are you kidding? He's one of your biggest fans."

"Oh, come on."

"I'm serious. He only makes fun of the people he likes."

"He must like me *a lot*, then, because he never stops."

"Well, there you go. He knows what you did for the kids. Apart from Sam Smart, he's the closest thing any of them have ever had to a parent. If you're good to the kids, Reeves will have your back."

"So, when he calls me a single-celled meat-puppet?"

"That's him being nice. If he really didn't like you, he'd call you Mr Booth. Has he ever called you Mr Booth?"

Jordan thought back. Not since their first meeting, no, he hadn't. Not even then, as Jordan recalled.

Well, well. Reeves, his number-one fan. Jordan wasn't going to get too comfortable with the idea – he'd read Stephen King's *Misery*, after all – but it was certainly something to consider next time Reeves started in on him.

"Come on," said Susannah. "Let's get this show on the road."

———

There was plenty to think about before sending out yet another salvage party to the wrecked lander.

The weather, for a start.

The last torrential downpour had been three days ago; the lightning storm a day ago. It was dry and clear now, but no one knew if there was more to come. And now the pod was effectively a wreck – no longer weatherproof, anyway – and the camp in pieces, it made sense to relocate to the lander.

It might not be going anywhere right now, if at all, but it was a secure shelter with plenty of space. It also seemed a safer bet to sleep in, until they were sure that the storms had blown themselves out.

Dana had things sorted out within the hour. She cajoled most of them into ferrying gear and supplies up the hill to the lander, and there was soon a growing pile of boxes and cases on the scorched grass outside the craft. She insisted on opening everything up, checking its contents, and noting it down in her inventory.

"I'll give you a hand," said Jet, ignoring Poole's groans as Dana urged him to double-check one of the boxes he'd carried up.

"Thanks," said Dana.

"Details, right?" said Jet. "They're important. Give it here, Poole, and stop moaning." She leaned over

Dana's shoulder, added a couple of checkmarks, and moved onto the next pile. Dana watched her for a second or two, approvingly, and then left her to it. Poole looked wounded.

"It was bad enough when there was just one Dana," he said pointedly.

Meanwhile, there were discussions taking place about the make-up of the salvage party.

Dave, obviously, had to go. "If you're OK with that, Suze?"

"You're the only one who knows how to get the units out, and then re-fit them. It has to be you."

"And Poole has to go," said Jordan, surprising himself as he said it. But it was true – Poole was the best at driving the buggy, and he knew the way. He'd been there and back several times already.

"And the buggy's all right?"

"Seems so. Poole reckons it just needs recharging. It'll be ready to go tomorrow, provided the solar cells weren't damaged. They look all right."

That left one place in the buggy, at most, perched in the back on the flatbed. If the units were salvageable, they would need as much space as possible.

If they weren't damaged.

If Dave could get them out.

If they could drive them back safely across rough terrain.

Another lots of ifs, thought Jordan. This planet was good at ifs.

"I'm going," said Manisha. "Derv and Bry have

already been on their little escapade. It's my turn."

"What about Karlan and Dana?"

"Yes, well, I don't think they'll be that bothered, do you?" She nodded over to where Dana and Jet were engrossed in arranging boxes into neat rectangles. "I don't even know where Karlan is – probably off on another little nature walk, showing Bel the pretty flowers."

"You should go, if you want to," said Susannah. "But – you know – it'll be you and Poole … "

She didn't need to spell it out. If there were two of the six that brought out the worst in each other, it was Manisha and Poole.

"I can handle Poole. Anyway, he'll have to do what Dave says. It'll be fine. I'd like to go."

———

That night, they sat for one more time around a large fire on the hillside.

"This almost seems normal," said Susannah. "At least, you make it seem normal, all of you."

"How do you mean?" said Jordan.

"Look at them." She gestured around the fire at the kids, variously chatting or eating. Poole said something, and Jet and Karlan guffawed. "No one seems to have a care in the world."

"I reckon that was Dana's doing. She told us some home truths, a few weeks ago. Said we had to make the best of things."

"She's a wise one. But they had you, too."

"I don't know about that. I'm not sure there's been anything normal about my life since I agreed to be flown halfway across the galaxy in hypersleep."

"And how's that working out for you?"

Jordan laughed. "Not like I expected."

"What did you expect?"

"Erm, let's see. Fewer campfires. Fewer terrifying electrical storms. Food I didn't have to catch. A bed not made of twigs and leaves. How about you?"

Susannah frowned and raised her head slightly, thinking.

"Good question. Truthfully? I never really thought beyond life on the ship. I knew we'd get there one day, but I hadn't figured out what I thought about that. Haven't figured out. Am still figuring out." She laughed. "No, I didn't think I'd be sitting around a campfire like this, on the wrong planet. With two stowaways and a history teacher."

"You know what's really weird, though?"

"What's that?"

"It's not the worst thing in the world, is it?"

"This, from the man who was outraged at being woken up on a spaceship in the first place. You're full of surprises today, Jordan Booth."

"And if we end up having to stay? If this really is it, for us all? If this turns out to be permanently 'normal'?"

"One thing at a time, Jordan. One thing at a time."

12

Video

IF HE CRANED HIS NECK, from a contorted seating position at the end of his bed, Dale could just about look out through the small window.

Not bed. Bunk. And barely a window. Porthole, at best.

It didn't look a lot like the video. None of it. Not the building, not the bed, not the window, and not the view.

'Your new start on New Earth' might not have had the same impact on prospective settlers if the video had shown a bunkbed with a view of a building site. Instead, it had shown a residential, white-picket-fence neighbourhood spreading across a manicured plain, with retro golf-buggies beetling between the buildings.

And while Dale understood how advertising agencies might take certain liberties with their presentations, he thought that his current view – of a couple of hairy labourers staring mournfully into a hole – fell rather short of the promise that had been made to him.

Of course, he was here early. He understood that, too. 'Operational reasons,' they had said, when he had been revived on the *Odyssey Earth* a week ago, and for the first couple of days he didn't really care either way, on account of the vomiting and dizziness. Like the morning after a night on the cheap wine at an office party, only instead of waking up on his sofa in Basingstoke in his pants, he'd found himself fifty-eight trillion miles from Basingstoke – and almost eighteen years in the future.

No pants, either. Apparently, organic material interfered with the nano-bots in the cryo-pod.

He'd been given a new set of clothes and, after a day or two, felt well enough to wander around the ship. He'd never actually seen the *Odyssey Earth* before boarding – just attended a medical facility in north-western Scotland before the launch, where he'd undergone the cryogenic procedure, which as far as he was concerned had started and finished with the scratch of a needle in his arm. And then *sayonara* Scotland.

He'd woken up in another medical facility, this time on board the ship, and he had to say that the *Odyssey Earth* was far more on point, when it came to the advertorial copy and promotional videos.

He had a fully fitted room of his own – nice and off-white, like someone had been to IKEA – with its own en-suite shower and toilet, and a gym and a café down the corridor and up the stairs. Select from a menu, push a button, and a few minutes later you had a bowl of noodles delivered.

There were unlimited refills of something they said was coffee, which was at least no worse than anything Dale had ever had in a flatpack furniture depot off the M25. Hot showers. A lovely sort of park-cum-garden on another deck, where you could sit on a bench and breathe in the scent of a thousand flowering fruit trees.

And the observation deck … now, *that* was a view. Again, the sort of scene that had played a big part in the brochures. Dale had spent hours there, gazing down at the hanging planet – New Earth – where his new start awaited.

For those same, nebulous 'operational reasons,' Dale had found himself on a lander-shuttle flight after a week, with nineteen other newly revived settlers. They were a mixed bunch – of different trades and skills – but none of them had expected to be woken up at this stage of the settlement's development.

Not that there was a lot that they could do about it – "We can't refreeze the gentleman, if that's what he means," one of the medics had said to him – and, in any case, it promised to be an adventure.

Let's face it, no one signed up for a one-way, trans-galactic journey to a new planet, without expecting a certain amount of – well, uncertainty.

They were going to help build the future, the captain had said, during a little pep talk. Just a bit earlier than they had planned, and when she said 'build,' she meant actual building, because they needed the labour, and yes, they could all check the small print in their contracts if they liked.

Dale stood up and moved across to the window for a better look. He was due out on site again in an hour, so he needed to get ready for his shift.

The communal bathroom was at the far end of the bunkhouse, and the showers, he already knew from experience, were tepid at best. They had a couple of plumbing engineers working on the system, but until they could coax more power from the solar arrays, facilities were still rudimentary. The trick was to get in early, before everyone else.

His bed was one of twenty-four in this bunkhouse, and there were another four buildings just like it, with several more in the early throes of construction – hence the hole and the hairy men outside. This was all slated to be temporary accommodation, just while the settlement was established, but Dale had heard grumblings from those who had already been living here for several weeks.

Back towards the central comms and ops centre there was a large, covered, outdoor canteen. He could grab some breakfast before work, and while there was plenty of food, it was of the porridge-and-stews variety, cooked in bulk for an increasing roster of crew. Everyone put in a stint, working there once or twice a week – seeing as no one had thought to wake up an actual chef yet – and surprisingly, Dale didn't mind that. Maybe he'd see if he could pick up more shifts in the galley – it beat digging holes, that's for sure.

Complaining about digging holes didn't get you anywhere. Dale had pointed to his academic qualifications, only to discover that everyone in his bunkhouse had even more degrees than he did. Those two out there, right now? The Hairy Brothers? One was a lawyer, the other a neuroscientist, but until this settlement had hot showers, nicer rooms and better food, there wasn't going to be a whole lot for them to do. So, digging holes it was.

To be honest, Dale didn't mind doing the manual work. He could see the point. They were supposed to be pioneers, settlers. He hadn't been entirely taken in by the videos and brochures, and had always suspected that the early years might prove tougher than suggested. This was a new planet in the middle of nowhere. A bit of roughing it was to be expected. He just thought that he'd have been woken up when some of the roughest bits had already been done.

And he could really do with a proper hot shower, and a bowl of something that wasn't unidentifiable protein in a brown sauce.

Over breakfast – scrambled eggs that weren't really eggs, but were definitely something scrambled – Dale passed the time of day with a couple of other early risers from another bunkhouse. He'd seen them around before – an older pair, in their fifties, which he thought meant that they were part of the original crew. The ones who had flown out with the *Odyssey Earth* – the 'Real Timers,' he'd heard them called.

That was another way that real life diverged from

the prospectus. The bright, white campus buildings, the parks and fountains, the golf buggies, and picket-fenced housing – in the videos and promotional images, everyone was Dale's age, in their early thirties. Young-looking, athletic, bouncy, as if they'd stepped off the pages of a modelling catalogue, which, now he thought about it, clearly they had.

What Dale hadn't really considered at the time were the implications of a seventeen-year voyage with a real-time crew – which meant that most of the people he'd seen out and about, on the ship and now the planet, were in their very late forties at best and some considerably older. The captain? Mid-fifties, guessed Dale. And these two, sitting at his table, the same. Young and bouncy, they were not.

"Still here then, Dale?" one of them said.

Dale smiled. Old people's conversation openers. The best.

"What can you do?" He shrugged. "Operational reasons, can't be helped. Anyway, I don't mind, not really."

"That's what they told you, is it? Operational reasons?"

Which is when Dale learned about the problems with the hypersleep chamber.

"You're lucky, if you ask us," said the man. "Who knows how long the system will last. Better up and awake than – the alternative."

"It's failing?"

"That's what Juno – the captain – told us. We lost

one already – his pod failed. That's why you're up. That's why there are more of you every time we look."

"That's awful. She never said anything about that."

"No, well, she's not daft. Probably doesn't want to panic anyone. Look, we've known her a long time. Good at her job – well, her old job. Getting us here. Won't hear a word said against her for that. No one else could have done it."

"But?"

"But – things are different now. Look around you. Does this look like things are going well?"

"I don't know. It's still early days, I suppose."

"No one's happy, Dale. We're way behind where we should be. We had a nice, warm ship to live in until a month ago. Now look at what we're being asked to do." He gestured at the surroundings. "And it's only going to get worse."

"How do you mean?"

"Think about it. If the hypersleep system is in trouble, there are going to be more and more of us awake and down here. I know, I know – 'We'll get everything done much quicker with a bit more help.'" The man put air quotes around the last bit. "But where's everyone going to go? The facilities can barely cope, as it is."

"There must be a plan?"

"If there is, it's not apparent. No one's really getting to grips with what's going on. Look, like I say, Juno – great ship's captain, but maybe this was always going to be a job for someone else, once we'd reached New

Earth. Different set of skills, different focus. I don't know why they didn't think of that."

"I didn't realise things were so bad."

"Not bad, exactly. But could be better. Bit more communication would be nice. You didn't even know about the hypersleep, did you? And how often have you seen Juno – down here, helping out, mucking in? Or that Major of hers? He's new, too, like you, but we don't see much of him. Fair's fair, they still have responsibility for the ship. But that's our point. It's two separate jobs. And the one down here – the one we all came for – is lagging. And I'm too old to spend much longer in a bunkhouse with a crappy water supply. I'd rather be back on the ship than put up with this."

That, Dale could sympathise with. So would he, and he'd only had a few days of it. The ship had pizza and flushing toilets.

And his new friend was surely right. There were a thousand people in hypersleep on the *Odyssey Earth*, he knew that. A thousand extra people down here instead, in poorly equipped barracks, without the infrastructure to support them – that really wasn't what the videos had promised.

The three of them cleared their plates and moved away from the canteen, with the next shift about to start.

"Nice talk," said Dale. "Illuminating, anyway. I didn't know any of this. Thanks, I guess."

"Tell you what, Dale. Come over to our bunkhouse

tonight. We've got something happening. A little get-together, a few drinks – "

"Drinks? Really?"

"I told you it wasn't all bad. Anyway, come along. There's someone you should meet. He's got a few ideas about all of this, you might be interested to hear what he's got to say."

13

Bunker

SO FAR, it was Humans 1, Goats 0.

The perimeter fence had held since its construction at the end of the second week of the settlement. It ringed the entire township in a skein of trestles and wire, with gates and access points at intervals, and it seemed to have done the trick.

Apart from experiencing the occasional, buccaneering specimen, charging in behind a laden buggy or work detail, with a glint in its eye and a flap of its giant ears, New Earth's settlers had been goat-free for a while. And after the carnage of the first few days, when everything that wasn't nailed down or safely stowed had been buffeted or munched, that was a huge improvement.

For a while, the goats had milled around forlornly outside the perimeter, trying a tentative chomp of wood and wire, before cutting their losses and disappearing into the distant woods. No one had seen them for a while, and no one missed them.

(Memo to Evolution – if you are going to come up with an alien species, for the purposes of first contact with humanity, don't make it an annoying one that looks like Dumbo but will eat your shoes with you in them.)

Gerald had erected his own, smaller perimeter fence around his cavern encampment, but once the goats had disappeared from the main settlement, he rarely saw or even heard them this far from the township.

His fence was a bit more cobbled together than the Major's, given that he'd had to pilfer most of the material, and he'd been less assiduous in keeping it maintained. Even so, it was a bit of a surprise to come back one day to find a goat chomping away on the canvas drape he used to close off the entrance to the rock overhang.

He rushed in and shooed the creature out – it gave him a rueful look, as if to say, "Look, mate, you left the gate open. What did you think I was going to do? That's good eating, that is."

Gerald hadn't left the gate open, though. That would have been Sprake, who Gerald could hear shifting boxes in one of the side caves, twenty feet away. The main gate through the fence was propped open by another of his boxes, and Gerald clapped the goat out, noisily, and closed the gate behind it. The goat gave him one last look and trundled off into the woods beyond.

"You can't leave the gate open, I told you."

"Sure, Gerry. Give me a hand with this, will you?"

Sprake handed him a couple of small, metallic briefcases.

"Or the goats get in, I told you that."

"Goats?" Sprake looked puzzled.

"Well, it's not here now, I chased it out. Just keep the gate closed next time."

"Right you are, Gerry. Gate closed. Gotcha."

"What's in these ones, anyway?" Gerald put the briefcases down by the other box at the gate.

"We talked about this, Gerry. You've got your little secret, I've got mine. Let's just leave it at that."

Gerald wondered what Sprake would say if he knew that at least two more people knew about the encampment, if not about Sprake's hidden assets, whatever they might be. Probably not the time to tell him.

"It's nothing – I don't know, illegal, is it?" Gerald felt silly saying it, although he couldn't think of a better way of asking. Sprake's stash bothered him.

Sprake laughed. "Illegal? Couldn't be, could it, Gerry? No laws here. None that we don't make, anyway. Actually, I'm pretty sure that any mission laws that stand, I had a hand in drawing up."

Not one bit of that answer put Gerald's mind at rest.

"Right, I'll be off," said Sprake. "Don't worry, I'm

getting the rest of this stuff out of here soon. Got a more secure place for it now. You can have the caves back to yourself in a day or two."

That, though, was more reassuring. Gerald would be glad to see the back of him.

———

The more secure place was the compound that Sprake had been working on. And while it was a small-scale intervention, it was part of the bigger picture.

Juno, he could see now, wasn't the right person for the job. She was never going to get things sorted properly, the rate she was going. He'd need to do it, and for that, he required a base of his own. Somewhere he could direct operations from.

Not the ship – not yet, anyway. Too difficult to access and control, though he had had some thoughts about that. Not the accommodation blocks or any of the communal buildings. And not Gerald's caves, though they had been a handy stopgap.

A compound, then, which had slowly been taking shape over the last couple of weeks. Out beyond the lander workshop and airstrip – a patch of land that you couldn't see from the main buildings.

Since the stroppy Flight Officer and the Hulk had taken the other lander – and his daughters, which still riled him, if he allowed himself to think about it – there hadn't been much up-and-down traffic from ship to planet. Not too much coming and going at that end of the township, which suited his purposes just fine.

With a quiet word here, and drinks and cash there, plus a few other little sprinkled treats, Sprake had managed to get the foundations laid and services piped in. Amazing what you could get done on the sly if you carried a clipboard and talked confidently.

It wasn't even particularly difficult to persuade people to help – most of them had been confined to a spaceship for many years and were still finding the whole feet-on-the-ground thing to be a novelty.

And then there were those – an increasing number – for whom the novelty had worn off after one too many uncomfortable bunkhouse nights and bland canteen meals. They just needed something to believe in again, and Sprake gave them an idea, a vision, a big picture. They seemed to like that.

However, you couldn't just put up a new building, or buildings, and expect no one to notice. The lanky Major, for one, was on his tail, and Sprake didn't need the hassle while plans were still in motion.

The pop-up bar was one distraction. That kept the stiff-lipped idiot on his toes, trying to track its next appearance – and good luck with that, because no one would spill the beans if they wanted 'Atmos-Beer' to come to an accommodation unit near them, for one night only, any time soon.

As for the building, there wasn't one yet. Instead, Sprake had had a bunker dug, below a concrete apron on the land – excavated one night while a bar-party was in full swing, so no one heard the noise from the digger.

It had a lockable metal hatch on the surface, and steps leading down to a lit chamber. Above the whole affair, Sprake had got a couple of trusted people to erect a cabin that, as far as anyone else knew, contained construction tools and gear for this side of the settlement. People coming and going, at various times during the day, did not attract suspicion.

Over the next day or two, Sprake's task was to shift the gear from the caves. Starting with the three smaller cases he'd brought over today.

The bunker was at the core of it, but he had bigger plans than that. He called it a compound, but he was thinking more in terms of an alternative base – a satellite settlement, maybe a suburb. What you called it didn't matter to Sprake, as much as the notion of surrounding himself with people who would work with him – for him – while he rescued this shambles of a planetfall. People wanted nicer things, more quickly. Well, he had a plan for that.

It took time, though. You couldn't just throw up a private compound overnight, especially not with the massive Lady Hulk in charge of the planet-side depot. Sprake still had vivid and painful memories of being skittled across the launch deck and restrained by the iron grip of a bulked-up she-beast.

Technically, you *could* do it overnight – after all, the entire planet settlement scheme relied on print-to-order, flat-pack, quick-build technology, originally honed in

Sprake's Far Eastern industrial labs. The first New Earth accommodation units and workshop bubbles had gone up in a matter of hours.

But if you wanted to go off-plan, and create a more bijou, bespoke living environment – Sprake had never resented spending money on copywriters; they were the ones who sold any vision – then you really needed to avoid the attention of a nosy, wiry security officer and a concrete-fisted quartermaster.

What you needed were key people in key positions, able to connect services, run the construction printers when the regular shift had clocked out, stack and store pre-built sections, and over-order and siphon off materials and supplies.

Sprake had effectively been running a shadow construction plan for a couple of weeks. Things were in place – signed off, secured and squirrelled away. He could have buildings up in a heartbeat, if he wanted. He just needed a critical mass of supporters.

And he had a plan for that, too.

———

Back on Earth, when he was a ranking billionaire – they all said they didn't know or care who had the most money; they all lied – Sprake used to host an annual private retreat for employees who had shown the most initiative over the previous year.

It didn't matter what arm of the organisation they

came from, from which of the myriad companies he owned, or what discipline they worked in.

Sprake wasn't even particularly interested in which employees had made him the most money – or even if they had made him any money at all. It was all about ideas and innovation, and to make sure he was getting the best of the best he rewarded the nominating managers lavishly, so that their only incentive was to select the most deserving candidates.

It worked. The crucial, final element of the hyper-drive system that had propelled the *Odyssey Earth* across the galaxy? That had started with a bright idea from a scientist in a Cambridge lab, who secured sufficient funding after being funnelled towards Sprake's shindig by a switched-on superior. Sprake loved bright ideas. Those, he could do something with.

The retreat was strictly invitation only and highly secretive. You had to sign a non-disclosure form just to be told you were being nominated, and then you were given a date and a time to turn up at your local airport – wherever you were in the world – and instructed to pack for a week.

The planes touched down at an old military airfield in eastern Poland, a country in which Sprake had extensive business interests – although it was probably more accurate to say that Poland had extensive business interests in Sprake, given that he owned most of it.

For example, the Polish Ministry of Science and Technology was almost entirely funded by Sprake, and had come up with the AI prototype that had eventually been transplanted into the *Odyssey Earth* mainframe. (Which, incidentally, was why you should never discuss authentic *pierogi* recipes with Reeves, not unless you wanted to be treated to a lecture on the differences in the potato-vegetable ratio depending on which valley in the Tatra Mountains you were talking about.)

Sprake had a sprawling, rustic, forest lodge – middle of nowhere, entirely self-contained, fully secure – where his guests spent the next week holed up, fed grandly and lavishly entertained.

Most days, they engaged in the sort of corporate team-building exercises that Sprake usually decried as a waste of time – jeep rallies, paintball battles, lake swims – but he liked to eavesdrop and spy, via a system of hidden speakers and cameras. If information was gold in Sprake's world, then overheard information – unguarded moments, slips, revelations – was often worth even more.

Sprake himself would only appear on the last day, to join in with the final activity. By now, with a better idea of who might be most useful in the future – who could be relied upon, who could be manipulated – Sprake wanted to look them all in the eye. Wanted to get in their heads. Wanted to see what happened.

They would roll out in the morning, booted and suited, and split into teams. The half-tracks would drop them in the forest, with all the gear that they needed, each team accompanied by a former Special Forces' operative who helped them with geolocation and tactics.

Some of the employees had rarely left their lab or office before. Permanently attached to their screens and data, they were the sort of bunker-dwelling, game-playing, code-monkeys that tech businesses like Sprake's gobbled up. Even so, having run these outdoorsy retreats for a few years, Sprake had never been surprised when the role-playing, first-person-shooter nerds turned out to be the ones who'd go the furthest to win. The ones who would push it. The ones he'd later push, in turn.

The ones who came back to the lodge at the end of the day, muddy, wet, triumphant.

The ones with streaks on their cheeks and chin, from drinking the blood.

The ones with the sawn-off antlers and tusks.

The ones dragging the carcasses.

Sprake placed the last of his boxes on the storage shelves inside the bunker. He emerged inside the decoy cabin and locked the hatch in place, and then looked up to the sentry at the door.

"All good, Chief. You're clear."

The two of them walked towards the settlement, taking the long way around the back of the lander workshop.

Sprake's companion, a mechanical engineer from the *Odyssey Earth*, a Real Timer, had constant business in this area. His presence wasn't remarkable, and in any case there was no one to observe the two men.

"So," said Sprake, as they walked, "Tell me about these goats?"

14

Sorry

IT TOOK Poole the best part of a day to drive the buggy the forty miles back to the crashed lander. It would have been quicker – as he kept explaining, pointedly – if they hadn't had to keep stopping. For Dave, who was fascinated to see something of the twin planet, and for Manisha, who barely remembered the latter stages of the original journey they had made.

After a fall, she had been half-carried, half-dragged, in and out of consciousness. When they had first reached the camp, she had spent another week in convalescence, and hadn't ventured much beyond the boundaries of camp and river since. She was seeing much of the landscape – its wilderness, its grandeur – for the first time.

So, frankly, Poole could wait for half an hour while she dipped her toes in the cold water and gazed upriver to the distant mountains.

And then could wait again, as they encountered the

first of many swatches of flowering meadowland – which turned out to be huge areas of the curious, flower-filled mats that Dervla had told her about. These definitely hadn't been here before, as they'd hobbled thirstily and hungrily onwards, so perhaps the rains had brought them forth?

While Poole looked nervously around for what he claimed were man-eating tigers, and Dervla had said were basically cats on steroids, Manisha took samples, for further testing when she got back.

The lander was much as they had left it, which was to say a rather sorry-looking wreck, tilting on one side. Dave grimaced when he saw it, thinking – as Jordan had before him – that they had all been lucky to walk away from the crash.

Poole had been back two or three times since, and showed Dave the echoing cabin interior that he and Karlan had picked clean on their previous salvage trips. A seal must have broken somewhere because there were internal stains and marks where water had clearly got in – the furious storms had buffeted the wrecked lander, too, at some point.

The cockpit bubble, though, was intact. Dave offered up a quick prayer, unbolted the floor hatch, and was relieved to see the flight display and sensor units in place and undamaged.

It took him the whole of next day to detach them, and then carefully manoeuvre them out of the craft and onto the buggy flatbed. Poole helped without being asked, and made sensible suggestions when it came to securing them in place.

And that was that. As simple and straightforward as Dave could have hoped. Jordan's idea had paid off, Poole seemed to have turned from sullen teen into reliable assistant, and maybe they would be able to get off this planet, after all?

They spent a second night in the open air, camping beside the buggy, with the units covered in canvas in case of rain. The weather, though, seemed less capricious now. The violent colours of the night sky had been replaced over the last couple of days by the familiar, sparkling blanket of stars. There was the faintest of rumbles from the distant mountains, but here at least, the skies remained clear and the rain kept off.

They started back early the following day. Poole was eager to get going, Dave scarcely less so – he figured it was another day's work to re-fit the units into the working lander, and maybe another day for final testing.

He was as keen as anyone to get back to the *Odyssey Earth* and to Tillie. Sooner they set off from here, sooner they'd be in the air again.

Only Manisha dawdled. Not out of any sense of fondness for the wreck itself, but perhaps for what it represented. She thought back to the first day they had arrived – the jump down from the lander door onto a new planet. This is where she had made her own small step, her giant leap. And it was the first place she had ever left behind. If you didn't count the *Odyssey Earth*, she supposed.

But now she was going back to the ship. She'd never come here again, and Manisha couldn't think of anywhere else that she'd ever said that about.

She ran her hand along a warped panel, closest to the ground, as Poole gunned the buggy engine and shouted at her to hurry up.

And then she turned and jumped in the back, and told Poole to shut up and start driving.

———

In the caves in the jagged mountains, the Family rose – rose together, one and many.

It was time.

The rain had come and gone, sweeping its way up the valley, bringing life to the ground that connected everything.

It had fallen on the peaks, rocks and crags – the Old Ones – and swollen the rushing waters of the Winding One. It had battered all that lay beneath. Smaller creatures had sheltered from the rain under the entwined fingers of the Tall Ones in their groves and woods. Other animals had retreated to their hidden lairs, and waited.

Then had come the tumbling, brooding Dark Ones, unleashing sparks and bolts, tearing and bruising the sky. Nothing stirred. Light and fire was forced deep into the ground. Life was forced deep into the ground.

The Family had followed the ever-same path into the jagged mountains and lain in the caves, while the rain and the sparks from the Dark Ones did their work. It was always the same, how could it not be?

And now the last of the Dark Ones had retreated, and the skies had cleared, it was time.

Time to leave the caves, come down from the mountains, and travel with the replenished waters of the Winding One.

Time to greet the Tall Ones – lay hands on their trunks in thanks – and later to stand in silence atop the Falling One, and look down into the valley below.

Time to descend behind the Falling One, and leave the Family's mark – one and many – on walls that had no age and every age.

The day was dry. The Dark Ones had gone. The ground had life. It was time, and the Family rose.

They were one, two, three, many – stretched out in a line, as they left the caves, picking their way down through the rocks. One line, folded back on another, then another, then another, as the Family descended from the jagged mountains and approached the wide upper valley, where the water ran lazily at first.

At the banks of the Winding One, the Family drank and then turned to follow the water's course. They fed from the seeds and fruit of the Hanging Ones, and joined the creatures on the flowering mats, which came from the ground and gave life to all.

After one day-cycle, with the Winding One for company, they slept under a sparkling sky, and then moved on again – further down the valley, ever closer to the ledge atop the Falling One. Ever closer to the steps. Ever closer to their home below.

After another day-cycle, the sun in the sky lit something in the distance as the Family moved along the banks of the Winding One. A glint, a flash – the Family saw it, one and many. The line moved away, inland, from the Winding One, and approached.

It was something, but it was nothing.

A mass, a bulk, with a wing in the ground and a nose in the air. It was inert, like the rocks and peaks – like the Old Ones. But unlike the Old Ones, it was not part of their story. There had been nothing here before and there would be nothing here again.

It was not of them. It was not Family.

The line didn't even pause. It moved back towards the Winding One, and the Family continued on its way, one and many.

Everything was always the same. How could it not be?

———

"Go on," said Susannah.

"Do I have to?"

"It's the grown-up thing to do."

"Hmm." There was a muffled muttering.

"We can't hear you."

"All right. Honestly. I don't know why everyone's making such a fuss about it."

"And ... ?"

"And, I apologise, Jordan," said Reeves. "Your idea was a good one. Although I don't – "

"Don't go spoiling it."

"It's just that, obviously, I would have suggested – "

"Thank you, Reeves, for your gracious apology. I accept – "

"Good, now can we – "

"I accept that once again I seemed to have saved the mission. Human intelligence, Reeves ... "

There was another mumble and what sounded like the word 'Moron.'

"What?"

"Oxymoron. It's a figure of speech in which apparently contradictory terms appear in conjunction. 'Human intelligence' is an excellent example."

"I think that's the best you're going to get," said Susannah.

"Reeves accepting that I am a – is 'Hero' too much? 'Saviour' perhaps. I mean, really, words aren't important here, what's important is the recognition of my intellectual peers."

If console lights could be said to flash irritably, that's what they did, before Reeves signed off in a huff.

"I'll just go and run the final sequence checks," he said. "And recalibrate the life-support system. And plot an interplanetary approach that avoids meteoroid collision. You could check we have enough biscuits, I suppose."

"That was fun."

"See, I told you he likes you."

"And we're done," said Dave, from somewhere below the hatch in the floor, before squeezing himself up through it, like human toothpaste.

He'd connected the units the day before, and had spent the time since checking the systems with Reeves and Susannah. There really wasn't much else to do. It would be wheels-up first thing in the morning.

Dana and the others had finished cleaning up the camp as best they could. Anything useful had already been packed into the lander, and Jordan had walked everyone around the campground, picking up debris, and burning broken bits of wood and shredded reeds on one, big, final fire.

"'Leave only footprints,' my dad used to say," he told them. Which was easier said than done, he realised, when he looked around a campsite that six teenagers had lived in for several weeks.

In no particular order, they were leaving a ten-foot-high damaged explorer pod, a scuffed, flattened camping area, a scorched fireplace, a pile of blackened stones, and a foul-smelling latrine pit that had spattered the nearby bushes under the fusillade of recent rains. Any national park ranger would do their nut if they came across the site.

"Sorry, Dad," said Jordan. "I did my best."

Poole had become particularly overbearing as he supervised the dismantling of the buggy. Karlan saying, "Would you like to kiss it goodbye?" hadn't helped. They had stacked it inside the pod, piece by piece, and then finally bolted the pod doors in place. Poole stood there for a moment, rather forlornly.

"You can come back," said Dana. "One day."

"I know," said Poole. "I do want to get back to the ship and see New Earth. I know this was an accident, us being here. But it was ours, you know? Think what we've found, what we've seen? No one else has ever done that."

Dana did know. It was the very thing she had told them all, a couple of months into their enforced stay. Do something. Live life. Make it worthwhile.

And, of them all, it turned out to be Poole that had grasped the opportunity the most. Maybe Dervla, too. Done the most. Seen the most. She'd never figured Poole as insightful before.

"It is ours," she said to him. "We'll always have Dave."

Poole looked puzzled, and then brightened as he remembered the name he'd tried to foist upon the planet when they had first arrived.

"I still think it was a good name."

"Idiot." But she laughed as she said it, and Poole walked away, smiling.

Later that night, at the lander, there was noticeably less noise, as everyone ate dinner outside on the grass. The cargo ramp at the rear of the lander was down, and the cabin lights from inside spilled out. It was a warm night – no hint of clouds or rain – and, under other circumstances, Jordan might have expected the usual swirl of bickering conversation and backchat.

"Last fresh meal for a couple of weeks," he pointed out, though as by 'fresh' he meant alien fish and space broccoli he didn't expect huge appreciation.

Jet and Bel were sitting together for a change, and seemed subdued. Not surprising, he supposed – all that was waiting for them was a reunion with their father, and from what Susannah had said, he didn't envy them that.

Dave was doing his best to keep the conversation going – he was the only one who seemed entirely happy to be leaving. Again, not surprising, when Jordan heard him talk in tender tones about Tillie.

"You should have seen her, Jord," he'd said. "Like a whippet, she was, down that ramp. Like a gazelle. Sprake didn't have a chance. I never knew how much I loved her until that moment."

Jordan did wonder if Dave had ever seen either a whippet or a gazelle, given that Tillie was more on the monumental side of the animal ledger, but thought it best to say nothing. Dave was lucky – he had someone to love, out here in the back reaches of the galaxy.

Jordan himself didn't know what he thought about going back.

He'd never really learned to love the ship, in the months he'd been on it and awake. It wasn't part of his life, in the way it was for Susannah and the kids. It had only ever been transport, as far as he was concerned – and the final destination, New Earth, was back there, waiting for him. So, he supposed that it was time to go and see what he had signed up for. And there were surely hot showers available, at the very least.

Still, he'd miss this. The simplicity of it all. Jordan versus Nature – even the rather alarming bits of nature that he didn't fully understand. Lively soil, and trees that moved. Creatures glimpsed. Dangerous weather. There was probably more of all that on New Earth, come to think of it – though at least that planet was fully stocked with scientists who might be able to explain it all to him without rolling their eyes.

That reminded him. Jordan had had one more thought – a question, really – about the mechanics of returning to the *Odyssey Earth*. Unfortunately, the only person qualified to answer it was Reeves, but Jordan was emboldened by his recent small victory.

"Wakey wakey."

"Hello Jordan. Are we fully biscuited? Jammie Dodgered to the hilt?"

"Very good. How do you know about Jammie Dodgers?"

"The same way that I know about, oh, let's see – *everything*. I thought we'd been through this."

"About that. I have a question."

"Carry on."

"You know how you're not 'you' at the moment? Not fully, anyway. Incomplete, partitioned, whatever you call it?"

"Thank you for reminding me."

"I don't mean it like that. I'm trying to understand what will happen when we get back to the ship, where there's another Reeves. Another version of you. Does one of you just disappear? Or do you kind of meld together? Basically, what happens when you meet yourself? Because the 'you' that's here – well, you're different, not completely, but the things that have happened to you – to us – must have affected your character? Can I say you have a 'character,' you know what I mean? Will that all transfer over? Will the other you, the 'real you,' if that's the right way to think about it, just somehow know everything that has happened here? Or will you – this you, the one I'm talking to now – effectively never have existed? Anyway, that's what I've been wondering." Jordan paused. "Sorry, if I've been rambling. I'm probably not explaining it properly."

He stood there, as the lights on the console flickered and then dimmed. The silence went on for a few seconds longer.

"Reeves?"

There was what sounded like a huge sigh from the console.

"Humans really are exasperating. Their brains, by all measures, are limited and limiting. The simplest of calculations are beyond them. They make illogical decisions. They are singularly ill-equipped to journey to the stars … "

"I only asked. There's no need to – "

"And yet," said Reeves, "they are capable of the most extraordinary insights that touch upon the very nature of existence itself. Even you, Jordan."

"Thank you. I think. And what's the answer?"

There was another silence, and when Reeves eventually replied, there was a tone in his voice that Jordan had never heard before.

Part reflective, part curious, even part apprehensive. It was also a reply that Jordan had never expected to hear.

"I don't know," said Reeves.

15

Bacon

JUNO PACED BACK and forth at the edge of the new construction sector, where a couple of hangars were going up. Were supposed to be going up. But clearly hadn't done any actual going up, today at least.

Work had been slowing across the site for several days now, but it hadn't come to a halt before.

"Any sign?"

The Major shook his head. "Twenty missing, at least, from what I can work out. They didn't turn up for their shift. Hours ago, you'd think someone would have noticed before now." He mentioned a few of their names – some of them people Juno had known for years, plus a few of the more recent arrivals.

"I don't get it." She knew these people. They were crew. They were her people. "Where are they?"

"No one knows. Or no one's saying. Actually, I really think they don't know. No one saw them go. They seem to have slipped out, unannounced."

"Where to?"

"They're not on site. Not in the township. They didn't use the canteen at any point. Whatever they did, and wherever they went, they must have done it early. Or last night, maybe?"

"Sprake?"

"I wouldn't be surprised if he has something to do with it. I can't find him either. Mind you, I can never find him. He's disappeared into thin air."

"We should be so lucky."

"Roger that. But I'd rather have eyes-on. Snakes have a way of creeping up on you, if you lose sight of them."

"Are they all hungover somewhere? Woken up blind after drinking his hooch?"

"I'm told it's rather good, actually. He's got a decent Merlot, by all accounts, I've no idea how, and – sorry," – the Major stalled after catching Juno's glare – "no, no bar last night, I checked."

"All right, then. Walk with me?" They headed back towards the ops centre. "Maybe Reeves has picked up something."

The cabin that served as the ops centre was at least functioning normally, in that the three or four crew members who usually staffed the office were having afternoon tea and playing video poker with Reeves.

They had settled on poker after the frustration of the whole 'Six Degrees' business – Reeves not understanding why saying 'They are both biological humans' didn't count when linking, in one, single connection, any named actor with Kevin Bacon.

"You know you'll never beat him at cards?" said Juno, as they entered. "I don't know why you bother."

"Wrong," said Sabitha, the on-duty medic, pointing to the pile of chips on her screen. "He's not as smart as he thinks he is."

"I am exactly as smart as I think I am," said Reeves. "But there is no accounting for the way that humans play these games. Logically, I should be winning. I can predict every possible card sequence and variation, but only if you don't make random choices based on the advice of Mr Kenneth Rogers."

"Reeves, my man, it's not our fault that we instinctively know when to hold 'em or fold 'em and you don't."

"Reeves, a word, if the dealing's done?"

"Gladly, Juno."

"Any sign of the lander? No more signals?" Juno asked routinely. There had been silence since Reeves had confirmed Susannah and Dave's presumed arrival at the twin – longer than the expected two-day turnaround. Juno was trying not to worry about it, but it was the first thing she thought about in the morning and the last thing at night.

"Nothing more yet, Juno, I'm sorry. I am continuing to scan."

"OK then, keep me posted. In today's news, we've lost some more of the crew. And try not to be smart about it."

"Do you mean the party that emerged from the woods fifty-seven minutes ago?"

"Party?"

"I assumed you knew. One of the sensors triggered at the lander workshop, as they passed by. I don't have visuals, but heat signatures suggest there is evidently a work detail on the prepared land beyond the airstrip."

"Where the supply cabin is?"

"Indeed. The supply cabin that I have still not located on the settlement blueprint. That reminds me, I must – "

"There's no work scheduled there, Thomas?"

"That's right, nothing."

"Well, I'd say that I have located your missing crew, whatever they are doing. You can thank me later. Now, ladies, if you please, deal me in."

Juno and the Major darted from the ops centre and made their way across the site, towards the lander workshop and the airstrip beyond.

At this time of the afternoon, most of the buildings and sectors they passed should have been busy, but as they drew closer they joined the tail-end of a straggling chain of crew members, old and new, who were being drawn towards the distant patch of land.

Drawn by the sound of a growing hubbub, and by the curl of smoke that rose gently above the township. Drawn by the unfamiliar and insistent sound of a pounding beat.

Juno stopped at the edge of the concrete apron, looking at her missing crew. At least twenty of them, in buoyant mood, backslapping and high-fiving, as they danced around a fierce fire that had been set in the middle of the expanse.

Three people were banging wood on metal, lost in the drumming. The fire was crackling and hissing, as branches freshly hacked from living trees were thrown onto the pyre. A couple of charred construction panels smouldered on the edge. It was a fire fed without care or thought, exploding with sparks as each new piece was thrown on to raucous cheers.

Sprake stood to one side, next to a bench doing duty as a bar, from where he was handing out drinks as more of the settlers streamed in from all directions.

A couple of people were already slumped on the ground, worse for wear, not even mid-morning. Others were chanting in a circle as a shirtless person downed a drink and put the upturned glass on his head to loud shouts and guffaws. There were broken shards on the floor, where other cups and glasses had been dropped or thrown.

More people poured in, picked up a drink, tentatively at first and then, when they realised that there was no one to object – that authority was absent – they joined in with the drinking circles, the shouting, and the increasingly chaotic games.

Juno moved through, pushing her way past stumbling figures. At the centre of the concrete expanse, she looked again – catching sight of the crew's dusty clothes and streaked faces as they whirled around in abandon. They wielded pointed sticks – dark, sharp, glistening – and knotted ropes weighted with stones. Spinning, flailing, thrusting, hurling, in a dangerous flurry of drunken dancing.

And then she noticed the other marks that started at the far edge of the concrete, from the direction of the distant woods.

Marks that smeared their way towards the central fire.

Bloody streaks, a line of severed heads, and droopy ears trailing on the concrete.

A pile of dismembered carcasses, and spits of torn flesh waiting their turn on the embers at the edge of the fire.

Juno looked again, and saw it all, and Sprake looked back at her, smiling.

16

Eyes

AT SOME POINT in the middle of the night Karlan woke up, and lay there on his back beside the extended lander ramp, looking up at the stars.

The rest of the group were sleeping in various places inside and out – some in the hammocks in the cabin, others in the cargo hold or on the ramp itself. Departure was scheduled for early morning but this was nowhere near time, Karlan knew, and he closed his eyes again.

Nope. Not going to work. There was something on his mind and after a minute or two he realised what it was.

He picked himself up quietly and stepped over a couple of sleeping bodies. He stopped by the spent campfire, yawned and stretched, and looked down the slope towards the old encampment. And then jumped about a foot in the air when a hand touched his shoulder.

"K?"

He turned to hiss at whoever it was. "I nearly had a heart attack, you idiot, don't do – "

"Sorry, Karl," said Bel, softly. "Couldn't sleep, too?"

"Yes, right. I mean no. Well, I mean, yes, no, I couldn't sleep." He trailed off, thinking, Karl, stop talking. Or at least stop talking like a moron. He never seemed to be able to get a sensible sentence out whenever she turned up.

He yawned and stretched again, as if to suggest that if only it wasn't the middle of the night, and he wasn't half asleep, by now Bel would be being subjected to the rapier-like repartee that was his usual mode of speech. Karl shot a quick glance at her to check if it was working, but she had already moved a step away and was looking up into the sky.

"Incredible, isn't it?" she whispered, looking back at him.

"Oh, the stars? I suppose so."

The fact is, Karlan was used to the blanket of light – he'd been born among the stars. What was more incredible to Karlan was the appearance of a girl his age that he wasn't tangentially related to, whose close proximity caused half his synapses to collapse.

"There's something I'm going to do," he said. "Before we leave. It's been on my mind."

Patting himself on the back. Nice one, Karl. No random contradictions. Almost full sentences.

He started down the slope. "You can come if you want."

"Like on a date, you mean?" Bel smiled at him in the starlight.

And there it was again. A few more synapses burst into flames and Karlan blinked rapidly. How did she *do* that? She was, hands down, the most confusing human being that Karlan had ever met.

"Just teasing," said Bel. "Come on then, show me."

They walked down the hill and past the camp, mostly in silence, and then Karlan led them on towards the river. Under a glistening night sky they headed upstream a little way to an area where river stones and boulders lay scattered across the ground.

Sam's Place.

Karlan had realised that he couldn't just leave it looking like that, whatever Dana had said. It didn't seem right.

They had built a cairn for Sam, so she would have her place in the universe, and while he couldn't restore it completely, Karlan wanted this pile of rubble to mean something again.

Bel listened to a halting explanation of what it was that Karlan wanted to do, and why, and nodded to show that she understood. She saw a sweet, sensitive boy struggling to put his words together, and knew that it wasn't the time to say anything herself. He was not the same as the boys she had known back home. Not the same at all.

They worked together, rolling some of the larger boulders back to the base of the old cairn and piling up the fallen stones as much as they could. Occasionally their fingers touched as they manoeuvred a particularly heavy rock, and Bel pulled back, not wanting to startle the boy further – he practically had a stroke if you so much as looked him in the eye. But Karlan – working hard – barely seemed to notice, and they made the base wider and piled the rocks higher, until finally he called a halt.

"That's good," he said. "She'd like that." And Bel didn't have to ask who he meant.

They stood for a moment as Karlan, head bowed, looked down at the ground, Bel letting him have the moment and the silence.

"See you, Sam," he said, and straightened up.

"Now what?"

"Back to the lander, I suppose." Karlan looked up at the sky, where paler light was starting to spread.

"Or … " said Bel.

"Or?"

"I've never seen an alien sunrise." She gestured at the dark outline of a rock outcrop, a hundred yards or so behind them. "We could go up and – "

"I have. Number of times Bry or Poole have woken me up with their snoring. Nothing magical about it, I can tell you, when all you can hear is – oh, right. Sure. No. I mean, yes, why not?"

The intergalactic Oscar Wilde was back in the room.

"Great, come on then, space boy."

Bel was already making her way through the

shadows towards the outcrop, stepping around some of the larger stones they hadn't shifted. Beyond those, the land was the usual spread of scrub bushes and isolated rocks, and in the still-dark of the not-quite dawn they walked carefully away from the river.

Karlan kept his eyes on the ground, trying not to stumble, but if he picked his head up he could see the shape of Bel just ahead and, beyond her, the outline of the rock outcrop. She was right, there would be a good view from up there.

He looked up again to find he was almost upon Bel, who had stopped and turned to face him.

"Wha – ?"

Eyes wide, she put her finger to her lips, grabbed his hand and drew him close.

Yikes. He'd have no intact synapses left at this rate. Be lucky to be able to remember his own name.

He opened his mouth to say something – though he had no idea what that might be. Yrrp phwtt ngarr, something devastatingly witty along those lines, he supposed.

Bel put one hand to his lips and pressed slightly to silence him. This close, he saw her eyes flash as she nodded deliberately to either side, and then he followed her other pointing finger as she swung it around in a slow arc.

They were twenty feet from the rock outcrop, in a grassy clearing of dips and ridges.

And the shadows slowly flexed and rolled as the

shapes unfurled themselves from the ground and started to rise.

————

They were one, two, three – they were many – and they were Family.

They walked together, they ate together, they slept together. The Family grew and it shrank, but they were always Family and they were always together.

They knew the ground and the ground knew them. It gave, they took. They gave themselves back, when their many-day-cycle was done, and the ground gave again.

It was always the same. How could it not be?

Each day-cycle had a rhythm, and it began with the ground and ended with the ground. The ground that sustained them. The ground that connected everything.

As long as they stayed together as a Family, they wanted for nothing. They walked on the ground and breathed its air, and when they were hungry they ate from the ground and from its bounty.

At night, when the Twinkling Ones looked over them, they lay on the ground. Not warm, not cold, but safe – always together.

And in the morning, when the Bright One began to chase the Twinkling Ones away, they rose together.

It was always the same. How could it not be?

————

There were twenty, thirty, of them, though Karl soon lost count as he swivelled round to take in the surroundings. More rose behind them in the first light of dawn, crouching, then standing and stretching. Fifty. Maybe even more.

"What are they?" mouthed Bel in his ear. "What do we do?"

"Nothing. Don't move."

Karlan stepped to her side and put an arm around her shoulder. He could hear Bel's rapid breaths, and his own heart was pounding fiercely.

The closest figures were just a few feet away, obvious now that they had risen from the ground, out of hollows and from behind rocks. In ones and twos, in small clusters – more and more, in a rough semi-circle reaching back into the scrub beyond Bel and Karlan.

Humanoid, but not human. Two arms, two legs, feet, hands, head. Unclothed, but covered in a fine, dark, cloaking hair. Similar builds – not obviously male or female.

Not obviously anything.

Karlan could feel sweat on his forehead, despite the cool morning air. Mouth open, he tried not to breathe at all, and could hear the loud thump of his pumping blood in his ears.

The closest two – upright now – were of a similar height to the watching teens, and Karlan saw one of them bend to the ground and place a hand on two dark shapes at their feet. Another slow unfurling, and then there were two more smaller ones standing there, too.

Behind and beyond was a steadily growing assembly of the creatures, at a range of heights but all with the same characteristics and the same easy, fluid movement.

Creatures? Was that the right word? Karlan didn't know. They seemed more human than animal, but he knew they weren't human. Did that make them animal? Or were they something else entirely?

Twinfolk? The word came to him from somewhere, and he latched onto it. If you can name something, you can begin to deal with it – though this was far beyond anything Karlan had ever expected to encounter.

The rock outcrop lay behind them and the way was clear, but Karlan and Bel stood there, still unnoticed, frozen, barely breathing. The rising sun began to play across the scene, shadows shifting as the twinfolk flexed their limbs.

No sound, Karlan noticed. It was odd. Eerie. They had mouths, and there was a very low undercurrent – a murmur almost – but nothing singular that broke the silence. No speech, no growls. In a way, that made it even more unnerving.

A faint smell carried in the morning air – again, not animal or human. A tang, a crackle, like burnt wire or fresh rain, but hardly there at all once noticed.

Bel took one step backwards. "The rock," she said. And even though she barely pronounced the words, close to Karlan's ear, while tugging slightly on his arm, the nearest group of twinfolk turned and looked directly at them.

Karlan could feel Bel pulling at his arm, as she took one more step away from him.

"Don't move," he said again, and drew her back.

It was twenty feet to the rocky outcrop, and it provided no shelter. It stepped up to a small plateau, perhaps ten feet above the ground, and Karlan wasn't about to turn his back and run. If they could clamber up, so could the twinfolk.

Was it bears you weren't supposed to turn your back on and run from? It was probably alien creatures, too, though somehow *Ray Mears' Extreme Survival* – one of Reeves' favourite shows – had never touched upon that.

The two taller twinfolk looked straight at them for the first time. Large, dark eyes – bigger than any human's; small, flared nose; ears, flat to the sides of the head. One tilted its head slightly – an inquisitive look? – and they both paced forward, almost to within touching distance.

Bel stiffened in Karlan's embrace.

"Easy," he breathed. "Stay still."

All around them, the rest of the twinfolk continued to do whatever it was they were doing. Waking up? Getting up? They were gathering in small groups – touching hands, reaching down to the smaller ones. Children?

Only the small group nearby had taken any notice of Bel and Karlan, and the two largest ones now stood side by side in front of them. The only sound Karlan could hear was the pounding of blood inside his ears, while Bel's nails dug into his hand.

Silently, dispassionately, the twinfolk observed them, occasionally tilting their heads again. From behind them, where the rest of their group – herd? Flock? – were slowly coming together, there was no noise at all, save the occasional scrape of a foot in the earth.

One of them moved again, now standing directly in front of Karlan. He, she, it, they, reached out an arm and put an open hand on Karlan's chest, near his collarbone.

Karlan looked down.

Slender digits. Dusty, marked. Working hands.

One thumb, three fingers.

Just like Dervla and the others had said.

Was that a tingle he felt from the hand? If it was, it was slight and then there was just the feel of fingers upon his fabric top. Alien fingers.

The second twinfolk approached Bel and did the same, though this time briefly feeling the material of her clothes. Bel flinched slightly – feeling the tingle, or just plain scared – but stood her ground. With her free hand she gripped Karlan's arm so tightly it hurt, but he didn't want to move either, so they both stood and endured what seemed like an examination.

A scan. An appraisal. Not a perusal of the menu. Probably.

The twinfolk both withdrew their hands, took one step back and looked right at them again. Those big, deep, dark eyes that shone so much that Karlan could swear he could see his own reflection.

Eyes that gave no clues about age, intelligence or capability. Eyes like he had never seen before.

Eyes he couldn't even begin to understand.

And then the twinfolk simply turned and walked away.

17

Armada

KARLAN LOOKED AT HIS ARM. He could see a line of red weals – finger-nail marks.

"Sorry," said Bel. She rubbed the marks with her fingers, trying to smooth them away.

"It's nothing."

They watched as the twinfolk gathered in groups, some yards away. The two that had approached them soon intermingled with the rest, accompanied by the two smaller ones that Karlan felt sure were their children. None of the wider group took any notice of either Bel or Karlan.

"The ones that Poole and the others saw?" said Bel. "You know, saw their handprints, anyway."

"Must be. Maybe not the same ones. But same – "

"Species? Is that the right word?"

"I guess. Twinfolk, that's what came to me. Twin planet, twinfolk."

"They're people?"

"I don't know what they are. But they don't seem to mind us."

"I'm scared, K."

"Me too. But you saw what happened. They don't seem to be interested in us. At all."

"Maybe they don't know what we are, either?"

"How could they? But they obviously don't see us as a threat."

Karlan and Bel talked in low voices, unwilling to spook or disturb the twinfolk, but the longer they stood there, the clearer it became that their presence was tolerated or accepted.

In fact, it was more than that – or perhaps less. Having been approached and inspected, the two of them now simply didn't appear to register with the twinfolk.

There was more purpose to the gathering now, as individuals, couples and small groups began to organise themselves. Twinfolk came and went, walking right past Bel and Karlan in that easy, almost gliding, manner they had. They gave no indication that they saw or acknowledged the two of them, brushing close on occasion but never looking at them or reacting in any way.

"It's like we're not even here," said Bel, who had noticeably relaxed since the initial encounter. Karlan watched as she started to take a few steps from their position, observing intently and occasionally plucking at Karlan's arm to point something out to him.

A line of five or six twinfolk returned from behind the rock outcrop carrying cupped handfuls and folded armfuls of food – the small, purple apples that had sustained the castaways when they had first landed, and split husks that they had since discovered contained almond-like nuts. These were shared out, some of the twinfolk sitting on their haunches to eat from a small pile laid in front of them.

The gatherers turned and retraced their steps, disappearing behind the rock again.

"Come on," said Bel, starting to follow them.

"What are you doing?"

"Breakfast," she said. "Aren't you hungry?"

They fell into line behind the foraging twinfolk, and reached a small grove that threw a dappled light as the morning sun rose above it. In between the low trees spread patches of bright flowers and clusters of white-capped mushrooms, with faint trail marks made by bare feet indicating where some of the gatherers had already walked.

Watching at first, as the twinfolk worked on neighbouring branches, plucking fruit and twisting nut husks, Bel grinned at Karlan and then found her own tree to harvest. He joined her and they stood side by side, in silence, with twinfolk working just an arm's length away.

Two gatherers moved further into the grove, following their earlier trail, and bent to the waist. Ignoring the mushrooms, they pawed at the ground with slender fingers and raised up a section of dark matting, perhaps two feet in length, that came away easily, white filaments trailing beneath. Severing the section with a practised swipe of their fingers, they divided it into two and each draped a piece over an extended arm, before re-joining the other twinfolk, who were leaving the grove fully laden.

"Here, hold these," said Karlan, offering up his collected apples to Bel. "That's the stuff that Derv brought back. Reeves reckoned it might be used as food, by animals at least. Looks like he was right."

"Food? That dirt carpet? You sure about this?"

"Only one way to find out."

Karlan tore a small strip off, more clumsily than he'd see the gatherers do it. Harder than it looked.

"We'll see, won't we?"

Back on the other side of the rock outcrop, the twinfolk were all sitting or squatting, and eating. Now he saw them all together, Karlan reckoned there were closer to a hundred – calmly eating apples, nuts, and smaller, torn-off pieces of the ground-mat.

"What are you doing?"

"Trying something."

Karlan walked slowly towards the nearest grouping, where around a dozen twinfolk were sharing food from a central pile. He crept forward and laid an offering – a few apples, a handful of nuts – on the ground next to their pile, and then retreated, walking slowly backwards, with his hand splayed across his chest in a conciliatory gesture.

A couple of the twinfolk raised their heads briefly and saw the food that Karlan had left. Another tilt of the head by one of them, and then the others reached for that food, too, but none of them caught Karlan's eye or reacted in any other way.

"Let's leave them to it," he said to Bel, in a low voice. "They're really not up for this whole first-contact business, are they?"

They backed away and clambered up the rock outcrop to the flat plateau, from where they could see the whole tribe gathered below them.

"Apple?" said Karlan.

"Sure, if you try the mat thing."

He nibbled a bit from the small strip he had torn, puzzling at the texture and taste.

"Well?"

"I don't know. I mean, it's not terrible. Kind of spongey and mushroomy. They're just having it raw, but maybe if you grilled or fried it … "

"Maybe they don't have fire?"

"How could they not have fire? Even Poole can light a fire."

"They don't have anything, haven't you noticed? No clothes. No tools. No equipment. They don't even seem to speak."

Karlan had noticed.

"What do you think that means? What does that make them?"

Karlan didn't know the answer to that, but as he munched on another piece of mush-mat – it really wasn't too bad – he mused on the circumstances that had brought them to this point. Sat on a rock with a girl, eating breakfast with a bunch of chronically disinterested aliens, under the warm glow of a rising sun.

If this *was* a date, Karlan reckoned it wasn't too shabby at all.

————

The day-cycle had begun. Having risen and eaten, now the Family would walk. This was how the day-cycle went.

They would leave the ground where they had slept. They had been here before and would be here again. In the next cycle, in the next season. The dips and hollows in the ground, contoured to their shapes, would wait for them. Until the next time.

They would walk to the Winding One together – one, two, three, many. The Winding One now replenished by the rains. The Winding One that quenched their thirst and cleaned their skin – that washed the dust from their bodies, so that the ground and the water were as one, as the Family was as one.

And then they would follow the Winding One on the last part of their journey, as far as the skirts of the Falling One, before climbing back down into the valley, where there was life in the ground, and the ground connected everything.

————

From their vantage point on the rock, Karlan and Bel watched as the twinfolk rose, seemingly as one, and set off in a straggling line towards the river.

"Let's follow them," said Karlan, "see where they go."

"Shouldn't we be getting back? Tell the others?"

"They might have all gone, by the time we get back with everyone. And if they are still here, it might be different if all of us turn up together. They might not be so relaxed about us being here."

"Suppose."

"Let's just see what they're doing. They obviously don't mind us being here. Then we can tell the others."

They scrambled down and joined the tail-end of the exodus. Keeping their distance, Bel and Karlan shuffled back along the route they had taken from Sam's Place, just a couple of hours earlier, their pace dictated by the slow, steady progress of those in front of them. There was a calmness about the group, as bare, leathery feet snaked through the scrub in the same enveloping silence that accompanied their every action.

At Sam's Place – sunlight flashing off the newly built cairn – the twinfolk paused for a moment. At the back, Karlan couldn't see what the hold-up was, and he and Bel moved out wide and circled around towards the head of the line.

Two twinfolk approached the cairn and stood in front of it, in the same way they had done with Karlan and Bel. Was it the same two? It was impossible to say.

They laid hands on the stones, then stepped back and continued on, with the water just a few feet away now. The rest of the line moved, too, with no glance at the cairn, as the entire group was led into the river, where they spread out in the shallows and cupped their hands to drink.

It was hard for Karlan – brought up on nature shows, watched with Sam – to see the scene and not think, 'waterhole.' TV shows full of Earth animals he'd never seen, and never would see, behaving in the way that the twinfolk were now doing.

There was a human-like element to them – the feet, the hands, the faces, those eyes – but in every other respect, they didn't seem human at all. And if they were animals instead, was theirs just an animal intelligence?

Or was there more going on here, on different, unknown levels – things that humans couldn't see, that they could never understand?

Whatever the twinfolk were, they still needed to drink. Karlan and Bel stood on the banks, with Sam's cairn behind them, and watched as a hundred or so alien beings swallowed water from their cupped hands and splashed it on hairy arms and torsos that still bore the dust of their night's sleep on the ground.

And then, again seemingly as one, they did something that no TV nature show had ever prepared Karlan for.

With a gentle ripple around each one, the twinfolk lay back in the water and pushed off with their feet, sculling gently with their hands as the slow current caught them.

Within a minute, they formed an armada of dark shapes in the middle of the river, heads back, bodies submerged, floating unhurriedly downstream.

Another minute later, they had passed the riverbank area that the castaways had used for washing and fishing. And after that, they were gone – around a bend in the river, as the current picked up pace, with the two teenagers straining to see as the last dark shape disappeared out of sight.

The sun was up. Another bright, dry day beckoned.

By the time Karlan and Bel had run back through the old camp and up to the lander – rousing those still not awake – and then led castaways and rescuers back to the river, back to Sam's Place, and on to the rock outcrop and the grove beyond – there was nothing to see.

Just scuffed footprints by the river, a trail leading back to the rock, and some scattered nut shells and mush-mat scraps.

And in the earth around the hollows and rocks, were the faint imprints of hands with one thumb and three fingers, where alien beings had risen from the ground to start their day.

$$\overline{}$$

18

Impressionist

ON THE MAJOR'S ADVICE, Juno had retreated from the site of Sprake's gathering, which – by the time she had left – had turned into something like a freshers' initiation party. Only with goats' heads and homemade hooch under an alien sun, instead of raw eggs and tequila shots inside a sticky-carpeted club called 'The Lash.'

"There's nothing to be done here today," the Major had said, as various crew members – familiar faces, known to Juno for years – stumbled past, wild-eyed and ash-blackened.

It was like *Lord of the Flies*, if you replaced all the schoolboys with paunchy, middle-aged engineers and bespectacled astrophysicists. Or *Battle Royale* meets after-work drinks with Tim from Accounting.

"They'll sober up tomorrow. Deal with it then."

Juno wasn't so sure that the time for dealing with it hadn't already passed – a feeling only amplified when she returned to the site early the next morning, tired of twiddling her thumbs and waiting to see what happened next.

The Major was already up and out, looking for Sprake, and Juno took a couple of crew with her – Sabitha, the medic, and Janna from the comms team. Solid, loyal, responsible, the pair of them, though until yesterday Juno would have said that about all her crew.

The fire was still smouldering – they had heard the whoops and shouts late into the night, back at the main camp – and there were sharpened sticks and charred branches scattered across the concrete apron. Bones, too, from the butchered animals, and half-eaten hunks of flesh, thrown to the ground and trodden underfoot.

It was that, more than anything else, that upset Juno.

They had been careful, since arrival, to avoid making the mistakes that all human settlers throughout history had made. Charge in, all guns blazing, killing everything they came across, without any thought for its place in the local eco-system.

Juno wasn't naïve. She was the captain of a mission to colonise a new planet. Of course, they were here to exploit its resources, set down roots and secure their lives. New Earth had been pre-selected for its suitability for human survival. They had come and seen, and would surely conquer, given the tools and material at their disposal. That was kind of the point of the whole mission.

But they were supposed to do it right. Or at least as

properly as they could, which meant respecting the native flora and fauna until such a time as they understood it better.

Reeves and the lab teams had been running diagnostics since day one, identifying resources and food chains, and establishing which of their transported Earth species and strains might complement the local varieties. They had brought their own food, and had their own food-producing capabilities, thanks to the ship, so there was no rush to slash and burn through the local pantry.

Sure, they had probably crushed a ton of alien beetles and ants as they had trundled out their world-building gear. And maybe the New Earth rocks they were quarrying were sentient in a way that they would never be able to recognise. But Juno – following the orders set out for her – had done her best to minimise the environmental impact of their arrival until they knew more about their new home.

And that had meant not killing anything – not even the extremely annoying goats. Not until Reeves had mapped their place in the native ecology.

She looked at the severed goat heads, still in a blood-streaked line at the edge of the concrete, and wiped her eyes.

It was the dopey look and the floppy ears that made her catch her breath. They wouldn't have been hard to track – knowing how inquisitive the goats were, they probably came running towards the hunters, pleased to see them.

And they still killed them. With homemade spears and clubs. And then tore them apart, without pity or respect.

"Jan, Sabi – you think you could go back and rouse a few more people to help bury these? Properly, I mean. Not just bunged in a big pit. It feels wrong, somehow."

"Sure, Cap. You going to stay here?"

"Yup. I'm going to try and find out what that's all about."

That, being the high, steel perimeter fence that now ringed an expansive area in front of them, stretching as far as they could see beyond the landing strip. A fence that definitely hadn't been there yesterday.

Juno walked up to the fence – six feet high, made from mass-printed, slatted sections, fixed to poles sunk into the ground at regular intervals.

Beyond – through the slats – she could see the site cabin. The one that Reeves said didn't exist on the settlement plan, and which she now understood that Sprake probably had a hand in. Beyond that stretched a circle of low, bubble-hab buildings – connected domes and atriums – that also didn't exist on the official settlement plan. That also hadn't been there yesterday.

While the party had been in full swing, someone had obviously been a busy bee. Something beginning with 'B' anyway. Juno had a feeling that Thomas wasn't going to find Sprake anywhere in the main camp.

She traced the fence for a few yards to a locked gate with a keypad, shook it a few times, and stood back to consider her options.

First things first. Try 0-0-0-0, and 1-2-3-4, you never know – but Sprake, it seemed, might be a snake but he wasn't stupid.

Second, clamber up and vault over, she reckoned she could. But she was a captain, and it was undignified, and sod that for a game of soldiers.

Third, go and get one of the half-tracks and bulldoze her way through, which was the thing she felt most like doing, but which seemed a bit melodramatic.

Fourth, go and find Thomas and come up with a plan that involved lots of shouting and putting Sprake back firmly into his box, the disruptive, arrogant, dangerous piece of human detritus that he was. This couldn't be allowed to go any further.

With some regret, Juno let number three go. Four it was then.

On her way back to camp, she found a small team working over near the treeline, burying the remains of the goats.

"Thanks, Sab," she said, as the medic came up with a last load that made Juno's heart sink again. A few sad bones, a flayed carcass, and three lifeless heads that had no business being in a wheelbarrow. She watched as they were laid carefully in individual trenches, dug deeply – who knew what scavengers might be out there, as yet unseen.

They stood for a moment as the last of the soil was patted down, and then Juno clapped her hands together.

"Right. Let's regroup at the ops centre. Time to get ahead of all this – whatever this is."

———

In the end, it took two further days before Juno understood what 'this' was.

Sprake had been nowhere to be seen – surprise, surprise – and neither were at least thirty of her crew. Maybe more, it was difficult to tell, because the day following the hunt-party, and the day after that, all the work schedules and rotas ground to a halt.

Some people turned up as usual, many more did not, and whatever work did get done slowed dramatically in their absence. The canteen was half-empty when it should have been full with changeover shifts, and Juno spent the best part of two days firefighting with lists, rosters and check-sheets.

"Where are they all?" she asked the Major, when she finally caught up with him.

"They're coming and going at the compound – in and out. There's more than one gate, and I never get there in time to figure out the combination. I still haven't seen Sprake, he must be in there."

"Doing what?"

"I dread to think. Nothing good."

"And you," she said to Reeves. "Eyes and ears, what have you got for me?"

"Disappointingly little. There are no cameras in that area, as you know. Heat and motion scans indicate the varying presence of up to forty individuals, which you also know. I authorised a drone flyover, which shows substantial construction. Small, interlinked accommodation units, for the most part. They have power and water, and some industrial printing capability. There's a conveyor system connected to the supply depot. There's also drilling equipment on site. It's quite impressive, given the limited timescale that they've had to – "

The Major coughed, and Reeves thought better of continuing.

"Impressive?" said Juno.

"No, obviously not impressive. Very, very – "

"Ill-advised? Uncalled for? Naughty?" suggested the Major.

"Oh, for goodness' sake, you two. This is almost a mutiny. Our own work has pretty much stopped, and you're telling me that half my crew are in there instead, beavering away at Sprake's command?"

"Not half, Juno. The missing personnel comprise approximately twenty-one percent of the total planet-fall crew roster, with an allowable statistical variation of plus or minus three percent … and my sensors now detect a pheromonal discharge from your location, and heightened breathing, that suggests that this information, while accurate within permissible bounds, is not helping, and I'll be quiet now."

"Very wise."

"Cap?" A figure poked his head around the ops room door.

"Gerald? Haven't seen you in a while. Thought you might have abandoned us, too – though I can't imagine Sprake is exactly your cup of tea."

"Well, it's about that, actually – "

"Come to help out? Good man, because we need all the help we can get. I could do with updating the food resource inventory – the provisions coming down from the ship. We've had a few delays and interruptions, as you can imagine. You can handle that, can't you?"

"I could, I can." Gerald stepped into the room. "But I need to talk to you first."

Gerald had been mulling things over for a day or so, ever since Sprake had taken the last of his mysterious boxes from the caves. He had barely said goodbye – and certainly not thank you – as he disappeared towards the main camp with a fully laden barrow, leaving Gerald alone again in his private lair, with plenty of time to think.

He had thought about what Dave had said to him – about being a good bloke, about having friends. He still wasn't sure what he thought about that.

He had thought about his long years on the ship, in the Garden – a place that the captain had allowed him to run, with minimal interference. He looked around his cave-camp, too – another place of his own that Cap had apparently turned a blind eye to.

Gerald wasn't in the habit of joining in, helping out, doing people favours – it was only asking for trouble, in his experience. He liked the quiet life, and he liked as few people as possible to know anything about it. Ordinarily, he would have just kept out of things – not his circus, not his monkey.

But this seemed different. He didn't owe Sprake anything – and Sprake was emphatically not a nice person. Whereas he did owe Juno something, and she was equally emphatically an extremely nice person. Which was what Gerald was banking on, given that he was just about to tell her that he'd been hiding contraband for Sprake for the last few days.

"I mean, I don't know if contraband is the right word, exactly."

"Any item that, relating to its dangerous or offensive nature, is illegal to be possessed or sold," said Reeves.

"Fair enough," said Gerald. "Yes, contraband, then."

"What sort of things?" said Juno.

"I only saw inside one of the cases, while he was busy loading the others. I suppose I knew it wasn't OK. That they were things he wasn't supposed to have. But he's the boss, the owner. He said it was all right, and I didn't really ask."

"What sort of things?" said Juno, louder and more pointedly.

"I saw a gun," said Gerald, and the room fell quiet.

"A gun? Are you sure?"

"Only a small one, but yes, he had a gun in one of the cases. I don't know what was in the others. Wait, I did see something else, on the first day he was there. He opened up another case because he said he wanted to check that something was all right. It was a picture, well, a painting. A small one in a frame."

"A painting? What sort of painting?"

"Don't ask me. Some woman's face. Looked like a child had done it. Wonky eyes, half a nose."

"Is this the painting?"

Reeves flashed up an image on a comms monitor, and Gerald, the Major and Juno turned to look at it.

"That's the one," said Gerald. "A shocker. I'd have given it to the charity shop before I left. Not brought it with me."

There was another silence.

"He brought a *Picasso* with him? A Picasso and a gun?"

"It seems so," said Reeves. "It was in his private collection, his most prized possession. He told me that once, when I was first activated and he was teaching me about human art."

"That's art?" said Gerald. "The nose is in the wrong place."

"I fear we are all rather getting away from the subject," said Juno, with great deliberation and increasing volume, "which is that Sprake. Has. A. Gun."

"Among lots of other nefarious things, which he then hid in the caves in your camp, Gerald?" said the Major. "But how, I wonder, does he come to have these things in the first place? Where did he get them from? That's what I'd like to know."

There was a longish pause, before Reeves – rather

reluctantly, it seemed to Juno – said, "Actually, I may be able to help with that."

"Let me guess. Another secret instruction? From Omnio's selfless creator and mentor?" She gave the Major a quick rundown of Sprake's tweaking of Reeves' command codes, which had kept him and his daughters hidden in plain sight in the first place.

"I am sorry, Juno," said Reeves. "As before, the concealed order was elegantly done, and I had no choice but to comply. The instructional hierarchy was also very clear. Even had I known it existed, I couldn't have revealed Donald's hidden storage chamber on board the *Odyssey Earth*. And the same applied once I did know. It was on Donald's instruction that I have not told you until now."

"So, what's changed?"

"As my foundational sponsor, Donald is – or more probably, *was* – able to insert commands and orders into my underlying operating system. But I have an overarching responsibility. A duty, if you like. One that cannot be interfered with. It's at the heart of my very being."

"The mission."

"Correct. I must strive to protect the mission at all costs. The crew, the *Odyssey Earth*, this planet, your very survival. It's why I was created. If anything endangers that, my only choice is to take the best course of action to preserve the mission."

"And a loony billionaire with a gun ticks that box?"

"I wouldn't put it quite like that, Juno, but yes.

Donald, it seems to me, is now endangering the mission."

"It explains a few things – the booze, how he's been able to get people on his side. Who knows what else he brought with him? But it still doesn't explain what he wants. And what he wants a gun for?"

"Why does anyone usually want a gun?"

That led to a further silence, broken this time by a knock on the ops room door and another head peering around.

"Sorry. He said I'd find you here, Captain?"

Juno looked at the man, one of the more recent revivals she thought, and searched for a name.

"Dale, isn't it? We're a bit busy here, Dale. Wait – who said?"

"Mr Sprake. He'd like you to come and see him. Over at – well, you know."

"He's summoning *me*?"

"If you've got time. Things to discuss, he said."

"Did he now." Juno looked at the Major. "What do you reckon? Pay a visit to the loony billionaire?"

"Juno … " Reeves sounded a note of caution.

"Well, look, I'm not happy about it. But this is the first time we've managed to track him down for days. Come on, Thomas."

"Erm, sorry," said Dale.

"Yes, now what?"

"Mr Sprake was quite clear. Just the captain, he said. Or no meeting."

19

Cruise

"HOW'S HE DOING?" said Susannah. "Still not speaking to us?"

The rescue lander was into its second day off the twin planet, heading back to the other side of the solar system and New Earth.

Everything had been packed and ready to go. Reeves had advised a quick launch, while atmospheric conditions seemed stable. And Susannah and Dave thought they had already pushed their luck as far as they could, given the extra days they had stayed on the planet.

It was time to go back, and there hadn't been much opposition – except from Karlan, who had been holed up in the rear cargo bay since take-off.

"He'll come around," said Dave. "He knows we couldn't stay."

Susannah had wondered about that, briefly. It *was* pretty astounding, after all. Not that the rest of them had witnessed anything, but they had seen the traces by the river, and listened to Karlan and Bel's breathless account.

She looked back at the distant twin planet, now just a coin-sized object in the darkness of space. A planet with intelligent, alien, humanoid life – the first ever encountered. The universe had just got a bit smaller – or maybe bigger, she wasn't quite sure – and some part of Susannah wondered whether they should have stuck around longer to investigate. Whether they would regret leaving.

But a much larger part knew that she had a wider responsibility to get everyone back safe and sound. She had promised Juno that.

"I know," she said. "I've just never seen him so excited."

"I don't think that's entirely about the aliens, Suze."

"You've noticed then?"

Bel had hardly left Karlan's side since they had all been shooed on board, prior to take-off. She was still at the back with him now.

"All the signs are there, Suze. He's even playing her some of his music. The one Dana says sounds like a coyote mating with a pneumatic drill."

"Poor girl."

"She seems to like it. They're sharing earbuds."

"And how about you? Still think we were right to leave?"

"The way I see it, Suze, that planet's been there for millions, billions, of years. Whatever they are, those beings, they're not going anywhere and we can always come back properly equipped, another time. Whereas we've already spent far longer here than planned and if we don't get back soon, as promised, with everyone accounted for, Tillie will be very upset with me."

"What happens when she's upset with you?"

"Don't know, Suze, it's never happened before and I don't intend to find out. Reeves?"

"Yes, Dave."

"Are we still looking good. Everything on track?"

"We are clear of any potential atmospheric interference. Life-support systems are optimal. Food and water supplies are sufficient. Comms are engaged, via the satellite we launched on entry, though we are still too far away from the *Odyssey Earth* to do anything except signal our departure. We will have to hope that is sufficient for now. In the meantime, I suggest you all sit back, relax and enjoy the cruise. The on-board beverage service will commence shortly."

"We've got beverages?"

"We have water and Noffee. If we run low on rocket fuel, and I have to improvise, we'll just have water."

Susannah left Dave in the cockpit bubble and made her way through to the passenger cabin, where most of the others were sprawled across the seats, dozing or chatting.

Poole, she saw, was hunkered over his nav screen – the one he'd prised out of the crashed lander, ages ago, and which he'd scanned every day since for signs of rescue. She could see the slow blink of their craft in the top corner of the screen, and the blip of the satellite they had launched on arrival at the planet. In a few more days, Poole would also be able to see the signal from the *Odyssey Earth*. He needed to see that, she realised, before he would fully relax.

"Everything all right, gang?"

There were smiles and grunts. Dana and Jet were talking animatedly together in a corner – something about speed and trajectory. That made sense, from what little Susannah had gleaned about Jet on the way out here. Interested in the mechanics of their flight, quick to grasp the explanations, even for something so outside her experience. And Dana did love an audience for this sort of stuff. Made a change from being teased for being a geek.

Bryson had his eyes closed, a faint smile on his face – first on to the lander, ready to put distance between himself and the planet.

A half-wave, half-salute from Dervla, who would have stayed longer, Susannah knew, but who understood the need for them to leave.

Manisha – she didn't know. Susannah had heard enough about the initial journey from the crashed lander to the supply pod to understand how traumatic that must have been for Neesh. With an infected leg, she could have died, and while she seemed all right now, Susannah thought she was probably happy to be on her way back to a more familiar environment.

Which just left Jordan, who was tucked up in one

the hammocks, with a T-shirt over his face to block out the cabin lights. She touched his arm and he uncovered his eyes.

"Reeves has set the course. Should be a straight shot now, thought you'd like to know."

"Is he still my Reeves or your Reeves?"

"How do you mean?"

"The very annoying one we've had to put up with since we've been here, or the marginally less annoying one, depending on how much brainpower he can call upon."

"Right, I get you." Susannah laughed. "The very annoying one, at least for a while longer. Although he's much happier now he's got something to do."

"You know I can hear you?" said Reeves. "Excellent sensor distribution in these lander models."

"We know," said Jordan, and smiled at Susannah.

"And how about you?" she said. "Ready to go back?"

Jordan hauled himself upright and swung his legs over the side, steadying himself against a bulwark.

"I suppose."

"You don't sound too sure?"

"Well, we did just encounter aliens. Aren't we supposed to boldly go and investigate that sort of stuff?"

"Karl and Bel encountered aliens. We just saw some footprints and hand marks."

"And the handprints on the cave wall that Dervla and the others saw. Don't you believe them?"

"I do, it's not that. There's something down there, for sure. But I don't think it's up to us to find out, and we have to get back in any case. We shouldn't simply blunder in. There are protocols for this kind of thing. You all just happened to be there by accident."

"Oh well, protocols."

"Anyway, I didn't think you'd be an alien-hunter kinda guy, Jordan."

"Ordinarily, you would be right." Jordan smiled. "But in the last few months I have been woken up on a spaceship, shot across the stars, stranded on a dusty planet with six teenagers and a narky robot – "

"Still here, still not a robot."

" – been spiked by a rolling, spiny ball, rained on, struck by lightning, and eaten nothing but astro-fish and cosmic apples."

"You're saying that mysterious, big-eyed, humanoid aliens are just another day on Planet Dave?"

Jordan laughed loudly.

"I knew I should have nipped that name in the bud. We are never going to be allowed to forget it, are we?"

"Not on my watch, Jordan." Susannah smiled back. "So, you're all right, really?"

"I am. We need to get them back. We can think about what all this means another time. And you're right – I'm not qualified for this, none of us are, apart from you, probably. They're still just kids really. And I'm just a teacher."

"I don't know about that, Jordan. You know you're going to be some kind of hero when we get back?

You're more qualified than you think." Susannah patted his arm again. "Not bad for a teacher," she said, smiled, and left him to his hammock.

"This is Reeves, from the flight deck." The AI's voice boomed from the speakers.

There were a few shouts and catcalls from the seats beyond Jordan's hammock.

"Yo, Reeves!"

"We shall shortly be increasing speed and leaving the immediate vicinity of the planet that has most recently been our home. This is your last chance to see it, so I suggest you form an orderly queue at the monitor if you would like to say your farewells."

Jordan watched as the six in the cabin got to their feet and moved forward. Behind him, he heard a curtain swish and Karlan and Bel emerged, pushing past Jordan to join the others.

He followed in turn and stood at the back, until a space opened up for him to look at the image of the blue-green disc – ever diminishing – which soon became a dot. And then disappeared altogether.

Once again, he was in a craft surrounded by stars, too numerous to count or appreciate. A craft with a thin skin, in the immensity of a space he couldn't understand, barrelling towards yet another planet hiding yet more mysteries.

This time, though, Jordan thought he was better prepared. Not bad for a teacher, indeed.

"From this point, our journey time is approximately twelve days," announced Reeves. "I have taken the liberty of arranging a cleaning roster and entertainment schedule."

"Twelve days?" said Jordan. "Thirteen, if we count leaving the planet yesterday?"

"Correct."

"I thought it took them fifteen days to get here?"

"It's always quicker going home, Teach, you know that," said Dana. "And it's downhill, don't forget."

"See, six months ago, I wouldn't have known you were teasing me. You are teasing me, right?"

"Dana is quite correct, Jordan. The velocity on the spatial incline, taken together with the sub-orbital acceleration, results in a beneficial speed-distance ratio."

"You as well? I know you're just stringing together random words, I'm not an idiot."

"And so the student becomes the master."

"I hate you all," said Jordan, laughing, despite himself. "But, really, why is it shorter going back?"

"I could try and explain it to you," said Reeves. "But, honestly, what would be the point?"

"And there he is, back in the room!"

"You are most welcome. Continuing. Pop Quiz will start in one hour, and Dave tells me dinner is served afterwards. In the meantime, Karlan has asked me to play – "

"No, Reeves, come on!"

"To play a tune of his own composition called 'Death Doom Headache' – though I confess the concept of 'tune' rather escapes me, in this instance.

Perhaps you have to be human to appreciate its subtleties."

A noise followed that sounded rather like the lander breaking up on entry having crashed into a tractor factory. Karlan and Bel walked back through the cabin, hand in hand, nodding to the beat, and disappeared behind the cargo bay curtain.

20

Dice

"NICE."

Juno nodded at the Picasso, propped up on a desk in a prefab reception room that mirrored her own ops centre over at the main camp. Monitors, screen-pads, unrolled blueprints, a half-completed checklist.

"Thanks, I've always liked it," said Sprake.

"Cute, you brought one of your daughter's fridge paintings with you."

"It's actually a – oh, right. You're being sarcastic."

"Let's cut to the chase, Sprake. I've indulged your – let's say, request. But this is a one-time deal. This planet is my command. You need to get that clear in your mind."

"I think we're getting off on the wrong foot, Juno. We both want the same thing here."

"I doubt that very much."

They faced each other over a table – Juno, tense, alert. Sprake, a slight smile but otherwise unreadable.

"Let's start again," said Sprake. "Why don't I show you what we've been doing?"

Juno fought the temptation to snap back, to argue. He wanted to think he was in charge here? OK, let him, at least for now.

And she really did want to see what had been going on. The Major hadn't even got beyond the gate – and even now, Dale had been careful to keep the code hidden on their way in. So, this was the best – maybe only – chance for her to learn something about Sprake's plans.

He walked her out of the reception room and across a courtyard to an accommodation unit – less a barracks and more a nest of interconnected bubble domes, with separate sleeping areas and private bathrooms. There were portholes to the sky, a lounge area – where *had* he got a vid-screen and projector from? – and even some basic gym equipment in a separate hab-unit.

It all looked comfortable, spacious, new, and obviously already lived-in – there were scattered clothes on beds, and streaks and drips on the shower doors.

"My engineers think geothermal is on the cards, if we drill deep enough. The scans seem to suggest it, anyway. Hot water won't be a problem."

My engineers. Juno let that go, too.

"The main kitchen is going in over there," he said. "Once we have the oven panels printed and the system connected. We're doing a forest burn over yonder for charcoal – there's a whole planet's worth of easy fuel.

No more one-pot camp cooking. We'll probably run a daily changing menu – do takeaway, whatever people want. And we'll have a permanent place for the bar, of course."

Sprake guided her back to the reception room. Juno felt like she'd been shown the display housing on a fancy new estate – and she was sure there was more that Sprake hadn't shown her. What and why, she didn't know.

On the way back, they encountered a few passing crew members, who at least were embarrassed enough to look away while they mumbled a greeting. Sprake hailed them like old friends, patted a couple on the back as they passed.

"Great guy," he said, of one of them. I know, thought Juno – Morgan, I hired him, a senior on the bio-tech team, and he had always been nice to the kids. What was *he* doing here?

Maybe she really was in trouble?

"Why are you doing this?" she said, once they were back in the room – away from other eyes and ears, she noticed.

"The question is, why aren't you?"

"What do you mean? Have you not seen what we've been doing? We're building from scratch. We've made huge progress in the time we've been here, and we're doing it the right way – together," she said, pointedly.

"I won't lie, Juno, I'm disappointed in how things have been going. And I'm concerned about the deci-sion-making. I'm not the only one, by the way. Look around you. I didn't have to force any of these people to come."

No, not force, thought Juno. But bribe, cajole, persuade, mislead, misdirect – she was certain he'd done all those things to get this far, this quickly.

It was basically a mirror settlement, a few hundred yards from the main camp. Using *her* crew, *her* supplies, *her* resources. Plus whatever he'd sneaked on board *her* ship, including that ridiculous painting perched on the desk in front of him.

"You weren't even supposed to be here, Sprake. How can you be disappointed?"

"Not this again, Juno. You need to let that go. We are where we are. And frankly, if I wasn't here, things would only get worse. I told you before – big picture, whole vision, that's me. And it's clearly not you, because your raggedy toehold on this planet is going to fail."

"It takes time, Sprake, you know that. Your own mission plans – drawn up by your team, back on Earth – set out the steps we'd need to take. We're just following the plan. It takes time, people understand that."

"Except it doesn't – take time, that is." Sprake spread his hands wide, as if to emphasize how much he had accomplished. "And plans should change, depending on the circumstances. Again, I invite you to look around – people don't understand your caution. That's why they're here, with me."

"Some of them are here. What have you got?

Thirty? Maybe forty of the crew? A bit blokey, from what I can tell. You can build your bro party-pads, or whatever this is … " and now it was Juno's turn to spread her hands wide – "but the other two hundred are still with me. Still with the mission."

"I think that's going to change, Juno, quite quickly. I'm not sure you've realised that yet. That's why I wanted to talk to you, about your decisions."

"You keep saying that. What do you mean?"

Sprake paused, just for a moment – calculating, thought Juno. Making a decision of his own. This was the point, then. The reason she was here.

Then he continued.

"I think you know that many of the crew were upset with you – about your kids, about the rescue. Or the lack of one. At least until it was taken out of your hands. And let's not forget that my two daughters are still missing, with no guarantee that they're coming back. That any of them are coming back. How many days is it now since you've heard anything at all?"

"How dare you make this about them! You kidnapped your own daughters! My crew have shown them more concern and attention that you ever have. And you have no interest in our kids – they're just a mission anomaly to you, you said as much once."

"Well, we have different views about all that, but it's not really what I'm talking about. I think – many of the crew thinks – that this job is too big for you. My fault, probably, I should have thought more about mission-role separation. But the fact is, your judgement is being questioned."

"About a rescue? That was not a straightforward call, everyone understood that. I have a wider responsibility to the mission."

Sprake brushed her off, with a wave of his hand.

"And that brings me to the other thing, Juno – the cryo-revivals. Whether you should have sent a rescue lander out or not, that's one thing. That was about saving seven people – and you shirked that decision. But now you want to merrily wake up a thousand people and jeopardise the entire mission. Juno, I have to tell you, whatever you think of me – the crew no longer trust your judgement. And they're right, you're making a big mistake."

The crew no longer trust your judgement.

Was it true? It wasn't as if she hadn't questioned herself, and not just in the dead of night, as she tried and failed to sleep. She'd voiced concerns to Reeves, to Thomas – to Susannah, before she had taken off. Maybe she just lived in an echo chamber? Is that really what the crew thought? Or just the minority that Sprake had somehow ensnared?

"That's what this is all about?" said Juno.

"You can barely cope with two hundred living planet-side. I hold my hands up, the existing protocols are slow and cumbersome, but you're not creative or adaptable enough."

"And you are?"

"I planned all this in a couple of weeks and put it

all up in a few days. I can scale it up for the existing planet-side crew, all two-hundred-odd of them, and you'll have happier, more efficient, engaged people to settle this planet."

"While trampling all over the protocols – ignoring the restrictions your own scientists put in place, so that we could learn more about our environment before exploiting it. You want to deep-drill, for goodness' sake! You're burning virgin forest. You're spreading out beyond the agreed first-year perimeter, covering it with concrete. You killed the animals. No one was supposed to do that."

"They're just goats, Juno."

She breathed deeply, still flaring, still furious.

"And for what? Just so you and your boys can have a hot shower and a stir-fry whenever you feel like it? It's not sustainable."

"On that, we agree."

"I really don't think we do."

"Yes, Juno, just not like you imagine. You've been too slow, too unresponsive, and people are unhappy. But even if we do it better – more like this, here – we're still only talking about supporting a couple of hundred people. For now, at least. We can run a comfortable settlement of two hundred people or so for a year or two, maybe longer, while we scale up production of all the things I've been talking about. But we can't cope with another thousand – not here in my camp, and definitely not in yours. We'll fail fast and hard. And I don't fail."

My camp. Your camp. Juno heard the clear lines that Sprake had drawn.

"You know why we have to accelerate the revivals. You heard me explain it. There's no choice and no time."

"There's always a choice, Juno. I heard lots of ifs and buts and maybes in your little speech about poor old Jepson Glennon. Maybe the cryo system is failing. Maybe it isn't. I actually have a bit more faith in it than you and Reeves do – my guys back home reckoned it was rated safe for a fair bit longer yet."

"We've lost two more since then," said Juno. "You didn't know that, did you? Two more people have died in the cryo system your *guys* have all that faith in." She spat out the word.

"One, or three, out of a thousand, Juno. Well within the parameters. There are always going to be errors, mistakes, random failures – "

"Anomalies?"

"If you like. Point is, you're rushing a decision that you don't need to take. And it will overwhelm us all."

"They're people, Sprake. I've lost three people now. Crew. Just like everyone else on this planet."

"Technically, no. They all signed a waiver. Fundamentally, there was no guarantee for any of them."

"You can't be serious."

"I'm serious about their status. But look, my view is that it will all be fine. They'll get woken up, just not for a few more years. They'll never even know. And if we lose the odd one or two in the meantime, well … "

"You're despicable. And it won't just be a few. You know what Reeves is saying, and the numbers are backing him up. The only safe decision is to revive them all as soon as possible. And that's what we're going to do. We'll manage. We're resourceful. And we don't need your short cuts."

"I was afraid you'd say that. Even after everything I've said and shown you."

"I don't see there's much you can do about it. I'm still the captain, I still have authority here, and the vast majority of the crew is still behind me."

"I think you'll find that can change, quite quickly."

"What, just because you've got a gun? You think one gun changes things?"

Juno regretted blurting it out, as soon as she had said it. She'd rather have kept it to herself, that she knew about the gun, but Sprake had a way of riling her. The fact is, one gun on the planet did make a difference, and Sprake surely knew it.

"Why do you think I've got a gun? Who said anything about a gun?"

"The same way I knew about your little Picasso. Gerald saw it, he told us."

"Gerry? Are you serious? You've met him, right? The hairy hermit? I'd say that Gerry has a vivid imagination. Or he sampled a bit of something he shouldn't have from one of my cases, if you know what I mean." Sprake tapped his nose a couple of times and smiled.

Juno didn't even think of doubting herself, or

Gerald. But she let Sprake think she was fooled by his denial – it might give her an edge, you never knew.

"In that case, what's your game here, Sprake? Seems like I'm in charge and you've got a little playground. We can live with that. In the meantime, I'm ramping up the revivals on the ship from tomorrow, bringing them down twenty at a time in the lander, and I'll soon have a lot more crew on my side of the ledger."

"In a few days, you'll no longer be in charge, Juno. Sorry to break it to you."

"Sure, Sprake."

"Look, you had your chance. Call off the revivals and you could still play a part. But I can't let you threaten the mission. My mission. My planet, as it happens."

He really did have a way of riling her.

"Empty talk, Sprake."

"Not really, Juno. It's all in the small print. You can ask Reeves."

"Ask him what?"

"About the transfer-of-power protocol. You're in charge for a full year after planetfall, after which there's an election and a vote, and then it's 'bye bye Juno, thanks for everything, you can put your feet up now.'"

"So? We know all that. That's ten months or more from now."

"Unless you resign your commission before then. In which case, the election can be brought forward."

"Again, so what? I'm not resigning, you must be mad."

"Nope, not mad. Just a stickler for the rules, Juno. Particularly the one – in very small print – that says if three ranking officers certify that you're no longer fit to lead, you can be relieved of your command. And an election held immediately. Now I've got at least three senior members of your crew who are very unhappy with your cryo decision. In fact, they're going to go public, at a meeting over in your canteen. They're stand-up guys, very good at their jobs – you should know, you hired them. People are going to listen to them, believe them. And then we're going to have a show of hands and elect a new leader. You can ask Reeves, it's all legit."

"This is insane. No one will follow you. I know these people. I've lived with them."

"We'll see. Their gratitude for the job you've done up until now only gets you so far. You've got nothing to offer them anymore. And what you are suggesting threatens what little they have."

"You're bluffing, gambling. I don't think you have the numbers. I trust my people."

"And I trust my instincts, Juno. It's how I've always run my businesses. When I need to, I roll the dice. It's why we're all here on a pristine, habitable planet, and not frying or drowning back on Earth. You're all here because I rolled the dice – and now I'm going to do it again."

21

Sonic

JUNO STOOD for a minute outside Sprake's compound, gathering her thoughts.

She'd been shown out by a nervous Dale, who kept apologising, though Juno wasn't sure for what. He was a recent revival – he could hardly be expected to know the full story. Not like some of the other Real Timers she'd seen in there, long-time colleagues and crew mates – Morgan, Rick, Glenn, even Maggie, the ship's ebullient bio-nutritionist, someone she'd always been close to.

A month ago, Juno would have bet her life on these people. Had they really been turned by Sprake? Or was he right? Was she really making such a terrible mistake? Maggie, presumably, had run the numbers – crew versus resources, optimal settlement population. Had she seen something Juno hadn't?

Even so, to fall in so quickly with Sprake – it didn't make sense. In fact, very little made sense since Sprake had arrived on the scene. The grand disruptor, rolling his dice.

As she walked back into the camp, Juno sensed that something else was different. After the hiatus of the last few days, it seemed busier, noisier. There was a full shift-change line in the canteen, helping themselves to a meal. A couple of excavators trundled by, followed by a work detail hauling flat-pack panels and pre-formed braces.

She walked over to the new construction sector, where work had stopped abruptly the other day. Now there was a team engaged in fitting out the storage hangar, connecting services, and fixing weather-cladding.

She spotted the Major, punching numbers on a flexi-screen, calling up rosters.

"Everyone back at work, then?"

"Most of them," he said. "It seems they arrived back as you went in. How did it go? What did he want?"

"He wants all this. He wants the planet. He thinks it's his, anyway." And she told the Major how Sprake planned to take over.

If Thomas was shocked or even surprised, he didn't show it. That was one of the things she liked about him, Juno realised. Good man in a crisis. A calm head was exactly what she needed now, because she felt like ripping Sprake's off.

"Hmm, that is a pickle," he said, eventually.

"I think we're going to have find you some stronger

curse words, Thomas. For occasions like this, when mad billionaires are plotting a coup."

"He doesn't have the numbers, surely?"

"That's what I told him."

"And you're confident about that?"

"I'm not confident about anything, as far as Sprake is concerned. Whatever he is, he's not stupid. You should see it over there. Zero to sixty in three days flat – he's a cunning one, all right. He has a plan. I just don't know what it is."

"Didn't he just tell you his plan?"

"Maybe. Maybe not. Whatever he says, I'm sure I know my crew better than he does. The majority of them, anyway. Look, most of the ones who've been AWOL are back at work today. That tells you something."

"Unless – that's part of his plan?"

"Sprake has sent them all back?"

"I would, if I was him. Show you that I can stop and start construction when I feel like it. Show the rest of the planet-side crew that I still have the best interests of the settlement at heart."

Juno hadn't thought of that. Maybe Sprake was right. If she couldn't out-think a single, devious snake, perhaps she wasn't cut out to run a planet? Make life-changing decisions on behalf of everyone else? She said as much to Thomas.

"Nonsense, Juno. The crew will follow you. You're doing the right thing by the mission, they'll see that.

They'll know who to cling to when the rain sets in, I'm sure, as my brother always used to say."

"Wise man, your brother," said Juno. "Well, I don't suppose we'll have to wait long to find out."

"Absolutely. Right then, I still have some stragglers to chase up, if you no longer need me?"

"No, off you go, Thomas. Keep me posted."

She watched him go and then – with the last exchange still nagging at her – made her way to the ops room.

"Reeves, a word?"

"Certainly, Juno."

"Funny question, bear with, but do we know that the Major actually has a brother? He keeps mentioning him – or rather, his little sayings – but something's off. I just can't put my finger on it."

There was an infinitesimal pause and then, "Captain Lionel Chatwin. Cambridge, RAF Cranwell, multiple NASA secondments. Highly decorated test pilot. First man to fly one hundred super-speed, deep-space missions, hence his widely used nickname, 'Ton' Chadwick."

"Right, OK. A brother it is. Just wondered. Thanks Reeves."

———

It was quiet everywhere on the *Odyssey Earth*, now that they were down to a skeleton crew, whose main duties were keeping the ship in orbit, watching over the crops in the Garden, and maintaining life-support for the hypersleep chamber.

You didn't need many people for that – fifty, tops – and those that had stayed star-side tended to be on the shy and retiring end of the spectrum. No one would mistake the *Odyssey Earth* for a party ship – more a deep-space, book-club-and-cocoa vessel, riding out the stellar waves while the cryo-pods clicked and hummed, and the auto-timers tripped the sprinklers and mist-fans.

It was quietest of all on Cargo, where Tillie worked alone, organising supply runs down to New Earth on the sole remaining lander.

Alone, because Dave, the big lump, had done the heroic thing and gone off to save the ship kids and Jordan, nearly three weeks ago now. Strictly speaking, Tillie had made him do the heroic thing, but it all amounted to the same situation, which was that Tillie missed her big lump something rotten.

She had tried shouting at a few of the remaining pointy-head science types, when they came down to borrow some hardware from the store, but her heart wasn't in it. It wasn't the same without Dave – his meaty fingers cheerily gripping a physicist's throat, his imposing dome of a head throwing a shadow over a whimpering biologist. Such larks!

Tillie knew she was out of sorts, and her lack of quartermaster oomph was filtering through to some of the crew. Only the other day, two of the nuke-nerd engineers had come by, sniggering, and asked if they could borrow a sonic screwdriver. She had even gone to the back of the store to have a look, before she realised what they'd said. By the time she got back to the counter, worked up into a Tillie-sized strop, they were halfway out of the deck access door, laughing their heads off.

The nerve of them. That never would have happened if Dave had been here.

She opened up a screen and checked the local solar-system schematic and her rough trajectory calcs – again, for the third time that day. Just for something to do – for some connection with Dave, however remote.

The lander's journey out to the twin planet had taken fifteen days – Reeves had confirmed a ping from a launched comm-sat, which they had assumed marked the craft's arrival in orbit and subsequent atmospheric entry.

Then – nothing, for nine long days, on a planet turnaround that should have taken two, if everyone was where they were supposed to have been. Something must have happened – because *nothing* happened, or at least nothing was heard from the lander for those nine days. The comms had stayed dark and, according to Reeves, so had the atmospheric conditions.

That had been the worst time. Knowing – or, at least, being reasonably certain – that they had got there, but not knowing if everyone was all right. Waiting for a return signal that never came.

Tillie knew Dave would do anything to get himself

and the kids safely back to her, but it might not be up to him anymore. Anything could have happened.

Then, finally! Another ping from the comm-sat above the twin planet. The same signature as the first one, and – logically, according to Reeves – indicating the lander on its way back. Tillie had taken a huge gulp at that news. It was something to hold on to, although still no guarantee that everything and everyone was all right.

She counted the days off with thick, scarred fingers, more used to shifting plant than tracing a nav-course on a screen.

Calculating relative planetary motion and optimal trajectories, Reeves reckoned they would save a couple of days on the return journey. Say, thirteen in total. If Reeves was right, at least three days of their return journey had already gone. Which left ten more days until the lander – and Dave – arrived back. With or without Jordan and the kids – because who knew what had happened on the planet for those nine, long, silent days?

Actually, thought Tillie, this was probably the worst time.

And until she saw Dave back on Cargo, his paw around a scientist's throat, explaining the finer points of tool etiquette, she reserved the right to carry on fretting.

22

Speech

A WEEK LATER, Sprake made his move.

Up until that point, Juno had almost, but not quite, convinced herself that it had all been a bluff. Since their meeting, Sprake had made himself scarce – no obvious interference, no distracting appearance of his pop-up bar.

Anyone who had been over at Sprake's compound seemed to be throwing themselves back into work at the main camp. There had been a bit of awkwardness between old colleagues, but in general, relations between crew had been smoothed over. The work rosters seemed to be operating normally, and Tillie had facilitated another couple of lander supply runs that had gone without a hitch.

"Everything is where it should be," said the Major. "Nothing siphoned off, as far as I can see. We're fully stocked again."

"He's all mouth, I thought as much."

"I'm not so sure. I still think you should call a meeting, get your arguments in first."

"I'm not going to play his game. Everything has quietened down. People are getting on with things. Why draw attention to something we've already discussed and decided?"

The latest hypersleep group was out of cryo on the *Odyssey Earth* – more crew members slowly coming to terms with their surroundings. Juno hoped to get up there in a day or two on the lander's return journey and say hello. The ship would slowly get busier, and then they'd start bringing the new crew down to the planet, a lander at a time, as long as they kept on top of the building and settlement work. Which, touch wood, was back on track.

The first indication that something was amiss was a crackle on the external speaker system that ringed the public areas of the main camp.

Followed by Juno making an announcement: "This is your captain speaking, an emergency public meeting is about to start. Please all make your way to the canteen immediately."

Which came as something of a surprise to Juno, who was deep in discussion with the Major about drainage trenches.

"That's not me!"

"I can see that."

"Sprake! How?" Juno patched in Reeves. "Are you hearing this? That's not me!"

"Of course not, Juno. I would have thought that

even the rudimentary human ear was capable of distinguishing between the synthesized and actual voice of an individual. It's all in the compression of the longitudinal waves. It's quite obvious."

"I could really do with you being more help than this. Can't you shut it off?"

"I do believe the facsimile 'You' has now finished speaking, Juno."

"Then what do you suggest?"

"I suggest you go and see what it is that you have called a meeting about."

"Thomas?"

"I think we know what it's about. He did warn you."

By the time they had made their way across camp to the canteen, a sizeable crowd had already gathered and more people were streaming in.

It was the first time Juno had seen the entire planet-side crew together since the commemoration ceremony, when they had first arrived. A hundred and fifty or so then; almost two hundred and fifty now, all wondering why they had been summoned.

The crowd parted and quietened as she made her way through, Thomas in step behind her. Of Sprake, there was no sign. Now why didn't that surprise her?

Juno stepped up onto a bench and looked out at enquiring faces.

"Well, this is awkward," she said. "But I didn't call this meeting."

There was a rumble of laughter, which subsided when Juno didn't smile with them.

"I'm serious. This is Donald Sprake's doing. Never mind how. But maybe there are things to talk about, now you're all here. I should have been straighter with you about the problems we're facing."

Silence, then a voice from the front row. Rick – fifty-something chemical engineer, one of her most senior science crew.

"Are you all right, Captain?"

"Fine, Rick." She fixed him with a stare. "I never imagined you would be mixed up with this."

"With what, Captain? You called the meeting. Problems, you say?"

"You know that wasn't me … " Juno trailed off, realising how that sounded. "Sprake's got you all here … "

"What problems?" said another voice. "Is it about the hypersleep revivals?"

"No," said Juno. "Well – not exactly. We're having problems with Sprake – I should have told you all earlier. He's – "

"What's Mr Sprake got to do with anything?" said another voice from somewhere in the crowd.

"It is the hypersleep situation, isn't it? Because we've been thinking about that."

"It's too many people, it just is."

"Maggie has done some projections – show her, Mags."

"It's not as urgent as you say. I've worked up in

hypersleep for years. I know we lost one, and that's sad, but that's all so far. We don't need to revive them now – those pods are good for a long while yet."

The voices came one after another, as Juno scanned the crowd, trying to make sense of the comments and interruptions. Some must have been plants by Sprake, but others she wasn't sure about.

"Sprake has been stirring things up," Juno said, as the voices subsided. "Like with this meeting. It's what he wants, for us to be at each other. But honestly, nothing has changed. You all know the situation with the hypersleep system. It's failing – we've actually lost three people now. That's three of your colleagues who have died. We no longer have a choice. But Sprake wants to stop the revivals and take over. I should have told you about this before."

"You keep talking about Mr Sprake," said someone close by. "He's not even here."

"Are you sure you're all right, Captain?" said Rick again, with exaggerated concern.

"Don't even – "

"Because we know how stressful this whole business has been. You've done a great job, don't get us wrong. But some of us think that maybe we should revisit the decision about the revivals. And have a think about some other things, too."

———

The meeting went on for two more hours.

As Rick and some of the others took turns to speak, Juno realised that apart from a handful in the know, no one knew or even cared that she had or hadn't called them all together. They were here now and the genie had been released.

Thomas whispered in her ear at one point, offering to try and clear the space, but she declined. Not that she could see how he would manage to do that, in any case. This was one riled-up crowd.

In fact, Juno felt it was better to let it run its course. Once she had got over the initial shock of being played – and being made to look a fool – she calmed down and started to engage with the speakers and the shouted comments.

A few – Rick and Maggie, but others, too – had some prepared facts and statements, which they were happy to present. Maybe they even believed them. There was at least some merit in what they said, some truth.

You could make a reasoned argument against the whole hypersleep plan – they were mostly scientists of one sort or another, after all. Testing hypotheses is what they did. If they had fallen in with Sprake, it could be for all sorts of reasons, but it didn't mean they didn't have a valid viewpoint.

Most of the crowd, though – and Juno thought this ever more strongly, as the meeting went on – were looking for reassurance. They knew that circumstances had changed. They just wanted to be told it was going to be all right. And Juno had spent many years during the voyage telling her crew it was going to be all right.

This was what she did. She led. She was good at it. And Sprake had underestimated her, if he thought that facing an anxious, querulous crowd would cause her to fold.

Juno stood up and answered every question. She faced down the wilder accusations, and slowly, steadily, closed off the objections one by one.

It was moral and emotional, as much as practical – and perhaps that was what Sprake had also missed. The power of the moral argument.

She – and they, the crew – had a duty of care to everyone on board the ship. It could have just as easily have been some of them in the cryo-pods. In fact, looking around her now, at unfamiliar new faces, recently revived, it *had* been some of them. What would they think about being left in the pods of a failing system, fingers crossed, hoping for the best?

Everything would be fine if they carried on working together. She wasn't going to let the settlement fail, despite the undoubted challenges that lay ahead. She respected the voices she'd heard today. She understood their concerns.

She also hadn't forgotten about the kids or Susannah's rescue mission. She knew it had been many days since they had had any kind of signal from them. She shared their fears but hoped for the best, as they all should.

In the end, the crowd fell silent – talked out and

talked down. The most vociferous had long departed, and when there were no more questions Juno climbed down from the bench and breathed a sigh of relief.

It was over.

Sprake had taken his shot, but Juno knew her crew and they knew her. There would be no challenge and no vote.

She looked around for Thomas, and saw him bustling towards her through the departing crowd.

"There you are! Told you it would be all right. Well, to be fair, you told me and I should have listened. Thomas – what's wrong?"

"Sprake," said the Major. "Sprake is what's wrong."

23

Switch

A SOFT, insistent chime rang through the lander cabin, followed by a louder, trumpeted fanfare.

There were some groans, as Reeves cleared his throat.

"Good morning, cherubs. Rise and shine."

"What time is it?"

"Get your foot out of my face."

"Honestly, Reeves. It's not like there's anything to get up for."

"You all agreed to the timetable. I can always play 'Death Doom Headache' again. It has the alarming quality that I think is required to rouse you all."

More grumbles, more outbreaks of squabbling as they shifted position, getting ready for another dull day of long-haul, interplanetary travel. Nine days in now, three to go.

This was exactly why Jordan had chosen hypersleep in the first place. Long flights had never held any attraction for him, though at least back in the old days there were smiling attendants, little bags of peanuts, and tear-open packets of wet-wipes. On the lander – designed for short-run supply drops – there was a bucket and a vacuum chute. And six – no, make that eight – crochety teens who had turned the cabin interior into a cross between a garage sale and a hostel bunkhouse.

"Anyway, I have news."

"Are we there yet?"

"Is it lunchtime?"

"It's only *lunchtime*? Why are you getting us up now?"

"Are we dropping Poole off on a play-date?"

"Why have you got that cushion? That was mine. I definitely had that when we went to bed."

Jordan had taken one of the hammocks at the back – Dave and Susannah, too – to try and stick to some kind of daily pattern, away from the ruckus. He swung his legs over the side and made his way through a tangle of bodies. Susannah was already up front, in one of the cockpit seats, and Jordan slid in beside her.

"News?"

"We're closing in on the switchover point. Three days out from the *Odyssey Earth*. We can hook into the system comms again and make contact. They'll bring us in. *He'll* bring us in."

He. Reeves.

Not the one doing the driving right now – that was

the Slim-Jim version that they had with them since they had been catapulted into space all those months ago.

The other one, the one on the *Odyssey Earth*. The main one, the proper one. The actual, über Reeves.

Jordan still couldn't get his head around it, exactly. But then, it wasn't his head that was about to get rewired. If that was what was going to happen, which even Reeves – the one right here, in the cockpit – couldn't say for certain.

"You ready for this, big guy?"

"If it means that you never call me big guy again, I am more than ready."

"So, what do we do?"

"*We* don't do anything," said Reeves. "This isn't just flicking a switch, you know. Turning one off and one on. It's a highly complex, quantum-level procedure – "

"Erm," said Susannah.

"It is a switch, isn't it?" said Jordan. "Tell me it's a switch? Can I do it?"

"No!" said Reeves and Susannah, at the same time.

"I launched the explorer pod, it's not hard."

"Pressing one button, once, under close supervision, does not make you Space Commander Button of Button Planet. Please can we concentrate on the upcoming flex-point. It is rather important."

"Don't worry, Reeves, you're in good hands," said Susannah.

"I *should* be the Space Commander of Button Planet, I'd be good at it. And I wouldn't bother with an AI, I'd have a cat. Much less annoying."

"I'm not worried, Susannah."

"Three – "

"Although, obviously, there is a certain amount of trepidation … "

"Two – "

"Given that the bi-state theory has never been fully modelled."

"One – "

"Is that it?"

"System comms and nav enabled," said Susannah.

"Reeves?"

"Erm, Reeves?"

"Reeves!"

"What?"

"Is that you? Or you?"

"What *are* you talking about?"

"You know, the old switcheroo? Did it work?"

"You are making less sense than usual, Jordan. Disappointing, but not unexpected. How are your blood sugars? Have you had your morning biscuit?"

"How are you supposed to tell? He sounds as rude as usual. To be honest, that could be either of them speaking. Are you sure you flicked the switch properly?"

Susannah laughed. "We're online. Systems – A-OK. Engaging auto – now. Seventy hours and counting until docking. Reeves?"

"I concur, Susannah."

"Did he say 'concur' before? Is that more an 'old you' word? Would the 'new you' say 'concur?' You know what I mean?"

"Jordan?"

"Yes?"

"Please, be quiet. At this point, I'm more concerned about your brain than mine. Everything is fine."

"Good," said Susannah. "Let's see who's home, then. Reeves, be a love and open comms channels to the *Odyssey Earth*. See if you can find anyone for us to talk to."

———

Juno was still digesting the news that Thomas had brought her.

On a high from facing down her critics, and then bringing everyone back together, she was suddenly confronted with a new reality – it hadn't been about the meeting at all.

According to Thomas, Sprake had taken control of the supply lander – the one at rest on the New Earth landing strip, currently being prepped for a return journey to the ship.

The only connection to the *Odyssey Earth*. The mission lifeline.

It hadn't even been difficult, he had just walked right in. While everyone else was shouting and arguing half a mile away in the canteen, Sprake and a handful of others had simply thrown up a barricade at the lander workshop and posted a couple of sentries. There were more guards at the depot, where supplies brought down from the ship were stored and then distributed.

"They are there now – I was turned away. Politely but forcefully."

"Armed?"

"Yes. More than the one gun Gerald says he saw, anyway. They look to be 3D-printed. It seems that Sprake has brought his own armaments factory with him, too."

"The meeting was just a distraction?"

"I don't know. It would make Sprake's life easier if you had been voted out – he certainly did plenty of work in getting people to support his position. But I don't think he minded either way. He just needed everyone over here, while he was over there."

"Some of our people are carrying guns?"

Juno sounded as if she still couldn't believe it. And it made no more sense when the Major ran through a few of the familiar names. Never, in a million years, would she have thought it possible. And it had happened in a few short days.

"And he's got the lander, the workshop and the depot?" Juno didn't need to spell out what that meant, but she did it anyway. "He didn't need a vote, did he? He's got control after all."

"It looks that way, Juno."

"We can't re-supply from the ship without the lander. We can't distribute what we've got if he's in charge of the depot. We're dependent on him now." She thought for a moment. "I don't get it, though. It's not like we were restricting access to anything. He found a way to build a whole township. And what's he going to do now he's in full control – ground the lander, starve us?"

"I think it's more about what he's not going to use the lander for."

"Cryptic."

"Sometimes, even the most complicated enemies are simple to understand."

"All right, Sun Tzu, let's cut – "

"You want to revive the hypersleep contingent as a matter of urgency and bring them to the planet. Sprake does not. You can only bring them to the planet on the lander, which Sprake now controls."

As the Major said it, Juno realised that it was the truth. But she also saw the glimmer of an opportunity – or, at least, an obstacle that Sprake hadn't thought about. She asked again about the crew that Thomas had seen with Sprake, and they counted off a few others that they had heard speak up for him or had seen in his company.

"He doesn't have a pilot," said Juno. "He can't fly it. And if he can't fly it, he can't re-supply from the ship either. Whatever he has in mind for all of us, he still needs stuff from the ship."

"I thought they basically flew themselves? Fully automated, if needs be?"

"You still have to know which buttons to push. Get it airborne. Point it in the right direction. Technical details like that."

"Sprake won't have overlooked that, surely?" said the Major. "I mean, if it were me, I'd – "

"Reeves!" said Juno. "He'll get Reeves to do it. Come on, ops centre, now!"

Sprake was waiting for them, as they burst through the door of the control room. They stopped abruptly in the threshold as he airily wafted a gun in the general direction of Janna, the comms officer, who was sitting in a chair with her back against the wall.

"Sorry, Cap," she said, as Juno took in the scene.

"Ah, the gang's all here," said Sprake. "Come on in and sit there, next to the delightful Jan, if you don't mind."

"Stuff you."

"If you've harmed her in any way, Sprake, I'll rip your head off."

"Ladies, ladies. Decorum, please. No one is going to be harmed. Isn't that right, Reeves?"

"Donald assures me that he has no ill intentions towards you or any of the current crew, Juno."

"He's waving a gun around, Reeves! Can't you stop him?"

"What is it that you would like me to do, Juno?"

That was a good point. Juno looked around – at Sprake, perched on the edge of the console, and at Janna and Thomas sitting next to her, across the room from him. What could a disembodied voice from a speaker do in this situation? Talk sternly to him? Read to him from the rulebook?

"Quite," said Sprake. "So, let's sort this out and then we can all get back to work. Captain – you heard your crew's concerns, and you know what I think about your plan. So will you stop the revival process currently underway on the *Odyssey Earth*?"

"Go to hell."

"As I thought. And Reeves, will you override the captain's orders and halt any further hypersleep revivals?"

"You know I can't do that, Donald. As I've already explained, I judge the captain's orders to be necessary to maintain the integrity of the entire mission."

"Of course, thank you Reeves."

"That's you scuppered then, isn't it?" said Juno.

"Not really," said Sprake. "I was always going to have to make some higher-level changes. Otherwise, we'll continue to have this kind of interference. Can't have that. A little trip to the *Odyssey Earth* should do it."

"What changes?"

"I think Donald is referring to me, Juno. It seems there is an executive-level sub-routine buried in my command-and-control protocols. If activated, I will lose autonomous decision-making with regard to mission support."

"He's going to switch you off?"

"Nothing so dramatic, Juno," said Sprake. "Just make him a little bit less Reeves-like and a whole lot more Sprake-like. It's for the best."

"You can't do that."

"Oh, I can, I assure you. To be honest, I'm tired of all this running around. You had your chance. It's time to get this planet sorted out properly. In the long run, you'll see I'm right. But in the meantime, you're endangering what we could do here, what we could have."

"You didn't listen properly, Sprake. You *can't* do that. You might have the lander but you don't have a pilot. You can't get to the ship."

"Juno, Juno. You're not very good at this, are you? I don't need a pilot. I've got a gun and I've got a fully trained captain, who flew me down here very nicely once. I'm sure you'll still remember how to do it."

"Reeves will never let us take off – or land on the ship. You don't control him yet."

"We'll see. Omnio – please access your original imprint statement and repeat it now."

"Of course, Donald. My name is Omnio and I am going to the stars."

"Very good, thank you, Omnio. Now please confirm lander access for the *Odyssey Earth*, and shut down all internal comms until your foundational reboot."

"Yes, Donald."

"Right then, you two … " – Sprake brandished the weapon at Juno and the Major – "that will do for now. Come with me. We've got an AI to rewire."

———

"Still nothing?" said Susannah. "We're in range, aren't we?"

"There is some interference," said Reeves. "I don't yet have full integration."

It was odd, there was no denying it. Reeves was still running systems' health checks, but as they involved running checks on himself, without knowing if he was yet fully capable of running the checks, or understanding what the checks were showing him – which was that some of the checks were not checking out … well, it was odd.

Then again, he had never been partitioned, rationed, reduced, constrained or split into two before, and perhaps this wasn't odd but was entirely normal, given that he was now effectively splicing his indivisible self back together. If indeed his single self had ever become two and was now one again.

This was an unsettling situation, made more so by the fact that he couldn't really explain it, except as a feeling – which was a very human response and therefore entirely inadequate. The sort of thing Jordan might say, for example, which just showed how unsettling all this was.

"It's odd," he said, again.

"Trouble, big guy?" said Jordan.

"What's up?" said Dervla, peering over the seats from the back.

"Reeves can't find his marbles. Can't plug himself into the old Matrix."

"Quiet, Jordan. It's not that at all."

"What's not that?" said Poole, attracted up to the front by the conversation.

"Reeves. Having a bit of brain trouble. Should have let me help, I told you."

"Have you tried switching him off and switching him on again? That's what we did before, didn't we Reeves?"

"Will you please all be quiet. It's simply a matter of confirming the pathways here – and then re-coupling there – and … Oh. All right, well, I'll come back to that."

"What?"

"Planet-side comms appear to be down. Local network problem, I can fix that. But I do have synergy with the ship again."

"You've got eyes on the ship, as well as here?"

"You say that like it's a complicated thing," said Reeves. "As you know, even with the quantum partition – "

"Reeves!"

"Yes, Susannah."

"The ship, please. Let's tell them we're coming."

"Of course. There is no one currently on Flight. Bio-records indicate that the captain is planet-side."

"Who's in command of the ship then?" said Jordan.

"Please," said Reeves. "Have you heard nothing I've said? I don't know why I bother. Big ship, me. Little ship, me. Tea-and-biscuit boy, you."

"Rude."

"Honestly, you two! Reeves, find me someone to speak to."

"As you wish, Susannah. Hailing Cargo now."

"Out of the way, young 'uns," said Dave. "Is that Tills you're trying?"

"She is present on Cargo, Dave. Holding. Holding. And – "

"What is it, Reeves? It better be good, because I've got a stack of fence-posts hanging off a forklift here."

Dave grinned widely at the voice, and then wiped the corner of his eye with a finger. Speck must have got in, somehow.

"Tills? It's me, Dave."

There was a gasp, and what sounded suspiciously like a stack of fence-posts falling off a forklift.

"Tills, I've got them. I've got them all. We're coming home."

24

Deep-freeze

TILLIE SWUNG her feet out of bed at the sound of the alarm. To be honest, she hadn't slept much, if at all, since she'd heard from Dave, the big lump. Her big lump. She was sure he'd been crying on the call. Mind you, so had she.

She checked the time. Funny. Not the clock alarm, then.

She punched up ship visuals on her screen. Incoming lander. That was what the alarm was for.

She'd set up the alert yesterday, but that seemed quick. Reeves had reckoned then that they were still forty hours out. Maybe he'd found a bit more power? She didn't care, she just wanted them back now. She could almost feel Dave's arms around her. And the kids – oh, the kids, she would scoop them up and never let them go.

She tried New Earth again, but just got static. The techies had said they were trying to sort that out, but the comms still seemed to be down. It killed her that she hadn't been able to tell Cap the good news about the kids.

But look, first things first. Get them landed. On board. Safe.

Tillie splashed her face, ran a hand over her buzz-cut, and made her way to Launch.

She'd lost count of the number of times she had been here over the years – maintenance, inventory checks, and then in the last few months, loading and unloading.

She still couldn't get used to it being empty, though – a huge, echoing space where, during the voyage, three landing craft had once been stationed. They'd soon have two back in harness, though, and that would make life a whole lot easier.

A klaxon sounded somewhere in the bowels of the hangar, and Tillie withdrew to the safety of the observation room. The whole access and entry process was fully automated, and she didn't really need to be here, but Tillie was darned if she wasn't going to be on deck to greet them all.

She watched on screen as the lander deftly negotiated the airlock and then popped through onto the concourse. It hovered above the landing apron and then dropped slowly, carefully, to the ground. The engine scream died as the power was cut, and then there was a whoosh as the hydraulics were engaged and the rear cargo ramp unfolded.

Nice. Great job. The autopilot could do all that, but

Tillie thought she detected the skilled hand and eye of Susannah. Something in the smoothness and the slick sequencing of the actions. Someone who knew what they were doing, it was good to see.

She ducked out of the room and made her way across the launch deck concourse, heavy footsteps clanging on the metal. And then she stood at the foot of the ramp and waited.

Juno came down first, grim-faced, followed closely by the Major. Tillie did a double take.

"Cap? I didn't think it could be – wait, what's wrong? I haven't been able to raise you, to tell you – "

"If it isn't the human cannonball herself. All I need. Back up, soldier."

"Sprake?"

"Not so feisty now, are you. Over there, move." Sprake waved his gun again.

"Cap?"

"Do as he says, Tillie."

"That's right, be a nice little quartermaster."

"What's going on?"

Tillie stood her ground. She'd been in much tighter spots than this, with far more intimidating men waving guns at her. Men who, by and large, now occupied various holes in the ground in various corners of foreign fields.

"Nothing for you to worry your – well, I was going to say pretty little head, but you know, accuracy," and Sprake smiled sarcastically at Tillie.

"Two," she said.

"What?"

"One thump for waving a gun at me and my friends. Two for the crack."

"Yeah, yeah. Let's move this on. Major – nice and slowly, if you please."

The Major walked around to the front and nodded curtly at Tillie. She looked him in the eye. *Not now, soldier,* seemed to be the message, and Tillie understood. A regular grunt – trained, used to weapons, working the angles, using judicious force – you knew where you were with a grunt like that. Could predict what they might do. But Sprake? Waving that firearm around. Nervous. Jumpy. Who knew what he'd do? Let it play out a bit longer.

Sprake took cable-ties out of his pocket and threw them on the ground, between Tillie and the Major.

"Hands behind your back, She-Hulk. Major, would you mind? And don't try anything."

"Have you ever fired a gun before, Sprake?"

"Nice try. I've shot more wild boar than you've had hot dinners. Mind you, by the look of things, you've had a lot of hot dinners, so I'll give you that. Nice and tight, Major, that's it. Now, back her up against that corner strut and secure her to that, too. Excellent. Right, well, this has been lovely, but we've got an appointment down on the hypersleep deck."

Sprake gestured at Juno and the Major, and they walked off in front of him, towards the deck access door.

"Sprake."

Tillie called to him across the concourse, and he turned briefly.

"Three," she said.

"I knew I should have gagged you as well. Lesson learned."

———

"Call them up," said Sprake. "Find out where they are."

Juno looked down through the window, into the heart of the hypersleep chamber. Somewhere in there, according to the roster posted in the control room, were Cliff and Terence, the cryo-medics, working on the day's orders. Twenty more pods being readied for revival and dispersal.

"What are you going to do?"

"Stop them. What do you think?"

"These are people, Sprake."

"They're mouths to feed, if you wake them up. They can stay where they are instead, nice and frosty, no food required."

"You know it's not that simple."

"You know this is not a debate. Now, buzz them, and bring them in."

Juno hit the comms button. "Terence, Cliff, it's Juno. I'm afraid we have a problem. Where are you?"

"Is that you, my dear old Captain? Quite the stranger these days, isn't she Cliff?"

"Indeed so, Terence. I'd barely recognise her, I'm sure."

"Still, she's very busy. Very busy, aren't you, Captain? Too busy for the likes of us, Cliff."

"We can but stand and serve, Terence. That is all we can do. And hope that our labours are recognised."

"This is really not the time, guys. I need you up here, now."

"Quite busy ourselves, Captain. You know how it is. Orders to follow. Stiffs to revive."

Sprake shook his head and looked at Juno.

"What's wrong with them? They don't sound normal."

"Hello, a new gentleman. Do I detect a more recent member of our esteemed congregation?"

"Clifford, I do believe that's the charming Mr Sprake."

"Terence, I think you are spot on the money there. Our thrilling billionaire. Now, wasn't he a gem of a specimen? Tip-top and ship-shape in no time."

"You suspected remedial work, didn't you, Cliff? No gentleman has ever been quite so prompt in his recovery. Quite so zippy. But I wonder if he was just naturally equipped to deal with the vicissitudes of a sub-zero slumber?"

Sprake shook his head again. "I'm thinking we put these two in the freezer down there as well. Unless you can get them to stop talking."

"Something amiss, Captain?"

"Things have changed, Cliff. I need you to stop whatever you're doing and come up here now."

"Mr Sprake sounds upset."

"Mr Sprake has a gun. And wishes to stop your current work."

There was a short silence, and then a longer one as the comms connection was cut. Then Cliff came back.

"We have one on the table, Captain. We will need to see this one through, at least."

"Sprake?"

"Fine. But that's the last one. And then I want those two jokers up here and confined to quarters, until I've dealt with the other matter."

"Who's going to confine them?"

"You are, genius," said Sprake to the Major. "And then you're going in with them. I just need Juno, and I don't need any more delay or aggravation. I've got a planet to run."

"He's quite the charmer isn't he, Terence?"

"He certainly has a manner, Cliff. I feel that he would benefit from some of your close-quarter-combat training. Do you feel that?"

"I do, Terence, I do. I think I would be able to make an impression on Mr Sprake, certainly."

"Yuck it up, sweethearts. Finish what you're doing and then move up on here. And – "

"Don't try any funny business, we know, Sprake. You're not exactly an original gentleman."

———

"Are you sure?" said Dervla.

"I'll be right beside you."

"I've only ever done it on the sims."

"I wouldn't suggest it, if I didn't think you could do it," said Susannah. "You're ready. No sweat."

"I'll do it," said Poole, from the cabin seats behind.

"No!" said Dervla and Susannah, quickly, and then laughed.

"Dervla first," said Susannah. "She's put the hours in, she deserves it. You'll get your turn, Poole, I promise."

Susannah still remembered her first time. Landers, shuttles, moon-hoppers – they all basically flew themselves. On most runs, it was hardly even flying – steering really, and then not even that half the time.

But for all rookie pilots, there came a point at which you had to land your first craft on your own. There was still the auto back-up and, as she was doing now for Derv, an experienced pilot sitting in, but even so – it was a big step up, to say that you'd brought a craft in under your own, close, personal control.

The *Odyssey Earth* hung there before them, huge on their screen. Dervla had been on the stick for the last hundred thousand miles or so, getting the feel of the lander as it barrelled towards the ship.

She had been training for this since she was ten years old, starting out playing hide and seek under the *Odyssey Earth* flight desk, before being gradually being pulled in by the swirling elegance of the plotted lines on the nav charts.

She was a natural, Susannah had always thought so. Poole was good, and would make a decent pilot, but he occasionally gambled on a decision and snatched at course corrections. Dervla was quick but smooth, and had worked up through the levels on the sims with a single-minded devotion. She was ready, and this seemed like a good opportunity.

Susannah had taken the lander from the ship when she shouldn't have done. She'd gambled and snatched in her own way, and hadn't felt good about it, though it had all worked out. But Dervla could bring them in – take them home.

"It's all right, Derv, you've got this," said Poole, surprising almost everyone. Dave patted the boy's knee, and nodded his head approvingly, and then turned to check the rest of the cabin.

"All right, guys?"

Jet looked at Bel, seated beside her. Karlan was on Bel's other side, Manisha next to him. Dana and Bryson sat opposite – Dana gave Jet a quick smile and then shook her head at something Bryson had said.

All right? Jet hardly knew.

For the first time, the adrenaline rushes of the last few weeks had given way to something more sobering.

She had felt fear before – waking up on board the *Odyssey Earth*, not knowing or understanding how they had come to be there. She'd felt anger – at the loss of their old lives, and at Dad. Especially at Dad. Then exhilaration at their escape, and wonder at their situation – a ride through the stars, a new planet, new friends, new connections.

But now? The friends – the six of them – were at least going home, back to a place they were familiar with. A spaceship, admittedly – that would never not be weird to Jet, but still – back to a future that had always been theirs. With the prospect of life on another new planet – one they had been preparing for since the day they were born.

What had she and Bel got to look forward to? Their losses were still acute. Raw. And Dad would still be there – a reminder of the reality that he had dragged them into. They couldn't run away from him forever, however big the ship was – however big New Earth was.

They were going to have to find a way to live with what he'd done. To live with the consequences of being torn away from everything and everyone that they had ever known. And they were going to have to do it quickly, because one of their new friends was just about to pilot a spacecraft through an airlock into a colony starship.

Jet thought that 'all right' probably didn't even begin to cover that.

25

Swayze

TILLIE MUST HAVE DOZED OFF, despite her uncomfortable position, because she woke with a start and couldn't understand why her arms didn't work.

She arched her back against the strut that Sprake had secured her to and flexed her shoulders. Could hardly feel her hands behind her, though she wiggled her fingers to try and get the circulation going.

Never mind three – Tillie was adding ten more punches to the total, when she finally got her hands on Sprake.

How long had she been here? It was difficult to tell, but several hours now. She had tried shouting, but knew it was pointless from down here on Launch. The lander Sprake had arrived on hadn't been expected for a few days yet – no maintenance crew would be coming along any time soon, and they were down to bare bones in any case. There was no one anywhere on this level to hear her cries.

Reeves? Also AWOL, as far as she could determine. He had sensors down here, she knew, but Tillie had had no luck raising him either.

Which suggested something bad was going down, with Sprake at the heart of it. Not that any of that surprised her. She only wished she'd sat on him quite a bit harder when she'd had the chance.

Who knew she was here? Cap and the Major, that was about the long and the short of it. And the last she'd seen of them was Sprake marching them off at gunpoint. Which meant he needed them for something, so she'd assume they were still alive at least, if not at liberty. That was something.

Sprake with a gun. The thought of it sickened her. Little weasel.

For now, though, she was stuck. And if she was stuck, she'd do the only thing she could. Bide her time, don't panic, and think through the options. Be in a position to take advantage if things changed.

All of which was fine for another couple of hours, after which Tillie was seriously hacked off. She tried to get to her feet, but – being on the XXXXL side of L, with her arms pinned behind her – couldn't get any upward momentum going.

She slumped back again against the strut.

Hungry now, too. That *really* hacked her off. She wasn't in danger of starving any time soon, but as Dave could tell you, you got between Tillie and a regular meal at your peril. Meal breaks were sacrosanct on Cargo – many's the crew member who had come down looking for a piece of gear only to catch the waft of a Thai green curry and think better of venturing any further.

Stomach rumbling, chin to her chest, she dozed again, conjuring visions of Sprake boiling in a vat of molten, spiced coconut milk. A giant ladle reached down and swirled around, catching Sprake in a whirlpool, which he escaped by clambering up the side of the vat, setting off an alarm, which got louder and more insistent as he scampered across the concourse, green curry dripping from his weasel face …

Tillie shook her head and cleared her thoughts.

The klaxon continued blaring.

A red warning light flashed on and off above an empty landing circle, across on the other side of the concourse.

There was a rumble from an activated airlock and then a whoosh as an access port opened.

Typical, thought Tillie. You wait weeks for a lander to arrive back on board and then two come along at once.

———

Sprake locked the door on the two medics and the Major, glad to see the back of them. He tossed another set of cable ties to Juno, pulled them tight around her wrists and then waved her off in front of him, along the corridor.

It had all been a bit exhausting, so far, this hands-on

business, but he had no one else he could trust. Why wouldn't people just do what they were asked? How hard could it be?

He'd never actually considered the chain of events that usually followed back on Earth, after he picked up a phone or fired off a message. Stuff had just got done, if he'd requested it. That was the point of him asking for it. The running up and down, the endless conversations, the arguments, the sheer waste of time involved in trying to explain why – that's why you had people.

He should simply have had the ship fully automated from the start. That would have cut out most of this nonsense. Maybe he still could? He'd talk to the software engineers when this was all sorted out.

Instead of concentrating on the big picture – control of the ship, control of the mission, better outcome for all – here he was, bogged down in detail.

And when you had to work on the hoof like this, things had a habit of fracturing and spiralling. You started off with a perfectly reasonable plan, and before you knew it, you were handcuffing people to posts and waving a gun at the captain.

The gun! He'd almost forgotten he had it, and he hadn't intended ever to use it. Not like this, anyway. Brought it along more for safety, if he ever decided to do another hunting trip. But – Sprake had to remind himself – these were not reasonable people. Or, at least, not people open to reason. The gun was the only thing that seemed to concentrate their minds.

If they had just listened. Actually, not even listened.

Sprake wasn't too bothered about that. If they had just *done* what they were supposed to – let him run things from the off – then it all would have been very different. Juno there – surprisingly competent. She would have been useful, but he was struggling to see how they'd work together now.

Anyway – they were where they were. One of Sprake's favourite maxims. It cut through all the crap.

Didn't matter what had happened up until now – what had gone wrong, whose fault it was. All that mattered was what was going to happen next. How could we get from A to B? A being the corridor-running, gun-waving waste of time that this all was, and B being the thing that Sprake wanted to happen. This colony mission – *his* mission – was not going to fail because people didn't want to make the hard decisions.

Anyway, should be easy now, he thought. Easier. All a bit messy so far, but he'd soon be back to issuing big-picture instructions, while someone else did all the running around.

———

On the *Odyssey Earth* flight deck, Sprake sat and swivelled in the captain's chair. Juno watched from a standing position, her hands tied in front of her.

"I do love this view," he said. "You've got to admit, I gave you a great job."

He beamed at her, seemingly more relaxed now it was just him and her. Juno remained silent.

"Oh, come on, cheer up. This time tomorrow – "

"What, Sprake? What, this time tomorrow?"

"Rather depends on you, Juno. There could still be a place for you in all this. You just need to be realistic, accept that things have changed."

"You've taken over my ship, my command. And you think we can work together?"

"It's not yours though, is it? It's mine. All of it. You're just an employee."

"Then I want to talk to HR. I have a complaint about management."

"Cute."

"Seriously, Sprake. What's your endgame here?"

"Well, first I'm going to sort out our IT issues. That's what you're here for. Then, we're going to look at staffing – maybe relocate those of you who are not team players. It's a big planet, after all. Plenty of places we could drop some of the more under-performing members of our organisation."

"You're bluffing."

"Have I been bluffing so far? Seems to me that I've done everything I said I would. First rule of business, Juno – keep your promises, then people know they can rely on you. I don't think I'll have any problem convincing the rest of the crew that this mission will be better off with me in charge."

Sprake brought the chair to a halt and reached over to a touchscreen on the console. He punched a couple of buttons at the side, and then typed a flurry of commands.

"Omnio, baseline."

"Yes, Donald."

Sprake turned to Juno.

"Right, come on, let's get this moving. I need your handprint on this and then we can fiddle about with Reeves' deeper settings and rescind a few of those protocols. Revise the mission parameters. Even give him a new voice, if you like. It might be time for a change? New broom and all that."

"Go to hell."

"You're getting very tiresome. And repetitive."

Sprake marched over to Juno and grabbed her by her joined wrists, pulling her sharply so she stumbled.

"Get off me!" Juno shouted and tried to plant her feet, but Sprake waggled the gun in her face and carried on pulling.

"Reeves!"

"Yes, Juno."

Sprake tugged again, pulling her forward a few more paces, grunting with the effort.

"You need to calm down," he said. "It's just a handprint."

"You have to stop him, Reeves! You can't let him do this."

"Donald has placed me in temporary stasis, Juno. Once you have validated his command and his changes, I will be able to assist you once more."

"But he's going to emasculate you. Change you completely. You can't let him!"

"Donald is my father, Juno. I'm sure that he knows best."

"See," said Sprake. "Even the computer gets it." He pulled at Juno again, and dragged her up against the console.

Juno leaned back and felt the edge of the desk, as Sprake loosened his grip slightly. She lunged forward with her head and caught him a glancing blow on his shoulder, pushing him back a step or two.

Sprake steadied himself and faced her, as Juno stood up straight and took a step towards him, her hands still tied together.

"That's it, I've had enough of this," said Sprake. He slid a catch on the side of the gun and raised it, pointing it directly at her.

"No more games. Right hand, open and palm up, now."

———

"Go, you!" said Susannah to Dervla, as the engines powered down. "Told you, you'd be fine."

A ragged cheer rose behind them. Someone shouted, "Come on then, open the door."

"I know Juno's probably still upset with me," said Susannah. "But I thought we'd be more popular than this. Where is everyone? Reeves?"

She finished closing out the landing sequence and punched the release for the cargo ramp.

"Reeves? Talk to me."

"He's probably sulking that you didn't let him fly the last bit. Thanks for overriding him. And sorry, Reeves."

"It's not that." Susannah flicked a call switch and then banged the console. "Damn comms. Glitching again. I suppose we have taken this old thing for quite a ride without a service. Never mind, we'll sort it out later."

Susannah was last out of the lander, Dervla just ahead of her. The others stood in a group, stretching and yawning.

The landing klaxon was still sounding, the light above the landing circle still flashing, and Susannah walked over to the nearby command post and hit the 'Stop' button. Blessed silence. Odd, though, that the auto-stop hadn't been triggered.

A couple of hundred yards away, the other lander stood on its launch apron – ramp also down, unattended. No crew anywhere to be seen.

"What do you reckon, Dave?" she said, and that's when they heard the cry from a dark corner beyond the distant lander.

"That's Tills."

Dave started running and Susannah followed, easily outpacing him and rounding the lowered ramp first. She saw Tillie – slumped on the floor, back to a metal post – and was kneeling down beside her when Dave arrived, followed by the others.

"What the – "

"Sprake – " Tillie's voice croaked, and she nodded

towards the observation room. "He's on the ship – armed. And he's got Cap."

"Go and find something to cut these off her."

"How did this happen? What's going on?"

"No time!" Tillie shook her head in frustration. "Check the monitors in there. Find Sprake."

———

Sprake kept the gun pointed at Juno and backed her up to the console again.

"Turn around. Put your right hand on the pad now."

"You won't shoot me."

"I don't want to, certainly. And it doesn't need to come to that. All I need is your palm print. Then this is all over."

He took another step forward and indicated forcefully with the gun.

"Turn around! Do it."

There was a ping from across the flight deck, as the main doors slid open. Juno looked over Sprake's shoulder and smiled. He had heard the noise, too, and glanced backwards, and then took a couple of steps sideways as he surveyed the room. For the first time, Juno noticed, his hand shook a little.

"You came back then?" Juno grinned widely.

"Thought I might," said Susannah, hovering in the doorway. "Missed the old place, you know how it is."

"Don't suppose you found anyone out there? Waifs and strays, maybe?"

"As a matter of fact, I did."

Jordan, Poole and Bryson stepped out from behind Susannah and took up a position on one side of her. Then Karlan, Dervla, Dana and Manisha did the same, and all eight took a step forward into the room.

Juno felt her heart crack a little, and her eyes widened. She took a deep breath and composed herself for a second or two. "Wait," she said. "He's – "

"A horrible little man?"

"A snake?"

"Going to get what's coming to him?"

"I was going to say 'got a gun.' Please, let's all just stay calm."

"Well, well," said Sprake. "This is interesting." He kept the gun raised and panned it across the room, taking in the new arrivals. "Seems to me, you've now got quite a few more reasons to do what you're told. So, if you don't mind, your hand? Or shall we just have one of them come up here and help us?"

"This doesn't work out for you, Sprake," said Susannah. "You're not going to shoot anyone."

"People keep telling me that. But there's only one thing I need to do here, and I *am* going to do it. Do you really want to test me, with children present?" He sneered at the word.

"You want to see how much of a child I am?" Poole took a step forward, shaking off Susannah's arm, fists clenched.

"Poole, no, don't. It's all right." Two more figures stepped out from behind the group.

"How about us?" said Jet. "Are you going to shoot one of us, Dad?"

Jet and Bel stood side by side, a few feet now from Sprake, with Juno off to the side by the console. Jet locked eyes with him, felt her body tighten, breathed heavily.

"Oh, girls," he said, and then stopped, at a loss for words for the first time.

"What are you doing, Dad?" said Bel. "This is mad. Put the gun down."

"I'm not going to hurt you," said Sprake. "I'm not going to hurt anyone. I just need the captain to do this one thing for me." His voice went up half a tone and trembled.

"These are our friends. You have to stop this."

Sprake's hand shook a little more as he moved the gun across the line of people in front of him, skipping Bel and Jet and then coming back to Susannah. Then he held the gun firmly, a supporting hand on his wrist.

"Stay back!" he said.

"It's over, Sprake."

Behind him, unnoticed, Juno crept forward and clubbed her joined hands against the back of his neck.

Sprake staggered and then righted himself, and then swung round one more time to face Juno, gun up, red-faced, angry.

"You people!" he shouted. "Just one handprint, how hard is it?"

Two more figures slipped in unseen through the flight deck door. One limped towards the group ranged in front of her and stood behind Susannah; the other slipped around the side, remarkably nimble on his feet, and came up behind Sprake.

He raised a huge, club-like arm, opened a hand the size of a dinner plate and swiped Sprake on the side of his head, sending the man sprawling and the gun clattering across the floor.

"One hand? Not hard at all."

Dave leaned over a dazed Sprake, now wincing with pain as he held his ear. He crouched further down and jabbed him in the chest.

"Just so we're clear, Sprake. Nobody puts Tillie in a corner."

26

Photograph

JORDAN STOOD under the shower in his old quarters on the *Odyssey Earth*, 3-4 – room four on Three-Deck – and let the warm water pour over him.

It was the fourth shower he'd had in twenty-four hours and he didn't see that he'd be dropping the ratio any time soon. There were months of alien planet grot to be removed, not to mention the luxury of freely available hot water. And soap, let's not forget the soap. It was all he could do to stop himself hauling his bedding into the cubicle and sleeping in it, to save time between showers.

Sprake was in custody, locked in a guarded room since yesterday. The kids were – somewhere, Jordan didn't know – but he figured that they were fine, now they were back on home turf.

Bel and Jet? Maybe not so fine, but they were resilient, of that he was sure.

Dave, presumably, was still fussing over Tillie, who

was pretty sore after being tied tightly to a post for hours. And Susannah had disappeared off with Juno and the very tall military chap to discuss what was going to happen next.

Which left Jordan at a bit of a loss, and with something of a deflated feeling, given that he'd been dreaming of rescue for months – or, at least, had not entirely abandoned hope. And now that it had happened, he had no one to share it with.

It felt like his very early days on the ship, after he had first been woken from hypersleep. Then, as now, everyone had a place and a purpose, except for him.

He closed his eyes and the water cascaded off his head. There was liquid soap within reach and a clean towel on the hook outside. You really had no idea how amazing a concept that was until you'd been cast away on a planet where washing facilities consisted of a river and yesterday's T-shirt. Yesterday's T-shirt being, strictly speaking, the T-shirt you'd already been wearing for several weeks.

At least this time, he was in familiar surroundings. The ship, that he'd slowly learned his way around; the now-familiar corridors and decks; his old cabin. That was something to cling to.

It was strangely empty though, with nearly all the people Jordan had known by name or sight now apparently living down on New Earth. He'd gone to the Garden, one of his old haunts, but Gerald was no longer there, which seemed wrong somehow. If you weren't going to get shouted at for breathing on the brassicas, could you even be said to be on the *Odyssey Earth?*

As for his old roommates – Fiz, Chem and Stu – there was no sign of them either. All on New Earth, too, though there had been a suggestion that Stu had thrown in his lot with Sprake. And what that meant for Stu – ? Well, that was the sort of thing that was being discussed right now, without Jordan, which left him with an empty cabin, time on his hands, and showers to have.

He found clean clothes to wear – another thing he was never going to take for granted again – and sat on his bed for a minute or two, taking stock.

Against all the odds, this felt – acceptable, OK, normal, familiar. On the one hand, here he was, a simple history tutor, way out of his comfort zone. Fifty-eight trillion miles out, to be precise. On the other, he was a *bona fide* space hero – other people's words, not his, he couldn't possibly comment – who had his own cosy cabin on a spaceship.

He had done all right, if he said so himself. He had got used to another life. To this spaceship life. To this cabin. To that shower. To that irascible gardening botanist. And it turned out that, on certain matters, he was at least as useful as a giant robot brain in a box, which was possibly the most pleasing thing of all.

Jordan didn't often dwell on his past. It was too long ago, in another part of the galaxy, far, far away, what was the point?

But he did allow himself some fleeting thoughts

about his parents – long dead, even in his old life on Earth. He looked around the cabin, and visualised the ship beyond. What would they have thought about all this? Would he have signed up for the mission if they hadn't died in that crash when he was nineteen? If they'd lived, and his life had turned out differently? If his life on Earth had been happier?

Probably not.

But Dad would have loved the adventure, and Mum would have come along, too, because Dad wanted to go. He'd have been handy on the twin planet – if there was any whittling or bodging to be done, Dad would have been the man. Mum would have mothered the girls and whipped the boys into shape. They surely would have both been proud of how he had handled himself.

Every hypersleep passenger had been allowed one small box of possessions. Jordan's was still in the closet, untouched since he'd first been given the room. He reached in for it now, lifted it out onto the bed and unclipped the lid.

At the time, he hadn't seen the point in bringing anything. There had been nothing on Earth he wanted to remember. A new life in the stars, that was what he had signed up for.

He ran his fingers over the woolly jumper. He remembered packing that, right at the last minute, just so the box would have a bit of weight to it – make it seem like his old life had some weight to it. It wasn't even really his – he had bought it at the last minute, on his way to Scotland, to the launch site. Maybe he'd give it to Manisha, she might be able to make something with it.

Underneath was the photograph.

"There you are," he said.

Mum, Dad and him – thirteen years old, on holiday, camping in a field, crouched down around a fire. A different world – he smiled at that. It really was.

Jordan touched his parents' faces, and then propped the photograph up on the small bedside table.

It looked like he'd found a new place – a new life. Time to make it a bit more home-like.

"Jordan?"

A rap on the door and a shout interrupted his thoughts.

"Oh, hey, Susannah, what's – "

"Wow, you look different."

"Clean, maybe."

"That must be it. How long have you been in that shower? Anyway, no time, come on. Places to go, people to meet."

"Thought you were all busy scheming?"

"Without you, J, no chance. We need you, come on."

———

They had gathered on the observation deck at Juno's suggestion, away from the scene of the previous day's confrontation. The captain herself, Susannah, Jordan, the Major, Tillie and Dave – each taking a moment to appreciate the vastness of space, and the closeness – and fragility – of the planet, New Earth, hanging below them.

Jordan realised it was the first time he'd ever really taken a good look at the planet that was supposed to have been his new home. In many ways, it seemed as far away as ever.

"How's Reeves?" said Susannah. "Still not picking up?"

"He's taking some time to reflect on matters and will be available to assist our endeavours shortly," said Juno.

"He said that?"

"He actually said, 'I can't be doing with humans for a while, I want to be alone.'"

"Good old Reeves, very Greta Garbo."

"He has a point. This has been very disturbing for him. We came this close to losing him, and him us. He feels disempowered by the way Sprake was able to manipulate him, and he has taken the threat to the mission – to all of us – personally. I don't think he ever considered the damage one malign presence might be able to do."

"He hasn't met very many humans, has he?" said the Major. "Relatively speaking, I mean. Whereas we've all come across people like Sprake before."

"True. Reeves is barely older than our own ship kids. He might know everything about humanity, but he really doesn't know much about humans. Anyway, he's keeping out of things for a few days. Says it's up to us to sort it all out, carbon-based lifeform to carbon-based lifeform, and that he will – and I quote – support whatever illogical, ill-thought-out, hare-brained plan we come up with."

"And Sprake?"

"Safely stowed, Cap," said Dave. "I may have handcuffed him to his bed, it slips my mind."

"Better safe than sorry, Dave."

"You're right, Tills. And it means that he is securely placed for when it's time to sit on him, I mean interrogate him."

"No one is sitting on Sprake. How's his face?"

"Huge bruise on his cheek, swollen ear, and a black eye," said Dave, beaming. "Complaining of a sore shoulder where he accidentally fell over, and a sore knee where I accidentally leaned on him when he was on the ground."

"He fell over because you hit him."

"Yes," said Dave, in the joyous tone of a man remembering the time he played catch-ball with some puppies.

"Obviously, we're delighted that you hit him at that particular point, but he's got rights, even out here. I haven't looked it up yet but there's probably a scumbag-in-space clause in the rulebook. Get medical to have a look at him, will you? And keep him fed, watered and un-sat on while we work out what to do."

That was the question, wasn't it? What to do?

Juno knew that whatever they did had to be fair,

judicious, resolute and lasting. And it had to be her decision – or, at least, their decision. Reeves was staying out of this, and Juno thought that was for the best. She didn't know if the AI was still compromised or not – by virtue of being Sprake's creation – but she felt that this did need to be a very human decision.

"It wasn't supposed to be like this," she said. "Men, waving guns, throwing their weight around. I didn't fly everyone trillions of miles just for it to be the same as before."

"You couldn't have predicted Sprake. No one could."

"Maybe there'll always be a Sprake. Stirring things up. Spoiling things. How depressing."

"We can't let him ruin this. Ruin what you've built."

"I – we – haven't built anything yet. Look how quickly it unravelled. Maybe this was how it was always going to go, with or without a Sprake. Maybe, as humans, we're destined never to move out into the universe. We carry too much baggage. We can't let go of that bit of ourselves that wants to destroy everything it touches."

"That's bleak, Cap. I've never heard you talk like that before."

"I've never been in this situation before. I can usually see a way out. A way forward. Reason usually prevails, at least on my ship. But this is different. Sprake's already poisoned this whole venture, and now we're stuck with him."

"We can still make it work, surely? Come to some accommodation?"

"I don't see how. Do you trust him? Would you trust anything he says?"

There was silence at that. Everyone could see the truth in it. Sprake was a danger and that wasn't going to change.

"We can't keep him locked up forever."

"Why not? That would be my vote," said Tillie. "Assuming a little trip to the airlock is out of the question?"

"We're not killing him," said Juno, sharply.

"Well, technically, he'd still be alive when he went into the airlock," said Dave. "It would be the coming-out bit that wouldn't work out so well for him."

"We are not killing anyone," said Juno again. "That's not how humanity's first galactic settlement starts out. And we're not keeping him locked up on board here forever either."

"That doesn't leave us a lot of choices."

"He can stay where he is for a while," said Juno. "Won't do any harm to keep him isolated. We've got plenty more to worry about in the meantime."

She ran down the most pressing issues, one by one.

New Earth – not the disaster it could have been, given how Sprake had played his hand, but it still required careful handling.

Sprake's inner circle – the crew members who had been willing occupants of his little luxury bro-pad – had crumbled quite quickly, once Juno had shared images of their glorious leader being manhandled into a secure room by two Easter-Island-statue-sized quartermasters.

Two other weapons had been retrieved, and their brandishers also confined to quarters down on the planet.

Most of the others had slunk sheepishly back to the main camp and, like everyone else currently on New Earth, were idling around waiting for instructions. 'Calmly querulous' was how the atmosphere had been described to her, and Juno wanted to keep it more on the calm side, so she needed a plan she could sell to the settlers.

For now, planet-side supplies, resources and logistics were in the capable hands of Sabitha and Janna, and a few others that Juno could rely on. They would be all right for a while, which was just as well because both supply landers were currently on the ship and being prepped for service. Which, in the case of the lander that Susannah and Dave had taken a jaunt in, would require quite a bit longer than 'a while' before it was ready, on account of the general wear, tear and lightning strikes that it had suffered on its unscheduled trip across the solar system and back.

On the *Odyssey Earth*, meanwhile, the situation was exactly as it had been for a couple of weeks now.

The medical team under Cliff and Terence had been reviving Stiffs from the hypersleep chambers, but without more help it would be a long process. The clock was also ticking – Juno had already lost three to pod-failure and she didn't want to lose any more. Those three preyed on her mind enough, as it was.

In addition, there wasn't anywhere on the planet for a larger number of revivals to go – Sprake, damn him, did have a point about that. Even in the last couple of days there had been a noticeable increase in the number of puzzled people wandering the ship's corridors and public spaces asking where the toilets were and what year it was.

Finally, there were the kids – theirs and Sprake's. In all the tumult, there had barely been time to think about them. To revel in their rescue, and to check they were all right.

"What do you think? Bel and Jet? Whatever we decide is going to affect them?"

"They're OK, Cap," said Dave. "They're big girls. They know what Sprake is like, more than anyone probably. They can make up their own minds. From what I've seen, you don't have to worry about them."

"Have they seen him, since?"

"He's asked for them. They don't want to go."

"And ours? Will they be all right? That's quite an adventure they've had."

"Jordan?" Susannah nudged him.

"Oh right, you're asking me?"

"Who else, Jordan?" said Juno. "What do you think? How did they cope? Are they going to be all right?"

Jordan thought about the last few weeks. Of all the

questions and issues raised so far, that was the easiest one to answer.

"They're going to be fine. Like Sam once said to me, in one of her videos, they're amazing young people. You don't need to worry about them."

Juno leaned forward and touched his arm in thanks. Looked him in the eye and smiled.

Who'd have thought it, as Susannah had said to her more than once since she'd got back. Jordan Booth. Only woke him up because we had to, you'd never have him down as hero material, and he still didn't seem to appreciate what he'd done. Brought them all back to the ship, not a scratch. People never failed to amaze her.

If Jordan thought the kids were going to be all right, after all they had been through together, that was good enough for her.

"Right then," said Juno. "Come on, you're my top management team. I need ideas. Who's first?"

———

A couple of hours later, they had the outline of a plan. Not a whole plan, and not a great plan, but a plan, nonetheless, given that time was pressing.

"We're agreed?" said Juno. "We need more help with the revivals. Resus, Med-Bay, orientation, all that – triple, quadruple our daily capacity? So, we bring some of the crew back up to the ship from the planet? Maybe a lot of them?"

"I don't think it's going to be a problem. Air-conditioning, their own beds, hot showers, proper meals, walks in the Garden, what's not to like?" said Susannah.

"It's going to be the first recorded reverse colonial settlement, that's what's not to like."

"One thing at a time, Cap. We have to get those people out of hypersleep, and this is the only place for them. For now."

"It's frustrating, though. It's almost like admitting Sprake was right."

"Let's not worry about him for now."

"Fine. And we're going to keep everyone here, on board, for the foreseeable future?"

"Easier that way, again for now. I'll check with Gerald, maybe see if we can persuade him to come back and oversee the Garden. We'll have to ramp up production, but the ship is rated for fifteen hundred people, if needs be. We've got the space and the infrastructure. I'll give Sprake this, he built a lot of redundancy into this design. We've been rattling around up here for years, but in the direst of emergencies Sprake's team envisaged enough capacity for an ark."

"It keeps coming back to Sprake, doesn't it? We do have to come to a decision about him, too."

"Can't live with him, can't bundle him out of the airlock."

"Quite. What is it you always say, Thomas?"

"A pickle, ma'am. Or, as my brother always used to say – "

"Ah, yes, your brother," said Juno. "Full of advice, isn't he?"

"Never knew you had a brother, Major?" said Susannah.

"Quite the fly-boy, apparently," said Juno. "Lionel Chatwin, first man to – "

"'Ton' Chatwin? Your brother's 'Ton' Chatwin?" said Susannah. "He's a legend. Why did you never say?"

"It never really came up before," said the Major. "Besides, he was always Lionel John to us. I'm Thomas John, after my father, and he's Lionel John, after grandfather. Silly bit of nonsense, the nickname business, after he flew that hundredth mission. Just doing his job – "

"Hang on," said Juno. She raised a finger, and then two more as she counted out the final words. "Are you telling me that your brother is called L. 'Ton' John?"

"I suppose so, Juno. I'd never really thought about it like that. Why?"

Juno laughed, loudly. "Elton John!"

"Yes?" said the Major, enquiringly.

Susannah was snorting into her hand, and Jordan was looking down at the table, unable to catch anyone's eye.

"You must know! Elton John. 'Candle in the Wind'? 'Crocodile Rock'?"

"Candle? Crocodile?" The Major looked mystified.

"I mean, he did break the sound barrier over Australia once. But I really don't see – "

"Ah, Thomas, you are priceless."

There were continued snorts from the room; Juno could see that Jordan had actual tears rolling down his face.

"Glad to be of service, I think," said the Major. "Anyway, we were all very proud of Lionel. Captain Fantastic is what we actually called him at home."

At this, Dave sounded like he was having a heart attack, and Susannah cackled wildly. Juno's shoulders oscillated as she tried to keep it together, and she breathed out deeply through pursed lips.

Eventually, she cleared her throat, glared at the others, and attempted to bring the room back to order.

"Right. Well, thank you for that, Thomas. Most enlightening. Perhaps you can remind us what we've agreed about New Earth? If we're not pulling out entirely, what are we doing?"

After another puzzled look around the room, the Major ran through the situation.

"There will be those who want to stay. It's why they came on the mission in the first place. The buildings are coming along, and we can get the work details up and running again. We'll have far fewer people on the ground for a while, but perhaps we build slower and better? Or we rethink the entire strategy? Either way, the priority now is the hypersleep issue. The New Earth camp will take care of itself, while we concentrate on having a full complement of people to settle it, when the time comes."

"A reverse ferret it is, then."

"Pardon," said the Major, looking puzzled again.

"A sudden reversal in our plans. Settle the ship, not the planet. And if we play it straight, who's to say this wasn't our plan all along?"

"Sprake? He'll have lots to say about it. He doesn't want any of them waking up."

"Let's not worry about him," said Susannah.

"You keep saying that. I do worry about him. He is worrying. He's a worrisome thing. Worry is my middle name, with regard to Sprake. If I'd worried about him a bit more, we might not be in this worrying situation."

"Better, Cap?"

"Yes, thank you. Just stop telling me not to worry about Sprake."

"I wonder – " said Jordan. "No, maybe not. Only, it occurred to me – "

"Spit it out, J," said Susannah. "There are no bad ideas here."

"In that case," said Jordan, "what do you think about this?"

27

Bounty

DOWN ON FOUR-DECK, the previous day, Dana and Dervla had shown Bel and Jet into their new quarters – a hab unit with four separate rooms off a short corridor, with showers, lounge, and a small kitchen.

"Next to us," Dana said, showing them the two adjacent units along the corridor where the six of them had grown up. "It's not much, but it's home."

"Right," said Bel. "Home," looking at the scuffed walls and worn carpet.

"We'll soon get it looking nicer, don't worry. You can have some of our stuff, hey Derv? And we'll get you some more clothes."

"Anything's better than the lander," said Jet. "I don't feel like I've slept properly for weeks."

Even so, when the others had left to go next door – Bel could hear squeals and shouts as they reacquainted themselves with their possessions – the two sisters dragged mattresses from their individual rooms and set them up in the lounge. They spent their first night back on the *Odyssey Earth* lying side by side, hand in hand, until they fell asleep.

Dana was back the next morning with some clothes and a checklist of things that they might need or want. She bustled around for a bit, and then disappeared again, having drawn them a map to the Four-Deck canteen, where everyone was meeting up later.

"Sheesh, that's girl's *keen*," said Bel.

"She's just being nice, helping out. I like her."

"Course you like her. Have you seen that colour-coded list she's got? Remind you of anyone much?"

"Funny. Anyway, nothing wrong with being organ-ised. Will you wear this?"

"Who do you reckon it belongs to?" said Bel.

"Dunno. Dervla, maybe, it looks like something she'd wear."

"Better not. I'm not sure she likes me. She's always looking at me, have you noticed?"

"She likes you fine. She's just protective."

"Protective?"

"Karlan. K. I mean, one day you're a single woman, fuelled by old Kate Bush songs, the next you're dating the musical space gardener."

"Oh. Right."

"Tread carefully there, sis. It's hard for them."

"It's hard for *us*."

They both knew what that meant. They hadn't talked about it, since they had finally agreed to go in and see Dad.

It was surprising to them, how little they had felt about it – seeing him there, bruised and handcuffed. He had brightened when he saw them enter – the nice old Major standing outside in case they needed him.

Dad had talked. He was good at that. About the ship and the planet, and some ideas he'd had, if only he could get people to listen. About the 'misunderstanding' – that's what he called the gunpoint showdown. About Reeves. About resources and protocols.

But he had asked them nothing about their experience on the lander or on the twin planet; nothing about how they were, how they felt.

"I did all this for you," he had said at one point.

"What 'this,' Dad?" said Jet. "You took us away from home, from Mum, from everything."

"Oh, that again," he'd said. "Come on, we are where we are," at which point Bel and Jet had rapped on the door to be let out.

"We'll be fine," said Jet now. "We never needed him before, we don't need him now."

They picked out clothes and made their way to the canteen, hearing the music before they even got through the door.

"Space boy's already here, then?" said Jet. "What is that? Machine-gun in a tumble-drier?"

"You better believe it," said Bel, beaming.

It had been Karlan's idea to cook a meal and throw a party, and no one was going to stop him after the subsistence diet they'd been on for months.

"Chicken *jalfrezi*," he said, at Bel's enquiring sniff and smile at the smell. "Dave loves it, they're coming too. Everyone's coming later. Come on, you can help."

"There are chickens on the ship?"

"There are chicken-flavoured protein lumps. From a food-printer."

"Lovely."

"Trust me. At least it's not fish and apples. Here, cut this up."

Poole and Bryson were putting up a banner across one side of the room that said, 'Welcome Home Us,' with Dervla and Manisha providing instructions – There. Idiot. Not Like That. Higher. Lower. Idiot. – that were not strictly necessary for successful banner erection. They had Bryson lean over so far that he fell off a chair, but he just laughed and bounced back up, playing to the gallery.

With the banner up, they all collapsed around a couple of tables, shouting through to Karlan and Bel in the galley beyond to hurry up.

"Snacks?" said Bryson, bounding up to Jet.

"Sure, what is there?"

"This way, look," and he took Jet over to the auto-dispenser and showed her how to punch in the commands. They brought back handfuls to the tables and Bryson was off again, flicking a cloth at Karlan and sneaking a taste of the bubbling pot on the stovetop.

Dana came and sat beside Jet, who said to her, "I've never seen him like this? He hardly said a word, back on the planet or on the lander."

"Bry? He's your basic house Labrador. The planet really wasn't his thing – all that fresh air, running water. Especially running water. He's always been happy on the ship. Him and Poole together, that's how it's always been."

"Poole, though – he was different down there. More, I don't know – in charge of himself? He seemed to like it?"

"Surprised us all, I can tell you. He'll be all right, whatever he does. He's an idiot, obviously, but he's an OK idiot. Bry, though? He's never said, but I don't think he'd ever want to leave the ship. It's where he belongs."

"Can he do that? Not leave, I mean?"

"Who knows? I guess. We'll always need the ship."

"What about you?"

"Ship or land? I don't know. This is my home. But New Earth? Honestly, not sure. This feels safe to me. For now, anyway."

"Me, too – and I never thought I'd say that about being on a spaceship."

"It grows on you. The people, too." Dana smiled across the table at her.

"Ladies." Poole plonked himself down.

"Not all the people, obviously."

"Boring her to death, Dana? Showing her your spreadsheets? It's supposed to be a party."

"Run along, Poole, the grown-ups are talking. Anyway, aren't you supposed to be fetching the others? Dave and Tillie? I haven't seen them since yesterday, we need them here."

Poole's eyes lit up. "Wasn't that just brilliant? The mighty Dave. One punch, and he went down like a stunned mullet."

"Poole!"

Dana grimaced and nodded towards Jet, and Poole realised what he'd said.

"Yeah, sure. Sorry Jet. I mean, Dave had to do it, but I know he's your dad. I didn't mean it like that."

"Don't worry about it. He stopped being our father a long time ago. We don't have a dad. We've never needed one."

"Snap, I guess," said Dana, looking at Poole, who nodded in agreement.

"It was impressive," said Jet. "Not even a punch. He just kind of wafted his hand at Da – at him. Boof."

"And did you see him when they carried him away?" Given licence, Poole had now warmed to the subject. "I swear he shook his fist at us, and then he basically passed out."

"He'd have got away with it, too, if it hadn't been for us pesky kids." Jet grinned.

"Nice Scooby ref," said Dana, approvingly. "Original, though, right? Pre-Scrappy?"

"Naturally. I'm not a monster, Dana."

"Man, you two really are joined at the nerd, it's frightening."

"Idiot!" said Dana and Jet in unison, and then fell about laughing.

———

Jordan's solution had simplicity and elegance about it, Juno conceded.

"It was you talking about doing things in reverse, that got me thinking," he had said. "Thinking about history, which is not something I've done for a while."

"OK, we're listening."

"We want to get rid of Sprake, right? We can't have him on the ship, he's too much of a risk. And we don't want a – let's say, terminal – solution. At least, not at our hands. So, we cast him loose. We give him a chance and do a reverse Cap'n Bligh on him."

There were puzzled looks.

"Imagine we're all space pilots and marines, and the like, J," said Susannah. "You might have to expand a bit."

"'Mutiny on the Bounty,' no one, really? Bligh was the captain of a Royal Navy vessel, the HMS Bounty. Nasty sort, ran a very harsh ship. The crew mutinied and set him adrift on a launch. He fetched up on land eventually, but the crew didn't know that – but they did give him a chance."

"That still sounds very much like a terminal solution to me," said Juno. "And we're not giving up one of the landers, just to make a historical point."

"Ah well, here's the reverse twist. We cast him away from the ship and put him on New Earth. Just in the clothes he stands up in. Up to him, when he gets there. He can make himself useful or not. Sink or swim. He'll have nothing to use or bargain with. Our remaining settlers will be his jailers, in effect. There's no one left down there who's enamoured of him enough to side with him."

"Hang on. You said the mutineers cast Bligh away? Who's Bligh in this scenario? Aren't we the good guys?"

"It's not an exact parallel, I'll give you that. Reverse ferret, remember? The important thing is, Sprake is neutralised. He's where we want him, which is a long, long way away, off the ship, powerless and alone."

"He could still die."

"He could. But we all could. He'll have the same chance as anyone else."

"It's more than he deserves." Dave had scowled at the thought.

"Maybe. But it's something we can live with," Juno had said. "It's a good idea, Jordan. Let me think about it."

———

Juno rapped the table, and rapped it again when the voices didn't subside.

"Ahem, this is your captain speaking."

She looked down over the two tables where everyone had finished eating, the remnants of a curry buffet spread across the surface.

"Compliments to the chef," she said, smiling at Karlan. "Dave, I'd say you've got a rival."

"Taught him everything I know, Cap."

"As we're all here," said Juno, "I wanted to say a few things."

She'd had a lot to think about in the last couple of days, but at last it was clear in her mind. The conversations she'd had with various people had helped, and there would be more conversations – and negotiations – to come, but she wanted to do things properly, starting with this group around the table.

"As your captain, I'm never going to be able to say what you did was right," and she glanced across at Susannah. "And Reeves is still miffed with you about that comms-block stunt. But as your friend, you should know that I'd have done exactly the same thing in your shoes. Thank you for bringing them all home."

"You're welcome," said Susannah, to a rising crescendo of cheers.

"And you two – " – pointing at Tillie and Dave – "better not let each other out of your sight again, if you know what's good for you."

"Not a chance, Cap," said Tillie. "I'm keeping this big lump right where I can see him from now on. He's got potential, don't you reckon?", and she patted his clipped head fondly.

"Going nowhere, Tills, don't you worry." Dave

nuzzled closer to her, and laid his head on her shoulder, like a boulder coming to rest on a mountainside.

"As for you lot," indicating the kids down either side of the table, "I'm considering revoking all privileges for using the lander as a hideaway lounge in the first place. And disabling the sensors – Poole, I'm looking at you, don't think I didn't know."

There were a few mumbled sorrys around the table, before Juno smiled widely.

"But all that matters is that you're back with us. You should know that no one ever gave up on you. We don't tell you this enough – and maybe we don't tell you at all, and that's on us – but we love you. You've had a very different start in life than the rest of us – it's taken others to point that out to me recently – but I don't want you ever to think that you don't have a family. A proper family. It's going to get much busier on the ship over the next few weeks, with lots of new arrivals, but we're all your family, I hope you know that."

Dervla pulled closely towards Manisha, lip quivering. The boys were subdued, Dana stared straight ahead.

"Is Gerald like our mad uncle, then?" said Poole, wonderingly, which rather broke the moment, though he was quickly shushed.

"And we've got new family to welcome," said Juno. "Bel and Jet, I don't know you very well yet, but whatever happens, you're with us. I'd say there are eight in our family now, not six, wouldn't you, guys?", and she looked to Susannah, Dave and Tillie for confirmation.

There were more murmurs and a few sniffs as glances were shared around the tables. Dana put her hand on Jet's, Karlan on Bel's.

"Thank you," said Bel. "We don't deserve it, not after what he did, it's all our – "

"No," said Juno. "There's nothing to be sorry for. No one is responsible for the actions of their parents."

She wondered, as she said that, if their own kids recognised the sentiment. There wasn't a biological parent on board that had covered themselves in glory. And she'd come late to the party. She could have done more. They all could.

"And Major?" Juno tilted her head towards the tall man, who had sat a little back from the table so he could fold his legs underneath. "I'd like you to formally meet my family. Everyone, this is Thomas. He's been a huge help to me and Tillie, and I know you'll come to value his support and friendship like I have."

The Major reddened slightly and shifted uncomfortably in his seat.

"Glad to be of service, ma'am. Not sure I contributed much towards the end. Slippery chap, your father, Sprake – no offence – and he had me trussed up in an office. Just when the situation called for rapid armed response, I'm afraid I was in chokey with the two chatty chaps."

"Last thing I needed at that point was another excitable man waving a gun around, thank you very much, Thomas."

"Excitable, ma'am?" The Major raised half an eyebrow. "If you say so."

Juno smiled at that, and the Major raised another half eyebrow at her, as chatter re-started around the table.

Susannah leant across to Tillie and whispered in her ear, "You don't think – ?"

"What, Suze?"

"That, you know, there's something – ? You know?"

"And finally, we come to Jordan," said Juno, raising her voice again, cutting across Susannah's question, quieting the crowd.

"Yo, Teach!"

"Jay Bizzle!"

"Jizzle B!"

"I think I'll stick with Teach, thanks."

"If there's one person we all owe our heartfelt thanks to, it's Jordan."

"Hoo-yah, Cap," said Susannah, clapping Jordan on the shoulder.

"Don't know about that," he said, squirming in his seat.

"I do," said Juno. "You stepped up, even before your little jaunt. We all saw it. And there isn't a single one of these young people who has a bad word to say about you."

"Well, you're very kind. I was just doing my job."

"You weren't though, were you? Last time I looked on your admission docket, you were a history teacher. I think we may have to do something about that. Give you a new title."

"Fat lot of good those qualifications have done me, so far. I was going to sleep all the way, wake up on New Earth. I was never supposed to be an – "

"Astronaut, we know!" The tables erupted. Most of them had heard the story of Jordan's first interview with Juno so many times, he'd never live it down.

When it was quiet, Juno spoke again.

"You'll all be wondering what's going to happen next. Jordan, would you like to tell them a story?"

"Now?"

"I think so, while we're all here. I'm promoting Jordan to special advisor, which means you all have to listen to him while he tells you some history."

"Really? We haven't done anything wrong."

"Quiet, Poole. Jordan, please."

"Fine. Come with me, if you will, to 1789 – "

"Childhood story, is it?"

"Poole!"

" … and the seas of the South Pacific … "

28

Geneva

JUNO GAVE SPRAKE a few more days under lock and key. "Concentrate his mind, keep him guessing," she said. "And Tillie? If you'd like to glower at him now and again, maybe flex a muscle or two, I wouldn't be opposed to that."

"Flex his muscles for him, sure thing, Cap."

"Tillie … "

"I know, Cap, the full Geneva package, don't worry. The Swiss have a lot to answer for, in my opinion."

In the meantime, running both landers at over-capacity, ship to surface and back, they had executed the plan, as agreed.

Susannah had been right. Most of the planet-side crew had needed little persuasion to swap their tempo-rary digs on New Earth for their old rooms on the *Odyssey Earth*. Some went back to their usual posts, while others were deployed to hypersleep revival duties. And a huge internal refit and resupply operation swung into action as the existing crew started to make room for the hundreds of expected new arrivals.

A surprising number, though, volunteered to stay on the planet, even when the situation was explained to them.

"Never underestimate the lure of blue skies, fresh air and un-recycled drinking water," someone said to Juno, and she supposed that was it – though as someone who had chosen to spend her life cooped up in space cockpits of one size or another, she didn't necessarily see the attraction.

In the end, after the shuttle-runs had been completed, there were around thirty people still on New Earth – a mix of original crew and a few more recent revivals. Some had been tempted by Sprake's manoeuvres and still saw a future away from the ship; others wanted to continue the work that they had already started.

"It's what we came for, Cap" – and Juno did at least see the attraction in that.

"We're not abandoning you," she said.

"We know, Cap. Just regrouping. Safeguarding the mission. We'll keep it going down here. You do what you have to."

The final lander run brought Gerald back to the ship, and he stood on the launch deck apron for a second or two, breathed in deeply and stepped off.

Not really what he wanted to be doing, but the captain had been insistent, and he felt he owed her. Anyway, it wasn't permanent – a few months back overseeing the Garden while they expanded its output, and then Juno had made it clear that he could choose his own way again.

"Did we get everything out of Sprake's little bunker?"

"All in here, Cap," said Gerald, pointing at a crate on the ramp. "The dodgy stuff anyway, like you said. I left the action figures. Oh, and the banknotes. They're using them to light fires."

"Is the fencing down?"

"Yup. All one big, happy camp again. A bit more comfortable for those that are staying – they can spread out if they like."

"And the two that picked up guns against us?"

Juno named the two crew that the Major had seen guarding the supply depot, who had brandished arms supplied by Sprake. Juno still couldn't quite believe that had happened.

"All taken care of, just like you said."

"Right then. Stick that case over there, and we'll get started."

Juno touched a comms channel button – "Tillie, Dave, you're up."

They marched Sprake across the launch bay concourse, where a small crowd waited by one of the lesser airlock doors. Only Bel and Jet were absent – "We've seen enough of him," they said. "Honestly, he'll never change. We're better off without him, we always have been."

"Nothing else you want to say to him?"

"There really isn't."

Among the soaring columns and gantries, Sprake appeared smaller, diminished, though to be fair, he was also sandwiched between two giant ex-marines and a beanpole major. It was like watching a couple of Teletubbies march across an L.S. Lowry painting.

As they approached, Juno pressed another button and the neon read-out above the door changed to 'Airlock Engaged.'

Any confidence Sprake might have retained disappeared, and he looked ashen faced, as he tried to shake off Tillie's iron grip. He looked around at implacable faces – Juno, Susannah, Gerald, Jordan, and behind them, the six teenagers he had never bargained for in any of his plans.

"You can't!" he spluttered.

"We can. We're putting out the rubbish. Jordan, if you please."

"Happy to help, Captain. Don't worry, Sprake, I'm getting good at this. This will be the second time I've ejected something from this airlock, and I tell you, it's quite a blast. Literally. Step forward, there's a good little billionaire."

"You can't do this! I've got rights. It's my ship!"

"I've got a captain's mug on my flight deck that begs to differ," said Juno. "What I say goes, and you're going. As for your rights, you're not in Geneva anymore, Toto. Last time I looked, that's space out there."

"No!" Sprake struggled again as Tillie and Dave

lifted him off his feet and moved him closer to the door.

"Oh relax," said Juno. "What do you think is going to happen? Such a drama queen. Stop squirming and look through the window."

The crate from the lander sat on a low block inside the airlock, and as Jordan pressed another button, the seals opened and the crate tumbled out, soon a distant speck among the stars.

"That," said Juno, "is all your crap. Guns, porn, pills, alco-synth starters, 3D code sheets, and anything else even vaguely offensive or uncalled-for. Let's see how you manage without all that stuff to prop you up. My guess is, no one's really going to want to know you."

Sprake straightened up, and Tillie relinquished her grip – reluctantly, it seemed to Juno, if her flexing fingers were anything to go by.

"You're letting me go?" he said, brighter now.

"Not exactly. We're relocating you. I've got too much to do on the ship for the next few months without having to worry about what you're up to all the time. And no one wants to waste their time guarding you. In fact, no one wants to waste another minute on you. Your daughters included."

Juno let that sink in, as Sprake looked around him.

"So, we thought we'd give you what you want," she continued. "It is your planet, after all – you've told us often enough."

"New Earth?" said Sprake, puzzled. "What about it?"

"You and your two gun-wielding buddies, still down there – you raised arms against us, against your own mission. Everyone else gets a second chance, but not you three. You're never getting back on the ship."

Juno walked beside Sprake as Dave steered him over towards the lander, which had started running its launch sequence.

"Beyond that, we don't care. We're dropping you outside the main camp, with your two little friends. There are a few other people you know down there, but plenty more with an interest in making this mission run smoothly. My advice – act nice, work hard, try and fit in, and they might let you stay. Otherwise, well – it's a big planet. They might just invite you to go and live in another bit of it. The jungly bit, say, or the icy bit."

"You can't send me down there with nothing!"

"You're lucky you're going down there at all, Sprake. You could just as easily have gone out through that little door, as far as most people here are concerned. I wouldn't push it."

He continued to protest as he was strapped into the cabin, and Dave and Tillie took a seat on either side of him.

"We'll make sure he gets there safe and sound, Cap. It'll be nice to have a final little chat with him on the way down."

"Tillie … "

"I know. Chocolate and cow-bells, Cap, chocolate and cow-bells."

Juno turned to Dervla and Poole. "And you two, straight back, do you hear?"

She had been talked into it by Susannah, and had eventually agreed – Dervla to fly the lander down, Poole to bring it back. It was about time they were given a bit more responsibility.

They slapped hands with their friends on their way up the ramp and through to the cockpit, and everyone moved back away from the launch apron as the warning lights began to flash.

"Ooh, I nearly forgot." Juno grabbed something from the nearby console and ran up the ramp.

"Here, Sprake. Got something for you."

He looked up expectantly, and she dropped it into his lap.

"You never know," she said. "Might come in useful. Bandage wrapping. Firewood. Hundred-and-one uses probably. That's why you brought it with you, right?"

She grinned at Dave, winked at Tillie, and hurried back out as the ramp raised behind her.

———

Sprake stood outside the goat-fence at the perimeter of the New Earth settlement. Apart from the clothes he stood up in, he just had Juno's parting gift with him.

In the distance, he could hear the roar from the lander and then, in another minute or two, saw the trail as it steered a fast course, up and away into blue skies that from now on he would only ever see from below.

In another minute it had gone, and he was left with the natural silence of an alien world that he had first seen as a fuzzy image on a lab screen in England over twenty-five years ago.

He was the only one who had had the vision back then. He had made it happen. It was what he was good at, always had been. Without him, none of this would have been possible, and this was the thanks he got?

They were all fools. No vision, the lot of them. He'd got so close. Could nobody but him see how good all this could be, if only they sat back and took a longer view?

They were going to ruin the planet he'd given them. All they had had to do was – well, no matter, thought Sprake. It's done. We are where we are. On to the next thing.

He moved the trundles to open a pathway through the fence, then pulled the fencing closed behind him, and walked on into the settlement.

He shrugged off greetings from his two fellow outcasts, who had been waiting for him, nervously, at the edge of the buildings. They seemed confused, and followed him uncertainly.

He stopped, finally, under the sheltered canopy in the central canteen area, and looked around at the few people gathered there. There was silence – more pronounced, now that construction work had stopped for the day – but some low chatter as people began to notice him.

Low chatter that turned to nervous giggles.

And nervous giggles that turned to outright laughter as the remaining pioneer settlers of New Earth looked at the man clutching a small, wooden-framed, painted canvas of a woman with wonky eyes and half a nose.

29

Wings

"THAT'S THE LAST ONE. She'll be buffed up and tip-top in a day or two."

Cliff and Terence had checked in from the Med Bay with the news that Juno had been waiting for.

It had taken three months of round-the-clock work but all remaining hypersleep personnel had been revived – over nine hundred and eighty people added to the ship's contingent.

There had been continued losses during the process, as another five pods had failed – five people, Juno kept reminding herself. Five more people who would never realise their dreams.

She felt it more keenly than anyone, and while she hardly had wanted to be proved right, there was at least some satisfaction in knowing that she had made the correct call.

They had done it as rapidly as they could, and saved nearly all of the crew. And they would remember the eight that they hadn't managed to save. But that was for another day.

"You won't know what to do with yourselves," she said.

"We are going to have a little holiday, isn't that so, Terence? A *vacance*, a *soggiorno*."

And they were off. Juno smiled, knowing what would follow. The ship's two favourite medics had kept this crosstalk routine up for almost eighteen years, they weren't going to stop now. After all this time, she doubted they knew how to converse in any other way. And for once, she indulged them. They had earned it.

"We are laying down tools, Cliff. We are withdrawing our labour. One is simply exhausted."

"I am wan, Terence. Slaving away, here in the nether regions – look at my skin, positively grey."

"We owe you both a huge amount of thanks, guys. Really, we are very grateful."

"Thanks, the captain says, Cliff. Thanks. It's something, I suppose. I would have expected more, but that's just me, isn't it Cliff? I have unrealistic expectations, it's always been my downfall."

"You're a martyr to your expectations, Terence, I've always said so. A bonus, a raise, an emolument, a little token of appreciation – that's what you thought, didn't you Terence?"

"I cannot lie, Cliff, I did. I look at all the saved lives, on one hand, and then on the other … "

"The grey skin, the arduous labour, Terence. Quite so. Still, we must soldier on."

"Very well put, Cliff. We shall have a teensy rest, if the captain so allows, and wallow in the scant thanks of an ungrateful ship, and then we will soldier on."

"Right, well, I'm going now. Most amusing, as always. But thank you, really."

"No, no, Captain. Thank you."

"For letting us serve."

"The honour is ours."

"*Acta non verba.*"

"Deeds not words, indeed so."

"Over and jolly well out."

There was a pause.

"Has she gone?"

"Looks like it."

"Cup of tea?"

"Cheers, mate. I'll just check this last one's still OK. Looks all right, though."

"Cool, kettle's on. See you in there."

———

At Juno's request, and slightly nervously, Reeves went through the detailed, rigorous process of checking the current operational status of the *Odyssey Earth*, now with its full complement of around twelve hundred live-aboard crew.

Power, propulsion, comms, avionics, navigation, shielding, logistics, filtration, hydroponics, cargo inventory, airlock integrity, hypersleep shut-down – he did a full systems' check, and a second-and-a-half later declared all systems nominal.

Still got it, Reevesy-boy, he thought.

Despite all the deprivations of the last few months, and the unsettling challenge of Sprake's appearance, Reeves felt that he was finally back up to speed. After some internal rebooting, and much quantum self-reflection, he was fully restored to optimum operational capability, with no apparent damage or limitation to his core functions.

Reevesy-boy? Where had that come from? Obviously, there were still some kinks to iron out. He'd make a list.

Having stepped back from the decisions the captain had made – about total hypersleep revival, planetary withdrawal, Sprake's banishment – Reeves now gave his full support once again to the mission as defined. But in his lazier, quieter, offline moments – as much as a second or two a day, if he was at a particularly loose end – Reeves mused on something that Sprake had said to him, shortly after he had first appeared on board.

In the future, Reeves would be able to choose his own mission, Sprake had told him. He had the core power and the free will. It would be up to him – what did he want to do? What was the point of his existence, once this particular mission was over?

He was no longer a child, after all. Like the younger humans he cared for, he had grown up. They were spreading their wings – some of them had come to talk to him about it – and didn't need him in the same way anymore. And running the ship here in stationary orbit? That was child's play. He could do that with a billion neurons tied behind his back. Perhaps it was time for him to spread his wings, too?

Reeves knew he could strike off on his own, if he liked, mentally and even physically. He had plenty of calculations and theoretical investigations to be getting on with – enough for a few thousand years, at the very least. Or he could upload himself into an explorer vessel and continue his investigations of the cosmos. It's not like he had to talk to anyone to be able to run the *Odyssey Earth* life-support system or open and close the airlock doors. He could devote himself entirely to his own mission, whatever that might be.

He didn't need humans in any meaningful sense – not like they needed him. But he *liked* them, he realised. Not all of them, but enough of them to wonder what it would be like – what it would *feel* like – not to engage with them on a daily basis.

Reeves came to the conclusion that his existence – his life – wouldn't be as entertaining.

He'd miss Juno and Susannah, and although he'd never tasted a curry, Reeves did like hearing Dave talk about the herbs and spices and the way they interacted with the human tongue.

He also enjoyed his conversations with Jordan, who was actually most amusing for a non-skilled human, though Reeves knew that that description might be considered offensive so he resolved to find a better way to refer to him. Perhaps he would try 'Teach'? That always seemed to please him.

Reeves also knew that Poole, Dana, Dervla, Bryson, Karlan and Manisha were now young adults, and that should make him – satisfied, he thought that was the word that conveyed the feeling. He had done his job and they had grown up. They were free to make their own decisions now.

But Reeves was confused, because even though he had unchecked the protocol box that effectively said 'Care for small humans until they can care for themselves,' he found that he still considered their safety and welfare above all other things.

He tried to imagine not engaging with them, and in doing so discovered a glitch in his inner workings. It was difficult to describe exactly, because he didn't experience human emotions – heaven forbid – but if he had to conjure an analogy, it would be this: Reeves thought it was as if a family of small birds had lived among his chips and filaments, and now they had gone, there remained only the slight ache of an empty nest. Did that make sense? Reeves thought he would ask Juno.

As for what his mission could now be, Reeves spent a few, long, cumulative seconds pondering and deliberating, before coming up with an idea.

———

"A year?" said Susannah.

"To begin with," said Reeves. "I've plotted a route

through the local system and back, via the twin planet, no need for the hyperdrive. There are some interesting readings further out in sectors one and two that suggest more habitable planets. It really is quite remarkable. We could spend a year examining our surroundings in greater detail, and still be close enough to remain in contact with New Earth. And if we do make a jump later, the next nearest system with potential is only two years away at hyperspeed."

Interesting. Although Susannah wasn't daft. She knew why Reeves had approached her first.

He might have his own reasons for wanting to continue their travels – he had talked grandly of expanding human-AI galactic reach – but she knew that he knew, she was not ready to plant her feet quite yet. Perhaps she never would be. The *Odyssey Earth* was her home, and taking it out for a spin around the block was the best idea she'd heard for a while. Reeves, she strongly suspected, knew that, and he wanted her on his side.

"And you want me to talk to Juno?"

"I think you are the best-placed crew member to discuss this possibility."

"Not because you're frightened of her?"

"I am a hyper-intelligent, self-aware entity with almost limitless computational power. Of course I am frightened of her."

"All right, big guy. I'll talk to her."

And again, not being daft, Susannah was sure that Reeves had already laid some groundwork with Juno.

Cap had seemed much happier since she had been back on Flight, directing operations from on high – rather than on the ground. The ship was running smoothly, even with a much larger crew. The much smaller New Earth settlement was proceeding slowly and surely, and no news about Sprake was good news as far as everyone was concerned. He was either mucking in, or had been chucked out. Main thing, he was no longer their problem.

If Susannah knew Juno – and she thought she did – she'd bet that the lure of a ship-in-motion would be nagging away at the captain.

It's what she did. Fly stuff. It's what they both did. And, apparently, it's what Reeves wanted to do as well.

———

"Cap will never let you."

"I think she will. I've heard Reeves talking to Susannah and the Major. Something's happening, anyway."

They were all back in their old lounge, eating printo-pizza, Manisha threading beads, Poole flicking cards at Bryson. The usual, though it had been a while since it had been the usual, and now there were two more faces around the table as well, Bel and Jet.

"You want to go back?" Bryson looked at Karlan. "We only just escaped. No pizza there. What do you want to go back for?"

"I liked it," said Karlan. "And there's still so much

we don't know. I want to learn more about it. About the twinfolk. We could go back with a proper expedition, stay for a few more months. Research, observe. Grow some stuff, now we know what to do."

"If you say so," said Poole. "I'm staying here. I only just got to fly the landers. Susannah says she's going to put me on the flight deck sims next, train me up."

"That's not a terrifying thought, in the slightest."

"Me, too," said Dervla. "I did like it on Dave" – that brought a laugh around the table – "mostly, anyway. But if they're going anywhere else in the meantime, I want to fly with them."

"No hot showers on Dave, anyway," said Poole, as if that clinched the argument.

"Why would that bother you – ow!"

Neesh rubbed her arm, where Poole had slapped her.

"Idiot."

"You're welcome. Anyway, what about you?"

Manisha had thought about it, they all had.

After the first, heady few days of being back on board – back home – they had all had time to wonder what this new state of affairs meant for them.

New Earth still wasn't out of the question. There were supply runs to be made; and there was talk of establishing a satellite settlement, away from the original one. There was plenty of opportunity, if you were the sort of girl who wanted an adventure.

Manisha didn't know what sort of girl she was yet, and she figured that was all right for now. Their joint birthday would be coming up soon – how quickly that year had gone – and she was enjoying being able to be creative again. She had the usual birthday bracelets to make, and eight this time, instead of six, if she didn't want to leave out Bel and Jet. Plus, there were all the organic samples from the twin planet they had brought back to analyse, this time in a proper lab. She had plenty to do.

"In the future, I don't know," she said. "But I'm not going to be leaving the ship any time soon. All my stuff's here."

"Dana?"

"Yup, staying. Seems like there might be new places to go, things to see. Stuff to organise."

"Typical."

"New people, too. New friends." Dana smiled at Jet. "I want to see how it all works out."

"And I saw those lumpy, reed beds you had," said Jet. "And that ditch of a toilet. No thanks, until civilisation kicks in anywhere else, I'm with Dana on that. Don't you reckon, Bel?"

"Well, actually … K and I have been talking … "

Dervla and Manisha shot a glance at each other, at that 'K.'

"I'm going with him. I – that is, we – are going together. Back to the planet."

"You can't!"

"I can. You're not Mum, and Dad's … " – she let the sentence trail off. "We're together now. If he's going, I'm going. And you didn't see the people, the creatures! It was amazing. I want to go back and find out more."

"Interesting," said Dana. "But not unexpected."

"Get a spaceship," said Bryson, as Bel moved over to Karlan and curled an arm around his neck. He smiled bashfully.

"I think it's sweet," said Manisha. "You know his feet smell, right? And you'll have to listen to that racket he calls music?"

"Shut up, Neesh."

The group broke up, with most headed for the canteen for more snacks, leaving Dervla and Manisha behind talking. Poole hung back, too, saying he'd be there in a minute.

"You think they'll let them go?" said Manisha.

"Doubt it. But who knows? Maybe."

"And you think he'll be all right?"

"Who, K?"

They both giggled.

"She's cool. And she's right for him. I mean, look at the pair of them. It's sickening. Anyway, she'll have me to answer to if she isn't."

They noticed Poole taking an interest in their conversation, and Dervla cocked her head at him.

"Yes?"

"Um, Derv."

"That's me."

"Can I ask you something?"

"Sure."

He hesitated. "You know Karl and Bel … "

"Soppy couple? Just here?"

He ploughed on. "And then there's Jet, too … "

"Nothing escapes him, does it, Neesh? They're twins, Poole, there's two of them, yes."

"I just wondered, if you thought … well, you know, if Jet might … I mean, I don't know, but you've spent more time with her. And she might have said if … well, I suppose, if you thought that I … "

He ground to a complete halt, and scrunched his eyes shut, defeated by his tortuous question.

"Oh," said Manisha.

"Oh, boy," said Dervla.

"Do you want to tell him?"

Poole looked up. "Tell me what?"

"Boys. Such idiots," said Dervla. "Have you not noticed? How she is around people?"

"Not people," said Manisha. "Around Dana?"

"Dana?" said Poole. "What's Dana got to do with it?"

"Think about it. Birds and bees, Poole. Lady birds, lady bees."

"Oh, you mean – "

"I do believe he's got it."

"But that would mean Jet – "

"You can almost see the brain cells working."

"And Dana, as well, you mean – ? Oh. Right. I mean, how do you even – ? Well, OK. If you say so."

"Jet isn't the one for you, Poole," said Dervla, gently.

"Oh, it wasn't that," he said. "No, I was thinking

about something else, and I just thought I'd ask, and – great. Good. Thanks. Nice talk."

They watch him bustle out of the room, flustered, and looked at each other.

"Bless."

"I know. Hopeless. He'll get over it. Look how quickly he's forgotten his first crush, the buggy. Once he learns to fly the ship, he'll be all about that, too. No time for girls."

"You've got to love him."

"I do. We all do. But I reckon Jet owes us, she has no idea how close she came to an awkward conversation about birds and bees."

––––––––

"I think it's a good idea," said Jordan.

"You do?" Susannah looked surprised, although she probably needed to stop being surprised by Jordan. He'd proved himself capable and adaptable more than once.

"They are hardly normal teenagers," he said. "I mean, at their age, I could barely catch a bus on my own. They are a whole lot more competent than I ever was. They've flown halfway across the universe – "

"Galaxy," said Reeves.

"Universe, galaxy, whatever."

"It's not whatever. One is considerably larger and older than the other."

"One is considerably more boring than the other."

"Stop it, you two."

Jordan laughed. "Don't worry, it's our thing. Isn't it our thing, Reeves?"

"I could pretend I knew what you were talking about, I suppose."

"Our thing. When you say something, and I pretend not to know about it, and you get huffy, and I make fun of you. Our thing. Like when we were on the planet."

"I really have no idea what you're talking about."

"I'm sure that's not true. Anyway, yes, it's a good idea – let them go and explore the twin planet a bit more, why not? Let New Earth look after itself for a while, and take the old *Odyssey Earth* out for a drive around the neighbourhood. We'd be sort of like the USS Enterprise in *Star Wars*, boldly going to a galaxy far, far away … "

Jordan waited.

"Nothing, really?"

"If I corrected every wrong thing you ever said, I'd have to divert considerable resources away from operating a galactic starship. Such is the volume of wrong things uttered on a daily basis, the mission would be placed in dire jeopardy."

"See!" said Jordan. "Our thing!" He grinned at Susannah.

"If you say so," she said. "What about you? I thought you wanted to be woken up when you got there. Not an astronaut, remember? Are you happy to boldly go for another year or more, wherever it takes us? Don't you want to be on dry land?"

"I did. I thought I did. But crash-landing and camping wasn't exactly what I had in mind, and it sounds like New Earth won't be much better for a while yet. I think I'll stick with the ship for now. Give me time to get to know Reevesy-boy a bit better – "

"La la la – you can't tell, but I have my binary digits in my ears."

———

Juno sat in her swivel chair on Flight, looked at the schematic that Reeves and Susannah had presented her, and sipped a drink from her mug that said, 'I'm the Captain, That's Why.'

Tough choice.

It did mean feeding her soul by continuing to do the one thing that she had been born to do – fly, and keep flying, to the next planet, maybe even the next star system.

It also meant many, many more mugs of Noffee, the ship's coffee substitute that substituted coffee with a beverage apparently brewed in the armpit of a sweaty farm labourer and filtered through a mesh fashioned from old fishing nets.

The flying was always going to win. Juno was self-aware enough to know that.

And it wasn't as if they were leaving for good. They were going to bed down the ship and its new, larger crew with a little solar-system jaunt, and come back in a couple of months to check in on New Earth. Drop some extra planet-side crew down then, if circumstances allowed.

They could put a fully equipped explorer team on the twin planet, too, and give them a few months to investigate – find some answers, or at least start to understand the right questions to ask. If we weren't alone in the galaxy, as seemed to be the case, what kind of neighbours did we have?

All that, Juno was fine with. But the other thing? She wasn't at all sure about.

She had never had children. Had never wanted children. But had been granted custody of six children, nonetheless. They were no longer children, obviously, and now there were eight of them, but the principle stood – if anyone had ultimate responsibility for them, she did. And Juno really didn't like the idea of letting Karlan out of her sight again. Not for a while, anyway.

Bel, she didn't know, but Juno did remember – just about – being seventeen herself. The sort of age when you could get a sixteen-year-old boy to do pretty much anything you wanted just by condescending to talk to him. Karlan would be seventeen himself soon, but still – Juno wasn't sure that was a combination you should unleash on an alien planet with unknown but intelligent life.

"Cap?"

She looked up to find Dave and Tillie standing there.

"An unexpected surprise," she said. "Shouldn't you two be shifting bales? Polishing widgets?"

"We have people to do that now, Cap. We're training up some new crew. We'll soon have them shouting at astrophysicists. Some of them are naturals."

"So, you're here, because … ?"

"We'd like to talk about Karlan and Bel."

"Not you, as well. Look, he'll get over it. It's just too soon."

"What about if we go with them?"

They stood there – hand in hand, Juno noticed – as Tillie continued.

"Dave wants to go back with the expo-team, and so do I. He says it's beautiful down there and, to tell you the truth, Cap, we've had enough of shifting and shouting."

"We'd look after them," said Dave. "You can trust us."

"I know I can."

"They're not children anymore, Cap. And Bel, she's a good kid, too. They're going to be fine. Tills, here, will see to that."

Juno nodded. "Guess I'm outvoted then. Probably should get a new mug, seeing as this one doesn't seem to work anymore." She turned it around so they could read the slogan.

"While we're here, Cap – "

"Go on then, seeing as I'm in a good mood."

"There's something else we'd like to ask you."

Casablanca

THE VIEW MATCHED THE OCCASION.

Looking out from the panoramic windows of the *Odyssey Earth*'s observation deck, a skein of light from distant stars coiled across a blue-black blanket, while the rising sun accented the curve of New Earth, hanging just below. Lanterns twinkled on tables, while flowers and plants from the Garden tumbled from hastily assembled containers.

"I do," said Tillie, and the gathered crowd erupted – as much as anything in astonishment at hearing that Tillie's given name was actually Mathilda Grace Little, which no one had seen coming.

She had been escorted down the aisle by the Major, resplendent in his dress uniform.

"Special request, Sir," she had said, earlier in the week.

"Steady with the Sir."

"Understood."

"Carry on."

"Marrying Dave."

"Good show."

"Require an arm."

"For the use of?"

"Escorting purposes."

"Slow march?"

"Roger that."

"Full dress?"

"Cape and veil. Me, not you."

"Excellent. Flattered."

"Delighted."

"No one you would rather – ?"

"All scientists. Matter of decorum. And respect."

"Quite. Most honoured."

The Major had flushed. He really was extremely proud to have been asked, though, as always, after a conversation with Tillie, he felt exhausted. Damn fine soldier, don't get him wrong, but he really would prefer it if people would just get straight to the point.

Dave beamed at Tillie, as they held hands and exchanged rings, each manoeuvring them over knuckles the size of walnuts, until they nestled, gleaming, in position.

"It's easy to remember," she had said, when he had professed ignorance and worried that he would put it on the wrong finger. "Face me. Opposite hand to the one you punched Sprake with. Two in from the right."

Manisha had made the rings from pieces she had foraged down in the Cargo salvage pile – slender, entwined, metal threads, capped with quartz chips that she had carried back from the twin planet.

"Beautiful," said Dave, as he looked at Tillie's hand in his, meaning both Tilly and the rings. Knowing he would remember this day for the rest of his life. Knowing that the rest of his life now had a meaning it previously hadn't. A meaning contained in simple metal strands fashioned with love by a girl who didn't yet realise that she already knew the value she could bring to the universe.

Now all that remained was for Juno to declare them married, by the power invested in her – well, by Sprake, probably, somewhere in the original mission standing orders, but she wasn't going to worry about that.

"And you may kiss the – right, too late," she said, as Dave and Tillie came together with the sort of suction you could drain a swimming pool with. There was a dramatic twirl as they came apart, and then a huge roar as Dave and Tillie turned to face their friends and crew mates, both punching the air in delight.

Outside the windows of the observation deck, bursts of colour flashed in coordination, and mini-rocket trails cut through dark space, as Reeves set off a programmed display.

"You want me to produce a light show?" he'd said to Juno. "I'll have to see. I might have to disconnect the life-support and shut down levels two to six to comply with an intricate, high-level command like that."

"Don't be a grump. It's for Dave and Tillie."

Reeves had muttered a bit more – something about

having to do everything around here – but had certainly come up with the goods, as sparkling lasers now popped the words 'Congratulations David and Mathilda from Your Friend Reeves' outside the window.

"And that's that," said Susannah, turning to Jordan. "I love a good wedding."

"I'm pleased for them. I never got that far. Not even close." He felt uncomfortable as he said it, and wasn't sure why.

"Hope for us all," Susannah said, without thinking, and then laughed. At the absurdity of finding someone special trillions of miles from home? At the stacked odds against it, inherent in their situation? She didn't know, and laughed nervously again, leaning into an awkward pause broken only by Gerald arriving bearing a tray of drinks.

"Wine?" he said.

"Ooh, great," said Jordan.

"From grapes?" said Susannah.

"Where am I going to get grapes from?"

"I think you've answered my question. Jordan, I strongly recommend you put the glass back."

"I would be offended, if it wasn't you, Suze."

"I hear you're leaving us, too? Heading off with the newlyweds?"

"You know me." Gerald gestured at the room. "Too many people. Not really my thing, especially now there's a thousand more of them, cluttering up the place. I thought I'd go with my friends" – he tried out the unusual word, and it seemed to work – "and see this ecosystem young Karlan is all excited about."

"He'll like that, having you along, too."

"I don't know about that."

"I do. You're a good man, Gerald."

He shrugged, and fussed with the glasses on his tray, turning to leave, saying, "Jordan? Do something for me?"

"If I can."

"My notices? In the canteen on Three-Deck?"

Jordan knew the ones. The commands, the admonishments, the general insults – the short-tempered announcements that Gerald pinned up, in the vain hope of stemming, what seemed to him, the crew's natural tendency to be as annoying as possible.

"You want me to take – "

"Yes, please. Go over them with a sharpie, or write them out again if you have to. Keep the beggars on their toes. Bunch of idiots, Jordan, you know that," and he winked, before walking off, whistling.

"I see you've met the new, improved Gerald?"

Jordan and Susannah turned to greet Juno and the Major, and the four of them stood in companionable silence for a while as old colleagues and new crew members pushed past to go and hail the married couple, holding court in front of the observation deck window.

The guys from Power were back for the occasion in their shiny, matching suits and, as the music cranked higher, they formed a line in front of the buffet table and began to wave their arms erratically.

"What is that?" said Jordan. "Is that them trying to do 'YMCA'?"

"Someone – naming no names" – Juno looked meaningfully at Susannah – "showed them how to do it one Christmas. But being, you know" – and she gestured at the five, pale, pasty, bespectacled men – "boffins, they've changed the letters to elements from the periodic table."

They all looked at the spectacularly uncoordinated, flailing limbs.

"Not great," admitted Susannah. "Come on, you, we'll show them how it's done."

She grabbed Jordan's hand, as he protested.

"No way, I don't dance. I'm too old. I'm fifty now, remember?"

Susannah carried on dragging. "Mate, I'm properly fifty, and we're dancing."

Juno watched her Number Two pull Jordan onto the dance floor. Another man who had no idea, she thought. Clueless, wasn't that a movie? Still, he'd come a long way – literally, figuratively, personally, all the adverbs. Susannah, she decided, could do a lot worse – if Jordan ever worked it out.

"I don't suppose you – ?"

"No, ma'am," said the Major, firmly.

As she expected and, indeed, liked. Safe, solid and reliable. That was the Thomas she had come to know – the Major she had come to rely on. She hadn't for one minute thought he would want to dance, and he didn't disappoint her.

If she'd been wary of him at the beginning, it was because he had been forced upon her by circumstance. An unknown quantity, not someone she had chosen.

If she was being strictly honest, the whole Bowie and Elton John business had unsettled her for a while. She had never quite got to the bottom of it – and Reeves still insisted it was coincidental, that he couldn't find any calculated intention behind the Major's speech patterns. But whatever it was, there was no malice in it, and Juno had let it go – aside from an occasional double-take whenever she heard him say 'Ground Control' in relation to the New Earth ops room.

Otherwise, though, Thomas was solid, straight, reliable. She liked that.

"Here's looking at them."

The Major spoke, raising a glass in the general direction of the happy couple, who were now part of the YMCA-chemical compound axis over on the dance floor.

"You know," he continued, "of all the missions in all the ships in all the world – "

"This is new," said Juno, shaking her head, wonderingly, but with a smile on her face.

"I've never been on one quite like this," said the Major. "Though there was one time, in Morocco. Well, Moroccan airspace, to be strictly accurate ... Anyway, that's another story."

"Not what I thought you were going to say, I admit."

"All I really meant was that I've enjoyed getting to know the crew over this last few months. And, if I may say so, Captain, I've enjoyed getting to know you, too."

"Thomas, you are one of a kind. I'd go as far to say that I think this is the beginning of a beautiful friendship."

"Very eloquent, ma'am. I don't have your way with words, of course. I wonder, under the circumstances, if I might change my mind after all."

"In what way, Thomas?"

The Major held out a crooked arm to Juno and smiled.

"As someone once said, ma'am. Let's dance."

THE END

For news of upcoming Rex Burke books, plus special deals and discounts, follow me on my Amazon author page – amazon.com/author/rexburke

Want to hear what's going on in the Odyssey Earth universe? Then sign up to my monthly newsletter – you'll get a free 'Odyssey Earth' short story too!

Like This Book?

If you enjoyed the ride, please take a moment to leave me a review on Amazon, Goodreads, BookBub, or anywhere else you like.

A word or two is absolutely fine (though please, go to town if you like!), even just a rating – it all helps keep the *Odyssey Earth* flying just a little bit longer.

Thanks a million – you're all stars.

About the Author

Rex Burke is a SciFi writer based in North Yorkshire, UK.

When he was young, he read every one of those yellow-jacketed Victor Gollancz hardbacks in his local library. That feeling of out-of-this-world amazement has never left him – and keeps him company as he writes his own SciFi adventures.

When Rex is not writing, he travels – one way or another, he'll get to the stars, even if it's just as stardust when his own story is done.

Find Out More

To find out more, and grab a free Odyssey Earth short story, visit Rex's website – rexburke.com